Grammar Guru

NEW EDITION 全新改版

Basic English Grammar Guide

英文文法入門指引

What you need to know about basic English grammar.
Simple, useful, and easy to understand.

呂香瑩　著

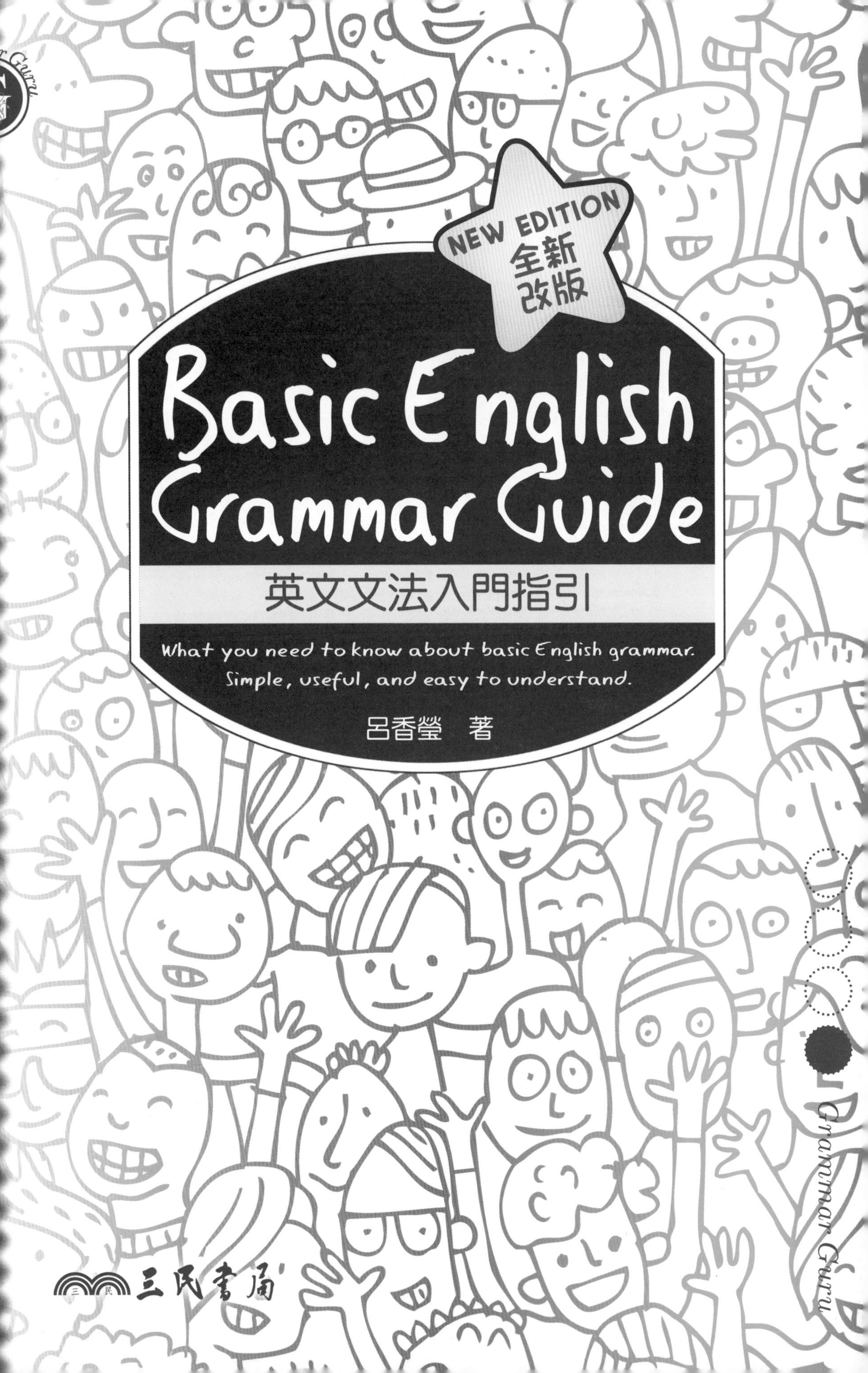

Grammar Guru

三民書局

國家圖書館出版品預行編目資料

Basic English Grammar Guide 英文文法入門指引／呂香瑩著.——修訂二版四刷.——臺北市：三民，2022
面； 公分.——（文法咕嚕Grammar Guru系列）

ISBN 978-957-14-6353-7 （平裝）
1. 英語 2. 語法

805.16 106021571

Basic English Grammar Guide (New Edition)
英文文法入門指引(全新改版)

著作人 | 呂香瑩
發行人 | 劉振強
出版者 | 三民書局股份有限公司
地址 | 臺北市復興北路 386 號(復北門市)
臺北市重慶南路一段 61 號(重南門市)
電話 | (02)25006600
網址 | 三民網路書店 https://www.sanmin.com.tw

出版日期 | 初版一刷 2009 年 4 月
修訂二版一刷 2018 年 2 月
修訂二版四刷 2022 年 2 月
書籍編號 | S807860
ISBN | 978-957-14-6353-7

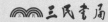

三民書局

序

如果說，單字是英文的血肉，文法就是英文的骨架。想要打好英文基礎，兩者實應相輔相成，缺一不可。

只是，單字可以死背，文法卻不然。

學習文法，如果沒有良師諄諄善誘，沒有好書細細剖析，只落得個見樹不見林，徒然勞心費力，實在可惜。

Guru 原義指的是精通於某領域的「達人」，因此，這一套「文法 Guru」系列叢書，本著 Guru「導師」的精神，要告訴你：親愛的，我把英文文法變簡單了！

「文法 Guru」系列，適用對象廣泛，從初習英文的超級新鮮人、被文法糾纏得寢食難安的中學生，到鎮日把玩英文的專業行家，都能在這一套系列叢書中找到最適合自己的夥伴。

深願「文法 Guru」系列，能成為你最好的學習夥伴，伴你一同輕鬆悠遊英文學習的美妙世界。

有了「文法 Guru」，文法輕鬆上路！

給讀者的話

在語言裡，文法扮演著如骨架對人體般的重要角色。然而，在許多人的英文學習過程中，英文文法卻是最困難的一環。面對瑣碎的規則與繁複的觀念，不少學習者因而感到挫折與卻步，最終將英文學習視為畏途，這著實讓人感到惋惜。

「英文文法入門指引」的編寫目標在於將文法規則化繁為簡，分為十五個章節，由架構分類切入，以點、線、面的系統順序帶領讀者認識英文文法，建構出完整的概念，適合文法基礎為零、觀念薄弱或希望高效率學習英文的讀者。

本書有以下特點：

條列重點：每章節的第一部分以條列的方式呈現基本概念，讓重點一目了然，幫助讀者快速掌握章節精髓。

表格呈現：將繁雜的文法重點歸納整理成表格形式，供讀者比較相似與相異處，提高學習效率。

實力演練：各小節末均附有實力演練，以多種題型讓讀者在閱讀完一小節後能立即檢驗學習成效，釐清模糊的文法觀念。

學習便利貼：提供記憶方法或便於背誦的口訣，使讀者能輕鬆找到快速學習且不易遺忘的秘訣。

英文文法並不可怕。讀者若能善用本書，按部就班學習並切實演練習題，相信能有效率地跨越學習關卡。在掌握文法要點之後，如再搭配運用多變化的句型與豐富的字彙，必定能提升文章閱讀與書寫文句的能力，進而將英文學得精、用得巧，在英文學習旅途中一帆風順。

contents

略語表

縮寫	名稱	中文	主要相關章節
S	subject	主詞	**Ch 1** 英文句子的基本概念
SC	subject complement	主詞補語	
V	verb	動詞	**Ch 1** 英文句子的基本概念、**Ch 5** 動詞的時態
VR	verb root	原形動詞	**Ch 5** 動詞的時態
V-ed	past tense	過去式	
V-ing	gerund	動名詞	**Ch 7** 動名詞與不定詞
V-ing	present participle	現在分詞	**Ch 5** 動詞的時態、**Ch 12** 分詞
p.p.	past participle	過去分詞	**Ch 5** 動詞的時態、**Ch 12** 分詞
vt.	transitive verb	及物動詞	
vi.	intransitive verb	不及物動詞	
O	object	受詞	**Ch 1** 英文句子的基本概念
OC	object complement	受詞補語	
DO	direct object	直接受詞	
IO	indirect object	間接受詞	
prep.	preposition	介系詞	
adj.	adjective	形容詞	**Ch 8** 形容詞與副詞
adv.	adverb	副詞	
N	noun	名詞	**Ch 1** 英文句子的基本概念、**Ch 2** 名詞
aux.	auxiliary (verb)	助動詞	**Ch 4** 助動詞
conj.	conjunction	連接詞	**Ch 9** 連接詞
etc.	et cetera	等…	

Chapter

1 英文句子的基本概念

1-1 句子的基本結構

1. 含有**主詞 (S) + 動詞 (V)** 的基本結構且意義完整的字串，稱為句子。
2. 句子可分為兩大部分：**主語部分 (S) + 述語部分 (V . . .)**
   主語為句子的發展中心，其他的字詞為述語。在主語中，最重要的字是**名詞 (N)**；在述語中，最重要的字是**動詞 (V)**。
3. 句首第一個字母得大寫，句末須加上英文標點符號，如句點 (.)、問號 (?)、驚嘆號 (!)。

- Jessica is a student. Jessica 是學生。
  (Jessica：主語；is a student：述語)
- The ancient Egyptians built the pyramids.
  (The ancient Egyptians：主語；built the pyramids：述語)
  古埃及人建造金字塔。
- Learning languages seems much fun.
  (Learning languages：主語；seems much fun：述語)
  學習語言好像很有趣。
- Taking exercise every day is good for your health. 每天運動有益你的健康。
  (Taking exercise every day：主語；is good for your health：述語)

學習便利貼

若無法判定主語和述語時，可先找出主要動詞。通常在主要動詞之前的字或字串就是主語，動詞及其後的字串為述語。

Try it! 實力演練

I. 畫底線並標出主語和述語

1. I am pleased to meet you.

2. The doctor suggests that the patient should quit smoking.

II. 選出句意與結構皆完整的句子

☐ 1. I'm sorry to have kept you waiting.

☐ 2. Some tree frogs may become extinct in the wild.

☐ 3. A lot of people in the restaurant.

1-2 五大基本句型

依據動詞的不同特性，可以歸納出五大基本句型，所有英文句子都是從這五大句型延伸變化而來。以下針對這五大基本句型做詳細的解說：

1-2-1 句型一：S + vi.

1. 此句型中，主要動詞為不及物動詞。**不及物動詞本身的意思完整**，不涉及行為對象，後面不須接受詞或補語。若有涉及行為對象時，用**介系詞**連接受詞。
2. 此句型後可接表示時間、地點或狀態的副詞，作修飾用，不影響句型結構。
3. 不及物動詞為數不少，常用的有：come、go、run、cry、sleep、sit、stand、listen、live、happen、rain、stay、rise、arrive、talk、agree 等。

S	vi.	prep. + O	adv.	中譯
The sun	**rises.**			太陽升起。
I	**agree**	with you.		我同意你說的話。
The hungry baby	**is crying**		loudly.	肚子餓的寶寶哭得很大聲。
Uncle Sam	**lives**	with his family	in Taipei.	Sam 叔叔和他的家人住在臺北。

Try it! 實力演練

I. 選出有不及物動詞 (vi.) 的句子

☐ 1. According to the report, a car accident happened yesterday.

☐ 2. Farmers grow rice in Taiwan.

☐ 3. Professor Parker is talking to her students.

II. 畫底線並標出 S 和 vi.

1. The nervous man spoke very fast.

2. The diligent worker works six days a week.

3. My brother goes to school by bus.

1-2-2 句型二：S + vi. + SC

1. 此句型中，主要動詞為**不完全不及物動詞**。此類動詞後面不接受詞，但因本身意思不完整，所以需要**主詞補語 (SC)** 來補充說明主詞的性質或狀態。
2. 本句型動詞以**連綴動詞**為主。連綴動詞用於連接主詞與主詞補語，主詞補語可以是**名詞**、**形容詞**、**分詞**、**不定詞**、或**介系詞片語**。
3. 連綴動詞有：

   (1) be 動詞：am、are、is、was、were

   (2) 表「感官造成知覺」(…起來) 的動詞：look、sound、smell、taste、feel

   (3) 表「變成；轉變」的動詞：become、turn、get、grow

   (4) 表「似乎；顯得」的動詞：seem、appear

   (5) 表「保持；維持」的動詞：stay、keep、remain

   ❶ be 動詞、stay 或 remain 後可以接地方副詞做為補語，用以表示「所處位置」。

S	vi.	SC	adv.	中譯
Emily Dickinson	**is**	a famous poet.		艾蜜莉・狄金森是有名的詩人。
These questions	**are**	quite easy.		這些問題相當簡單。
The sad girl	**remained**	silent	all day.	這傷心的女孩整天不說話。
This plan	**sounds**	interesting.		這計畫聽起來很有趣。
The manager	**will be**	here	soon.	經理很快就會到這裡。
The team's goal	**is**	to win the game.		這支隊伍的目標就是贏得比賽。
My brother and I	**stayed**	at home.		我和弟弟待在家裡。

Try it! 實力演練

I. 畫底線並標出 S、vi.、SC

1. Tim's answers are unexpected.

2. Everything looks fine.

3. After the show, the audience remained seated until the lights were on.

II. 選擇

______ 1. To those who don't know her well, Camilla seems very ______.
(A) unfriendly (B) unfriendliness (C) friendliness (D) friends

______ 2. The old man stays ______ by doing regular exercise.
(A) health (B) unhealthy (C) healthy (D) healthily

1-2-3 句型三：S + vt. + O

1. 此句型中，主要動詞為**完全及物動詞**。此類動詞涉及行為對象，後面必須接**受詞**才能使句意完整。
2. 此類動詞的受詞可用**名詞**、**代名詞**、**動名詞**、**不定詞**、**名詞片語**或**名詞子句**。
3. 此類動詞為數不少，例如：love、hate、like、eat、drink、catch、know、find、enjoy、watch、write、say、spend、prefer、bring、forgive、announce、believe、wear 等。
4. 有些及物動詞固定接續動名詞 (如 enjoy、mind、keep、consider 等)，有些則固定接續不定詞 (如 want、decide、intend、expect 等)。相關用法請見動名詞與不定詞 (CH7)。

❶ 如果受詞為人稱代名詞時，必須以受格形式出現。

S	vt.	O	中譯
I	**love**	her. (代名詞)	我愛她。
Chloé	**ate**	two hamburgers. (名詞)	Chloé 吃了二個漢堡。
The police	**caught**	the thief. (名詞)	警察抓住小偷。
The children	**enjoy**	picnicking. (動名詞)	孩子們喜歡野餐。
The committee	**decided**	to cancel the plan. (不定詞)	委員會決定取消計畫。
The smart boy	**knows**	what to do. (名詞片語)	這聰明的男孩知道該做什麼。
The referee	**announced**	that we won the game. (名詞子句)	裁判宣布我們贏得比賽。

Try it! 實力演練

I. 畫底線並標出 S、vt.、O

1. The thirsty athlete drank much water.

2. Many people believe that the mayor will make a wise decision.

3. The angry mother didn't know what to say.

II. 句子重組

1. told/Grandma/a ridiculous story

____

2. forgot/Judy/to bring an umbrella

____

3. do you/where your brother is/know

____

1-2-4 句型四：S + vt. + IO + DO = S + vt. + DO + prep. + IO

1. 此句型中，主要動詞為屬於及物動詞的**授與動詞**。授與動詞需要**兩個受詞**才能使句意完整 ， 可分為**間接受詞** (IO = Indirect Object) 和**直接受詞** (DO = Direct Object)。
2. 間接受詞多指人，直接受詞多指事物。間接受詞與直接受詞的位置若調換時，必須在間接受詞 (IO) 前加上特定的介系詞。
3. 當兩個受詞的排列順序為 **IO + DO** 時，不須加介系詞，記憶口訣為「人物」；反之，順序是 **DO + prep. + IO** 時，口訣為「物介人」。介系詞須特別背誦。
4. 此類動詞可依與其搭配的介系詞加以分類：

介系詞	授與動詞
to	give、tell、show (出示)、send、teach、pay、bring、pass、lend、offer、deliver
for	buy、prepare、choose、get、make (製作)、leave、cook
of	ask

• Father gave(vt.) me(IO) some pocket money(DO).

→ Father gave(vt.) some pocket money(DO) to(prep.) me(IO). 爸爸給我一些零用錢。

• My boyfriend bought(vt.) me(IO) a bunch of flowers(DO).

→ My boyfriend bought(vt.) a bunch of flowers(DO) for(prep.) me(IO). 我男朋友買了一束花給我。

• The teacher asked(vt.) her students(IO) a difficult question(DO).

→ The teacher asked(vt.) a difficult question(DO) of(prep.) her students(IO). 老師問學生一個難題。

Try it! 實力演練

I. 畫底線並標出 IO 和 DO

1. Remember to show the security your ID.

2. Victoria left her husband some food.

3. The president's speech brought the people some hope.

II. 將上述各句改為 S + vt. + DO + prep. + IO 的句型

1. ______________________________

2. ______________________________

3. ______________________________

1-2-5 句型五：S + vt. + O + OC

1. 此句型中，主要動詞為**不完全及物動詞 (vt.)**。不完全及物動詞後除了接受詞，還必須接**受詞補語 (OC)**，以補充說明受詞的性質或狀態使語意完整。
2. 受詞補語可用**名詞**、**形容詞**、**分詞** (表示主動意義用現在分詞 V-ing；表示被動意義用過去分詞 p.p)、**不定詞**、**介系詞片語**。
3. 常用的此類動詞有：
   (1) 表「認為」的動詞：think、consider、believe、find (覺得)
   (2) 表「使役」的動詞：make、have (使)、get (讓)
   (3) 表「感官」的動詞：see、watch、observe、hear、overhear、feel
   (4) 表「要求」的動詞：ask
   (5) 表「稱呼」的動詞：call、name
   (6) 表「任命」的動詞：elect、choose、appoint
   (7) 其他：keep、leave、find (發現)、catch、paint (油漆)

S	vt.	O	OC	翻譯
Everyone	**considers**	Oliver	a tough guy. (名詞)	每個人都認為 Oliver 是個硬漢。
Lila's poor grades	**made**	her parents	angry. (形容詞)	Lila 考不好讓她父母很生氣。
The nervous boy	**felt**	his legs	shaking. (分詞)	這緊張的男孩感覺腿在發抖。
The teacher	**asked**	her students	to concentrate. (不定詞)	老師要求學生專心。
Hank's friends	**call**	him	a genius. (名詞)	Hank 的朋友稱他為天才。
We	**elect**	May	chairperson. (名詞)	我們選 May 當主席。
Susan	**found**	her purse	stolen. (分詞)	Susan 發現錢包被偷。
The child	**kept**	the water	running. (分詞)	這孩子讓水流個不停。
They	**painted**	the wall	light blue. (形容詞)	他們把牆壁漆成淡藍色。

注意

a. call、name、elect、choose、appoint 只能接**名詞**當受詞補語。

b. keep、leave、find 有讓受詞維持某種狀態或發現受詞是某種狀態之意，故常接**形容詞**或**分詞**當受詞補語。

Try it! 實力演練

I. 畫底線並標出 S、vt.、O、OC

1. We consider Tina suitable for the job.

2. They kept themselves warm by using hand warmers.

3. The members elected Eric president.

II. 句子重組

1. made/the teacher's explanation/the question/easier

____

2. painted/the room/pink/the workers

____

3. Angela/her purse/on the bus/left

____

1-3 標點符號的應用

使用正確的標點符號可以使文意更清晰，讓文章更為通順，也更能表達出說話者或書寫者的意思。

句 號 .	用法	置於句尾，表示句意完整和句子的結束。 ❶ 英文的句號為實心的小點。
	範例	• An earthquake took place five minutes ago. 五分鐘前有地震。 • The best way to explore this town is on foot. 探索這小鎮的最好方式是步行。
逗 號 ,	用法	(1) 分隔多個片語、子句或詞性相同的字。 (2) 用於分詞構句和非限定用法的關係子句。 (3) 分隔主要子句和插入語、同位語和附加問句。 ❶ 逗號不可代替連接詞，沒有連接子句的功能。
	範例	• The man is smart, kind, and generous. 這男人很聰明、仁慈且慷慨大方。 • Getting up early, Lucy caught the first bus. 因為早起，Lucy 趕上第一班公車。 • My boyfriend, who is an engineer, writes computer programs. 我的男朋友是個工程師，他寫電腦程式。 • Taipei, the capital of Taiwan, is highly populated. 臺北是臺灣的首都，人口稠密。 • The Nintendo Wii system is seen as a revolution in video games, isn't it? 任天堂的 Wii 被認為是電玩界的革命，不是嗎？

分號 ;	用法	(1) 可用於連接兩個意思相關或對比的獨立句子，此時通常不再加連接詞。 (2) 可置於轉折語前，用以分隔轉折語與句子。
	範例	• Most girls like dolls; most boys like toy cars. 大部分的女孩喜歡洋娃娃，而大部分的男孩喜歡玩具車。 • Allen had a headache; therefore, he took a sick leave. Allen 頭痛，因此他請病假。
問號 ?	用法	(1) 置於問句後。 (2) 口語中，在直述句後加上問號並提高語調，也可表示疑問。
	範例	• Have you ever been to London? 你去過倫敦嗎？ • You have been to London? 你去過倫敦？
冒號 :	用法	(1) 置於完整的句子後。 (2) 冒號之後的部分用於舉例、說明或解釋前面的句子。
	範例	• The campers will need the following equipment: a tent, a compass, walking sticks, and flashlights. 露營者會需要以下裝備：帳棚、指南針、手杖和手電筒。 • I always believe in the saying: God helps those who help themselves. 我一直相信這句諺語：天助自助者。 • After a sleepless night, Alex made the final decision: He would quit the job. 在徹夜難眠後，Alex 做了最後決定：他要辭職。
破折號 —	用法	(1) 表示文意的中斷或語氣轉折。 (2) 前後兩個破折號可以代替括弧，做補充說明用。
	範例	• An honest politician—if such a creature ever exists—would never agree to such a proposal. 一個誠實的政客——如果有的話——絕對不會贊同這樣的提案。 • Helen's favorite food—snacks and cakes—will be sold in this newly open bakery. Helen 最喜歡的食物——點心和蛋糕——將會在這家新開幕的麵包店裡販售。

<table>
<tr><td rowspan="2">連字號
-</td><td>用法</td><td>用來連接二個以上的字以形成複合字。
❶ 連字號的長度比破折號短。</td></tr>
<tr><td>範例</td><td>• William gave his girlfriend a heart-shaped chocolate cake.
William 給他女朋友一個心型的巧克力蛋糕。
• Todd is hard-working and reliable. His boss thinks highly of him.
Todd 工作認真又可靠。他的老闆很看重他。</td></tr>
<tr><td rowspan="2">驚嘆號
!</td><td>用法</td><td>置於句尾，表達說話者的強烈情緒或加強語氣。</td></tr>
<tr><td>範例</td><td>• What a hot day! 多熱的一天啊！
• How adorable the baby is! 這嬰兒多可愛啊！</td></tr>
<tr><td rowspan="2">引號
“ ”</td><td>用法</td><td>用於表示對話內容或引述他人所說的話。
❶ 英文的句號、逗號和問號大多置於引號內。</td></tr>
<tr><td>範例</td><td>• The spokesperson said, “The project will be finished in time.”
發言人說：「這計畫會及時完成。」
• “When will your cousin arrive?” “I have no idea.”
「你的表弟何時會到？」「我不清楚。」</td></tr>
</table>

Try it! 實力演練

填入適當的標點符號

Have you ever visited Hualien ______ Hualien is a wonderful place for sightseeing ______ In recent years ______ more and more people have traveled there for a relaxing weekend ______ There ______ tourists can visit Taroko National Park ______ where they can see amazing cliffs and gorges ______ In addition ______ hiking down the path is something that tourists should not miss in Taroko National Park ______ An exciting alternative that Hualien offers the tourists is whitewater rafting along Hsiuguluan River ______ Rafters may enjoy the excitement while appreciating the gorgeous sights ______ What a joyful trip it seems ______

Notes

Chapter

2 名詞

指**人**、**事**、**物**或**抽象概念**的字，稱為名詞 (Noun)，可做為句子的**主詞**、**受詞**或**補語**。在使用上必須注意「格」與「數」的變化。

2-1 名詞的格

1. 名詞的格可以分為主格、受格與所有格。
2. 使用時，名詞的主、受格不須變化，而所有格則有變化，可分為有生命名詞與無生命名詞的用法。

	用法	位置	範例
主格	當主詞，表示執行動作者	置於動詞前	• **The children** are playing in the park happily. 孩子們開心在公園裡玩。
	當主詞補語，表示主詞的性質或狀態	置於連綴動詞後	• Professor Huang is **the special guest** tonight. 黃教授是今晚的特別來賓。
受格	當受詞，表示接受動作的對象	置於動詞或介系詞後	• We all know that **long-haired girl**. 我們都認識那個長髮女孩。 • Amanda is interested in **baseball**. Amanda 對棒球有興趣。
所有格	當形容詞，表示名詞的所有權	置於名詞之前	• **Jack's** father is an engineer. Jack 的爸爸是個工程師。

1. 有生命名詞的所有格

名詞		構成法	範例
單數	結尾非 -s	字尾加 -'s	girl's、boy's、baby's、farmer's
	結尾為 -s	字尾加 -' 或 -'s	James'/James's、Thomas'/Thomas's
複數	規則變化	字尾加 -'	girls'、boys'、babies'、farmers'
	不規則變化	字尾加 -'s	men's、women's、children's、mice's

2. 無生命名詞的所有格

(1) 無生命名詞的所有格為「所有物 + **of** + 所有者」的結構。

例：the legs **of** the desk (桌腳)、the cover **of** the book (書的封面)、the power **of** knowledge (知識的力量)。

(2) 此結構也可用於有生命名詞。

例：the singer**'s** album = the album **of** the singer (歌手的專輯)、Bruce Willis'(**s**) signature = the signature **of** Bruce Willis (Bruce Willis 的簽名)。

• J.K. Rowling wrote the *Harry Potter* books.
（J.K. Rowling：主格；the *Harry Potter* books：受格）

J.K. 羅琳撰寫《哈利波特》的系列書。

• Steve and Kim are watching an interesting program.
（Steve：主格；Kim：主格；an interesting program：受格）

Steve 和 Kim 正在看一個有趣的節目。

• The dentist's clinic is located in the downtown area.
（The dentist's：所有格；clinic：主格；the downtown area：受格）

這個牙醫的診所位於市中心。

• Men's Department is on the third floor in this department store.
（Men's：所有格；Department：主格；the third floor：受格；this department store：受格）

這家百貨公司的男裝部在三樓。

Try it! 實力演練

I. 改錯 (在錯誤的字下畫底線，並將正確答案填在空格中)

1. My sister boyfriend won the lottery! → ________________

2. Mr. Jones teaches music in a boys high school. → ________________

II. 翻譯填空

1. 沒有人知道這女孩的名字。

______ knows the ______ name.

2. 這房子的窗戶被二個調皮的孩子打破了。

The ______ of the ______ is broken by two naughty kids.

2-2 可數名詞

1. 一般可以計算出個數的名詞，稱為可數名詞，可分為**單數名詞**與**複數名詞**。
2. 使用單數名詞時，必須在其前加上**冠詞** (a, an, the)、**指示形容詞** (this, that) 或**所有形容詞** (my, your) 等。
3. 數量為二個以上的可數名詞，必須用複數形。

2-2-1 單數名詞與冠詞

1. 單數名詞與不定冠詞 (a/an)

(1) 以單字的實際音標來決定使用 a 或 an，而非由拼字決定。

	說明	範例
a	用於以子音開頭的單數名詞前	a book, a chair, a holiday, a Taiwanese, a unique shirt, a European [jurə`piən]
an	用於以母音開頭的單數名詞前	an apple, an orange, an old man, an armchair, an hour [aʊr], an honest [`ɑnɪst] man ! h 不發音

(2) 不定冠詞可以指「同類中的任一個體」，未限定對象。

- The magician needs **a** volunteer to help him.

  該魔術師需要一名自願者幫忙。 Note 指眾多自願者中的一個，未限定對象。

(3) 不定冠詞與單數名詞也可以代表「全體」。

- **A** barking dog seldom bites. 【諺】會叫的狗不咬人。

  Note 泛指一般會吠叫的狗。

2. 單數名詞與定冠詞 (the)

(1) 定冠詞可以指同類中的「特定」個體，有限定的作用。

- **The** actor is rehearsing for **the** show for tomorrow.
  這位演員正在排演明天的表演。
  Note 指特定的演員與特定的表演。

(2) 定冠詞也用於獨一無二的自然物或方位、方向前，如：the sun、the moon、the earth、the right、the left、the north、the west、the east。

(3) 定冠詞接子音開頭的字時，唸 [ðə]；接母音開頭的字時，唸 [ði]。

- We'll arrive in Taipei in **the** [ði] evening.
  我們將在傍晚到達臺北。

注意

1. 指示形容詞 (this, that) 與所有形容詞 (my, your, his, her, our, your, their, Mary's . . .) 都有限定的作用。請參見 CH8。
2. 指示形容詞、所有形容詞和冠詞有相同的功能，所以只能擇一，不可連用。
   - [O] **That** girl plays the guitar well. My sister does, too. 那女孩很會彈吉他。我姊姊也是。
   - [X] **My this a** skirt is expensive. 我這一件裙子很貴。

Try it! 實力演練

I. 填空 (根據中文意思，在空格中填入正確的冠詞)

1. 我生日時，爸爸買了一個禮物給我。
   Father bought ______ present for me on my birthday.
2. Alicio 來自歐洲，他是歐洲人。
   Alicio comes from Europe; he is ______ European.
3. 太陽從東方升起。
   ______ sun rises in ______ east.

II. 改錯 (在錯誤的字下畫底線，並將正確答案填在空格中)

1. Max is a honest man.→ ______________________
2. Charles keeps three pets, including a dogs and two turtle.
   → ______________________, ______________________

3. A comic book I borrowed from Frank is interesting.

→ ______________________

2-2-2 複數名詞與名詞的數

複數名詞必須在字尾做變化，可分為規則變化與不規則變化，務必牢記。

名詞的數	單數	• I heard that Cathy bought a new **car** last week. 我聽說 Cathy 上週買了一部新車。
	複數	• I have two **tickets** for the concert tomorrow. 我有兩張明天音樂會的票。
	不可數	• Would you like some **coffee**? 你要來點咖啡嗎？

1. 規則變化

條件	變化	範例
一般規則	字尾加 -s	• dog → dog**s** • car → car**s** • skirt → skirt**s** • candle → candle**s** • purpose → purpose**s** • requirement → requirement**s**
字尾為 -s、-ss、-x、-ch、-sh	字尾加 -es	• bus → bus**es** • class → class**es** • box → box**es** • torch (火把) → torch**es** • church → church**es** • brush → brush**es** ❶ 字尾 -ch 發音為 [k] 時，複數為字尾加 -s，如：stoma**ch** [ˋstʌmək] → stomachs
字尾為 -f 或 -fe	去 f(e)，加 -ves	• wolf → wol**ves** • thief → thie**ves** • life → li**ves** • wife → wi**ves** ❶ 有些加 -s 即可，如：proof → proof**s**、roof → roof**s**、chief (首領) → chief**s**、dwarf (侏儒) → dwarf**s**。 有些加 -s 或 -ves 均可，如：hoof (馬蹄) → hoof**s** 或 hoo**ves**、handkerchief → handkerchief**s** 或 handkerchie**ves**。

字尾為 -y： (1) 子音 + -y	去 -y 加 -ies	• story → stories • fairy → fairies • country → countries • party → parties • university → universities
(2) 母音 + -y	字尾加 -s	• day → days • key → keys • boy → boys • ray (射線) → rays • delay → delays
字尾為 -o： (1) 子音 + -o	字尾加 -es	• tomato → tomatoes • potato → potatoes • hero → heroes ❶ 有的字尾為子音 + -o 的字，複數為字尾加 -s，如： • photo → photos • cello (大提琴) → cellos • piano → pianos
	字尾可加 -s 或 -es	• zero → zero(e)s • volcano (火山) → volcano(e)s、 • mosquito (蚊子) → mosquito(e)s • tornado (龍捲風) → tornado(e)s
(2) 母音 + -o	字尾加 -s	• zoo → zoos • radio → radios • bamboo → bamboos

2. 不規則變化

變化	範例
單複數同形	sheep、deer、species (物種)、series (系列)、Chinese、Taiwanese
母音字母變化	• mouse → mice • foot → feet • tooth → teeth • goose → geese • man → men • woman → women • gentleman → gentlemen
字尾加 -en 或 -ren	ox → oxen、child → children
其他	• datum (資料) → data • medium (媒體) → media • basis → bases • crisis → crises • emphasis (強調) → emphases • phenomenon (現象) → phenomena

Try it! 實力演練

完成下表，填入下列名詞的單數或複數形

單數	複數	單數	複數
mosquito	1.	person	2.
branch	3.	woman	4.
activity	5.	6.	sheep
tooth	7.	child	8.
puzzle	9.	box	10.

2-3 不可數名詞

1. 不可數名詞常指物質、抽象物體或無固定形體的物體，分為物質名詞、抽象名詞和專有名詞。
2. 不可數名詞前不可直接加冠詞 a、an，亦不用複數形。

2-3-1 物質名詞

物質名詞多是指食物、液體、氣體、材質等的名詞：

食物：meat、pork、beef、fish、chicken、rice、wheat、butter 等。

液體：water、milk、juice、wine、beer、tea、coffee、soup 等。

氣體：air、gas、wind、smoke 等。

材質：wood、stone、paper、iron 等。

用法	範例
物質名詞屬不可數名詞，無複數形，不加冠詞 **a**、**an**	• Drinking **milk** can help you sleep better. 喝牛奶可以幫助睡眠。 • **Air** is necessary for living creatures. 空氣對生物而言是不可或缺的。

計算物質名詞須用單位詞，用法為：數量 + 單位詞 + of + 物質名詞。表示複數時，將單位詞改為複數	• a glass of milk → two glasses of milk • a cup of coffee → three cups of coffee、 • a piece of paper/cake → four pieces of paper/cake
常修飾物質名詞的詞語有：**much**、**a lot of**、**lots of**、**plenty of**、**a large amount of**、**a large sum of (金錢)**、**enough**、**some**、**a little** 等	• The hungry child ate **much** bread. 這飢腸轆轆的小孩吃了很多麵包。 • The poor man had **little** money left. 這窮人只剩下一些錢。
有些物質名詞兼作普通名詞，欲表示不同種類時，可有複數形	• We had chicken and fish for dinner. 我們晚餐吃雞肉和魚肉。 Note chicken 與 fish 指雞肉和魚肉，屬於物質名詞。 • There **are** many chickens on the farm. 農場裡有很多雞。 Note chicken 指的是雞隻，屬於可數的普通名詞。 • Most fish **are** cold-blooded animals. 大多數的魚是冷血動物。 Note fish 指的是魚隻，屬於可數的普通名詞。 • You can see many fishes at the aquarium. 你可以在水族館看到各式各樣的魚類。 Note fish 的複數形有兩種，一般使用 fish (單複數同形)，但若表示各式各樣的魚，則用 fishes。

Try it! 實力演練

I. 選擇

______ 1. Austin makes it a rule to drink ______ before going to bed every night.
(A) some milks (B) plenty of milks
(C) a glass of milk (D) a large sum of milk

______ 2. In certain areas of France, people eat ______ as a delicacy.
(A) horse meats (B) horse meat (C) a horse meat (D) many hose meat

II. 翻譯填空

1. 空氣和水維持生物的生命。

______ and ______ support the lives of living creatures.

2. 今天早上，David 吃了一塊蛋糕和喝了兩杯咖啡。

David ate ______ ______ ______ cake and drank ______ ______ ______ coffee this morning.

2-3-2 抽象名詞

抽象名詞可以表示「狀態」(如 childhood、friendship)、「性質」(如 kindness、honesty)、「動作」(如 action、advice)、「學科」(如 history、mathematics) 等沒有具體形態的名詞。

1. 大部分的抽象名詞可以由其他詞類衍生，大略整理如下：

類型	範例	
形容詞 + -ence, -ness, -ty, -th	• patient → patience	• convenient → convenience
	• diligent → diligence	• shy → shyness
	• great (偉大的) → greatness	• polite → politeness
	• happy → happiness	• rude → rudeness
	• real → reality	• honest → honesty
	• responsible → responsibility	• cruel → cruelty
	• wide →width	• dead → death
名詞 + -ship, -hood	• friend → friendship	• relation → relationship
	• child → childhood	• adult → adulthood
動詞 + -tion, -sion, -ment	• complete → completion	• delete → deletion
	• celebrate → celebration	• appreciate → appreciation
	• impress → impression	• express → expression
	• develop → development	• punish → punishment
	• treat → treatment	• move → movement

2. 抽象名詞的主要用法，整理如下：

用法	範例
抽象名詞屬不可數名詞，不加冠詞 (a/an)，沒有複數形	• That child has **difficulty** walking. 那孩子走路有困難。 • Vincent van Gogh had suffered **loneliness** all his life. Vincent van Gogh 一生飽受孤獨之苦。
抽象名詞常用的修飾詞：**much**、**little**、**some**、**any**、**no** 等	• The teacher listened to the student with **much** patience. 這老師很有耐心地聽學生說話。 • The students paid **no** attention to the teacher. 學生們沒注意聽老師講話。
抽象名詞可與介系詞連用，具有形容詞或副詞的功能	(1) **of + 抽象名詞 = 形容詞** **of** + **great** + 抽象名詞 = **very** + 形容詞 **of** + **no** + 抽象名詞 = **not** + 形容詞 • Sarah Brightman is a singer **of talent**. → Sarah Brightman is a **talented** singer. Sarah Brightman 是個有天份的歌手。 • The headquarters just made a decision **of great** importance. → The headquarters just made a **very important** decision. 總部剛剛做了非常重要的決定。 • Judging from her performance at work, Natalie is a person **of no responsibility**. → Judging from her performance at work, Natalie is **not** a **responsible** person. 從工作表現來看，Natalie 是個沒有責任感的人。 (2) **with, in, by, on + 抽象名詞 = 副詞** • The teacher teaches students **with patience**. → The teacher teaches students **patiently**. 這老師耐心地教導學生。

* The girl looked at the broken music box **in despair**.
  → The girl looked at the broken music box **despairingly**. 女孩絕望地望著壞掉的音樂盒。
* Mr. Chen locked himself out of his house **by accident**.
  → Mr. Chen locked himself out of his house **accidentally**. 陳先生不小心把自己鎖在家門外。
* According to the announcement, the flight will arrive **on time**.
  → According to the announcement, the flight will arrive **punctually**. 根據廣播，班機會準時抵達。

Try it! 實力演練

I. 將下列各詞改為抽象名詞

1. different → ______ 2. silent → ______ 3. evaluate → ______

4. delete → ______ 5. express → ______ 6. argue → ______

II. 選擇

______ 1. With the worsening of global warming, environmental protection is an issue ______ great significance.

(A) with (B) of (C) on (D) at

______ 2. To everyone's surprise, the ten-year-old boy solved the problem ______ ease.

(A) with (B) of (C) on (D) at

______ 3. Caroline is a girl ______, who always says what she means and means what she says.

(A) of no sincerity (B) of great sincerity

(C) with no honesty (D) with great honesty

2-3-3 專有名詞

專有名詞指人、事、物專有的名稱，如：

人名	Angus, Sandra, George Bush, Nicole Kidman, etc.
國名、地名	Taiwan, Germany, Taichung City, Jen-ai Road, etc.
機關、機構名	University of London, FBI, Bank of Taiwan, etc.
星期、月份、節日	Monday, Wednesday, February, Dragon Boat Festival, etc.
星體、山河	Sun, Moon, Earth, Mars (火星), Saturn (土星), Pluto (冥王星), Mt. Ali, Sun Moon Lake, the Yellow River, etc.

專有名詞的主要用法，整理如下：

用法	範例
專有名詞的字首必須大寫，但書名、文章名或機關行號名稱有介系詞時，介系詞不用大寫	• Taroko National Park 太魯閣國家公園 • *The Adventures of Tom Sawyer* 《湯姆歷險記》 • Department of Education 教育局
專有名詞大多不加冠詞，也沒有複數形	• Timothy speaks with a British accent; he must be from Britain. Timothy 說話有英國腔，他一定來自英國。 • Sandra held a party to celebrate her 16th birthday last Tuesday. Sandra 上週二開派對慶祝她 16 歲的生日

Try it! 實力演練

翻譯填空

1. 中東人通常不吃豬肉。

   People from the ______ ______ usually don't eat ______.

2. 在除夕夜和家人一起吃水餃是中國的習俗。

   It is a ______ custom to eat dumplings with their family members on ______ ______ ______ ______.

3. 宮崎駿 (Hayao Miyazaki) 是著名的日本動畫家，製作了許多精彩的動畫片。

______ ______ is a famous ______ animator, who has produced many extraordinary animated films.

2-4 集合名詞

1. 集合名詞指**同種的人、事、物**所組成的集合體，依意思不同，有單數與複數形。
2. 當集合名詞被視為整體，用法和普通名詞一樣，兩個以上用複數形。當表示**整體的**組成份子時，集合名詞雖是單數形，但作複數用，後面接複數動詞。

集合名詞的類別比較，整理如下：

含意			範例
family	整體	家庭	• Lisa's **family** is a big one. Lisa 的家是個大家庭。 Note 指的是一個家庭整體，當單數用。 • Twenty **families** live in this village. 這村裡住著二十戶人家。 Note 指的是家庭整體，兩個以上用複數形。
family	組成份子	家人	• My **family** are all very well. 我的家人都很健康。 Note 指家庭的組成份子，family = family members，為複數名詞。
class	整體	班級	• This **class** consists of 35 students. 這班有 35 個學生。 Note 指一個班級整體，當單數用。 • There are thirty **classes** in my school. 我的學校有 30 個班級。 Note 指的是班級整體，兩個以上用複數形。
class	組成份子	班級成員	• This **class** are all smart. 這班學生都很聰明。 Note 指班級的組成份子，class = class members，為複數名詞。

people	整體	民族	• The Chinese are a peace-loving **people**. 中國人是愛好和平的民族。 Note 指一個民族整體，當單數用。 • There are many different **peoples** in the world. 世界上有很多不同的民族。 Note 指民族整體，兩個以上用複數形。
	組成份子	人們	• Five **people** were injured in the accident. 五個人在意外中受傷。 Note 指個別的組成份子，為複數名詞。

注意

1. 集合名詞除了上述「形式為單數，意義可為單數與複數」一類外，另有其他常見的兩類：
   (1) 形式為單數，意義恆為複數，例：cattle、police。
   • The **police** are responsible for maintaining social order. 警方有責維持社會秩序。
   (2) 形式為複數，意義恆為複數，例：goods、clothes。
   • There are a lot of **clothes** in the model's closet. 這模特兒的衣櫥裡有很多衣服。
2. **the + adj.** 可作集合名詞，指「全體」，如：the poor、the deaf 等。
   • The **elderly** tend to catch a cold in winter. 老年人冬天容易感冒。

Try it! 實力演練

I. 選擇

______ 1. Of all the ______ in this neighborhood, Wyatt's ______ is the largest one.
(A) family; family (B) families; families
(C) families; family (D) family; families

______ 2. Teresa's family ______ all interested in hiking and camping.
(A) are (B) is (C) am (D) be

______ 3. This ______ ______ composed of 20 girls and 20 boys.
(A) class; are (B) classes; is (C) classes; are (D) class; is

II. 整句式翻譯

1. 我妹妹的班上有四十個學生。(. . . consist of . . .)

____

2. 不同的民族有不同的文化和習俗。

2-5 複合名詞

由兩個以上的字組合成的名詞，稱為「複合名詞」。

1. 複合名詞有三種型態：

(1) 由兩個名詞組成，有些可分開寫或合併成一個字，如：brick house (磚房)、color television (彩色電視機)、bookstore (書局)、salesperson (售貨員) 等。

(2) 由名詞與其他詞類組成，且以連字號連接，名詞是主要要素，如：father-in-law (岳父)、passer-by (路人)、looker-on (旁觀者) 等。

(3) 由名詞以外的詞類組成，以連字號連接，或合併成一個字，如：grown-up (成人)、forget-me-not (勿忘草)、push-up (伏地挺身) 等。

2. 複合名詞的複數形大略有以下規則：

條件	變化	範例
複合名詞的組合字皆為名詞，且視為整體時	最後一個名詞改為複數形	brick house**s**、African American**s**、color television**s**、bookstore**s**、sales**people**
名詞與其他詞類組成的複合名詞時	將主要的名詞改為複數	father**s**-in-law、daughter**s**-in-law、passer**s**-by、looker**s**-on
由動詞與其他詞類組成，視為整體時	將字尾改為複數形	push-up**s**、grown-up**s**、forget-me-not**s**
複合名詞包含 man 或 woman 時	兩個名詞都改為複數形	man-dancer → men-dancer**s**、woman-doctor → women-doctor**s**

Try it! 實力演練

I. 用底線標出錯誤，並改正

1. The couple are just passer by; they don't know what happened.

→ ____________________

2. Adam goes hiking with his father in law every weekend.

→ ____________________

3. Fiona is already a grown up, but she acts like a child.

→ ____________________

II. 完成下表，填入下列名詞的單數或複數形

單數	複數	單數	複數
firefly	1.	mother-in-law	2.
policeman	3.	push-up	4.

2-6 個別所有格與共同所有格

個別所有格表示兩個主詞各自擁有某人、事、物；共同所有格表示兩個主詞共同擁有某人、事、物。

兩種所有格的差異，比較如下：

	個別所有格	共同所有格
形式	A's and B's	A and B's
意義	A 與 B 各自擁有某人、事、物	A 與 B 共同擁有某人、事、物
說明	因表示 A、B 各自擁有，所以 A 和 B 都須用所有格。	因表示 A 和 B 共同擁有，視為整體，故 B 後加上 -'s 即可。
使用方法	後面的名詞常是複數形，動詞變化視名詞的單複數而定。	共同所有格後面的名詞可用單數或複數形，動詞變化視名詞的單複數而定。

• **Stuart's and Elaine's** fathers **are** architects.
Stuart 的爸爸和 Elaine 的爸爸都是建築師。

Note 表示個別所有：兩人各自的父親。使用複數名詞 fathers 和複數動詞 are。

• **Jill and Shannon's** father **is** a designer. Jill 和 Shannon 的爸爸是設計師。

Note 表示共同所有：共同擁有一個父親。使用單數名詞 father 和單數動詞 is。

- **Craig's and Sarah's** daughters **study** in the same school.
  Craig 的女兒和 Sarah 的女兒在同一所學校就讀。
  Note 表示個別所有：兩人各自的女兒。使用複數名詞 daughters 和複數動詞 study。
- **Ariel and Johnathan's** daughters study in college.
  Ariel 和 Johnathan 的女兒們在讀大學。
  Note 表示共同所有：共同擁有女兒們。使用複數名詞 daughters 和複數動詞 study。

Try it! 實力演練

I. 依據句意與提示字，填入正確的所有格

1. Ben and Cindy are brother and sister. ______ and ______ (Ben/Cindy) father is a manager.
2. ______ and ______ (Ben/Greg) fathers work in the same company. They are friends.
3. Apparently, Helen doesn't agree with Meg. ______ and ______ (Helen/Meg) opinions are different.

II. 選擇

______ 1. Lucy and James are neighbors. ______ daughters both major in Chinese.
(A) Lucy and James' (B) Lucy's and James
(C) Lucy's and James' (D) Lucy and James'

______ 2. ______ daughter is an English major. She studies in the university.
(A) Joanne's and Eric's (B) Joanne and Eric's
(C) Joanne's and Eric (D) Joanne and Eric

Notes

Chapter

3 代名詞

1. 代名詞可以分為**人稱代名詞** (含所有代名詞與反身代名詞)、**指示代名詞**、**不定代名詞**、**疑問代名詞**及**關係代名詞** (請參見 CH 10)。
2. 代名詞的主要功用在於代替名詞，與名詞屬性相似，可作為主詞、受詞或補語。
3. 在「不知對象為誰」、「不願透漏某人身分」或「無特定對象」的情況下，也可使用代名詞。

3-1 人稱代名詞

1. 人稱代名詞用於**代替前文**已經提過的人或事物。
2. 人稱代名詞的功用和名詞相同，也有數、性、格上的區分，作主詞和受詞用。

3-1-1 人稱代名詞的數、性、格

	第一人稱 (I)		第二人稱 (II)		第三人稱 (III)	
定義	指說話者本身		聽話者		第一、二人稱之外的對象	
數	單數	複數	單數	複數	單數	複數
	I (我)	we (我們)	you (你)	you(你們)	he/she/it (他/她/牠、它)	they (他們/她們/牠們/它們)
性	陽性、陰性名詞均可		陽性、陰性名詞均可		陽性：he (他) 陰性：she (她) 中性：it (牠 / 它)	
主格	I	we	you	you	he/she/it	they
受格	me	us	you	you	him/her/it	them

人稱代名詞的主要用法，整理如下：

用法	範例
作主格： 數、性與人稱須相符	• Leslie suffers from disconnect anxiety. **She** feels nervous when she has no access to her smartphone. Leslie 有離線焦慮。不能使用手機時她就覺得很不安。 • Barbara is overweight. **She** decides to cut down on junk food. Barbara 過胖。她決定要減少食用垃圾食物。 • Many people thought that lucky man was **he**. 很多人以為幸運兒是他。(作主詞補語)
作受格： 人稱代名詞置於動詞或介系詞後	• Sophie and Shirley are such adorable kids; no wonder everyone likes **them**. Sophie 和 Shirley 是很可愛的小孩，難怪大家都喜歡她們。 • Ever since Ronan moved to Ireland, I have been in contact with **him**. 自從 Ronan 搬去愛爾蘭，我一直跟他保持聯絡。

注意

1. 三個人稱代名詞同時作主詞時，有特定的順序：

(1) 單數：順序依 II、III、I 人稱排列。

• According to the coach, **you**, **he**, and **I** are in the same team.
根據教練的安排，你、他和我在同一隊。

• **You**, **she** and **I** are all born under water signs. 你、她和我都是水象星座的人。

(2) 複數：順序依 I、II、III 人稱排列。

• **We**, **you**, and **they** will finish this task together.
我們、你們和他們將會一起完成這項任務。

2. 二個人稱代名詞同時作主詞時，有特定的順序：

(1) 第一人稱代名詞 (I) 必須置於其他名詞或代名詞之後，以表示尊重其他人，即順序為 II + I 或者 III + I。

• **You** and **I** are in the same boat. We both need to work hard to make ends meet.
你和我的處境相同。我們都必須努力工作才能讓收支平衡。

• Both **my sister** and **I** are interested in animations and comedies.
我和妹妹都喜歡動畫與喜劇。

(2) 第二人稱代名詞 (you) 必須置於其他名詞或代名詞之前，以表示尊重聽話者，即順序為 II + I 或 II + III。

- **You** and **I** must take turns sweeping the floor. 你和我必須輪流掃地。
- **You** and **Sue** are both invited to the party. 你和 Sue 都受邀參加派對。

Try it! 實力演練

I. 將畫底線的名詞改為適當的代名詞

As a Hollywood heartthrob, Brad Pitt has starred in over 50 films in his career. [1]Brad Pitt has played almost every type of characters from a vampire to an assassin. [2]Brad Pitt's superb acting performance in films and has not only won [3]Brad Pitt numerous awards but also made him elected as one of the 100 most influential people in the world. Blessed with natural good looks, Brad Pitt is also cited as the world's most attractive man.

1. ______ 2. ______ 3. ______

II. 將提示的人稱代名詞做正確的排列

1. ______ and ______ (I, Hank) are both enthusiastic baseball fans.
2. ______, ______, and ______ (he, I, you) will have to finish this project together.
3. It's interesting that ______, ______, and ______ (they, we, you) are all dog lovers.

3-1-2 所有代名詞

1. 所有代名詞由所有格變化而來，也有人稱、數、性的區別，等於「代名詞所有格 + 名詞」，可用於**表示前述的人、事、物**，以避免文字重複。
2. 所有代名詞中，除了 mine、his 和 its 之外，其他是由所有格 + s 變化而來。

	第一人稱 (I)		第二人稱 (II)		第三人稱 (III)	
	所有格	所有代名詞	所有格	所有代名詞	所有格	所有代名詞
單數	my	mine	your	yours	his her its	his hers its
複數	our	ours	your	yours	their	theirs

所有代名詞的用法，整理如下：

用法	範例
所有代名詞在句中可作為主詞、補語或受詞	• My favorite ice cream flavor is vanilla, and **hers** is chocolate. 我最喜歡的冰淇淋口味是香草，而她的是巧克力。 Note hers = her favorite ice cream flavor 作主詞。 • This is our itinerary and that is **theirs**. Hopefully, these will help you plan **yours**. 這是我們的旅行計畫，那是他們的。希望這些能幫助你計畫自己的。 Note theirs = their itinerary 作主詞補詞。yours = your itinerary 做受詞。
專有名詞的所有代名詞與人稱代名詞用法一樣，由專有名詞 +'s 構成	• Ron's diet is healthier than **Kevin's**. No wonder Ron looks stronger than Kevin. Ron 的飲食比 Kevin 的健康。難怪 Ron 看起來比 Kevin 強壯。 Note Kevin's = Kevin's diet。
所有代名詞可以代替單數名詞，也可以代替複數名詞	• Their proposals are rejected, but **ours** are accepted. 他們的提議被拒絕，但是我們的被接受了。 Note ours = our proposals。

注意

所有代名詞之後不加名詞。

Try it! 實力演練

I. 將畫線部分改為所有代名詞

_____ 1. My hobbies are reading and cooking. What are <u>your hobbies</u>?

_____ 2. Are these mugs <u>my mugs</u>?

_____ 3. Fiona's computer skills are better than <u>his computer skills</u>.

II. 選擇

_____ 1. These are Abigail's earrings. Where are _____?

(A) my (B) mine (C) I (D) me

______ 2. Is this wallet ______?

(A) yours (B) your (C) you (D) you're

______ 3. Your painting received more praise than ______.

(A) her (B) Nicole (C) his (D) it

3-1-3 反身代名詞

1. 反身代名詞表示動詞作用的對象是主詞自身，即主詞與受詞為同一人或事物。
2. 反身代名詞也有人稱、數、性的變化，須與指稱對象一致，不可當主詞。

	第一人稱 (I)		第二人稱 (II)		第三人稱 (III)	
	所有格	反身代名詞	所有格	反身代名詞	所有格	反身代名詞
單數	my	myself	your	yourself	his her its	himself herself itself
複數	our	ourselves	your	yourselves	their	themselves

反身代名詞的主要用法，整理如下：

用法	範例
動詞的受詞	• I took the difficult job in order to challenge **myself**. 為了挑戰自己，我接受了這困難的工作。 • God helps those who help **themselves**. [諺] 天助自助者。
介系詞的受詞	• The woman looked at **herself** in the mirror. 那女人看著鏡中的自己。 • The lonely man often talks to **himself**. 那孤單的男人常常自言自語。
放句尾或主詞後，以強調「自己」之意	• We completed the challenging task **ourselves**. → We **ourselves** completed the challenging task. 我們自己完成這很有挑戰性的任務。 • You should take the responsibility **yourself**. → You **yourself** should take the responsibility. 你自己該負起責任。 Note 反身代名詞置於主詞後比置於句尾的語氣強。

Try it! 實力演練

I. 選擇

______ 1. Mr. Hiddleston built the doghouse ______.

(A) him (B) his (C) himself (D) he

______ 2. They ______ are to blame for the accident.

(A) them (B) their (C) themselves (D) theirs

______ 3. Tina hurt ______, not ______, so she was sent to the hospital.

(A) herself; myself (B) herself; me

(C) hers; me (D) her; myself

II. 文意選填

oneself	myself	himself	themselves

1. The spy always stays alert; he trusts no one but ______.
2. The workers were so careless that they hurt ______.
3. I ______ figured out the solution to the problem without others' help.

3-1-4 人稱代名詞 he、it 的特殊用法

1. he

用法	範例
用 **he who + V** 表示「凡是…的人」之意 = **one/anyone + who + 單數 V** = **people/those + who + 複數 V**	• **He** who laughs last laughs best. 最後笑的人，笑得最開心。 • **He** who is proud will have a fall. 驕者必敗。 → Anyone who is proud will have a fall.
字首大寫時，指上帝	• Tina is a Christian. She firmly believes in **Him**. Tina 是基督徒。她篤信上帝。

2. it

用法	範例
不知道或不必要說出所指涉者的性別時	• The baby is crying. Is **it** hungry? 嬰兒在哭。他餓了嗎？ Note it 多用於指動植物、無生命的名詞，但指嬰孩時，因為外觀上性別不明顯或無特別區分的必要，可以使用 it。
指天氣、天色或季節	• In the desert, **it** is burning hot in the day but freezing cold at night. 在沙漠，白天酷熱，晚上酷寒。 • **It**'s getting darker and darker. We had better call it a day. 天色越來越暗了。我們最好結束今天的工作。 • **It** is spring now. The flowers in my garden are in full bloom. 現在是春天。我花園裡的花都盛開了。
指距離	• **It**'s 2 kilometers from here to the downtown area. 這裡到市區有 2 公里。
指時間或日期	• A: What time is **it**? A：幾點了？ B: **It**'s quarter to four. B：現在 3:45。 • **It** is Tuesday. Daniel has an appointment with his dentist. 今天是星期二。Daniel 和牙醫有約。
作虛主詞，代替後面的不定詞、動名詞或名詞子句	• To talk with your mouth full is impolite. → **It** (虛主詞) is impolite to talk with your mouth full (真主詞 (不定詞)). 吃飯時講話是不禮貌的。 • Crying over spilt milk is no use. → **It** (虛主詞) is no use crying over spilt milk (真主詞 (動名詞)). (諺) 覆水難收。 • **It** (虛主詞) is strange that Logan didn't come to school today (真主詞 (名詞子句)). 真奇怪，Logan 今天沒來上學。 ❗ 主詞太長會讓句子顯得頭重腳輕，不利閱讀，此時可用 it 當虛主詞，將真主詞移至句末。

作虛受詞，代替後面的不定詞、動名詞或名詞子句	• Ed makes **it** a rule to listen to English radio shows every day. **it**：虛受詞；to listen to English radio shows every day：真受詞（不定詞） Ed 習慣每天聽英文廣播節目。 • The kids find **it** fun painting with their fingers. **it**：虛受詞；painting with their fingers：真受詞（動名詞） 孩子們發現用手指畫圖很有趣。 • I think **it** true that Naomi is a two-faced liar. **it**：虛受詞；that Naomi is a two-faced liar：真受詞（名詞子句） 我認為 Naomi 真的是雙面人。 ❗ 受詞太長會不利閱讀，可用 it 當虛受詞，將真受詞移至句末。
用於分裂句。句型結構：**It+ is/was + 強調部分 + that + 其餘部分** **(請參考 CH 15)**	• Wesley came across his old friend on the street. Wesley 在街上巧遇老友。 → **It** was his old friend that Wesley came across on the street. Note 強調受詞 his old friend。 → **It** was on the street that Wesley came across his old friend. Note 強調副詞 on the street。

Try it! 實力演練

I. 填空 (填入正確的代名詞)

1. I consider ______ a good deed to help people in need.
2. ______ was the young singer that won the talent show.
3. How far is ______ from your house to the library?

II. 引導式翻譯

1. 科學家讓複製動物成為可能的事。
   Scientists made ______ possible to clone animals.
2. 在山頂上觀看流星雨是個好點子。
   ______ is a good idea to view meteor showers on the mountaintop.
3. 就是 William 讓 Kate 對運動產生興趣。
   ______ was William that made Kate interested in sports.

3-2 指示代名詞

指示代名詞用於指示事物。最常用的指示代名詞有：this、that、these、those。

指示代名詞的主要用法，整理如下：

用法	範例
指示代名詞的單數用 **this** 和 **that**，複數用 **these** 和 **those**	• **This** is my umbrella and **those** are their umbrellas. 這把是我的雨傘，那些是他們的雨傘。
指示近處的名詞用 **this** 和 **these**，指示遠處的名詞用 **that** 和 **those**	• **This** is my brother, Edward. **That** is my sister, Cathy. 這位是我弟弟，Edward。那位是我妹妹，Cathy。
在句子中表示對比意思時，指示代名詞 **that** 與 **this** 可以表示「前者…，後者…」 ❶ 後方名詞雖意為「後者」，相當於 the latter，但因較靠近第二句，故以 this 指稱；前方主詞雖意為「前者」，相當於 the former，但因距離第二句比較遠，以 that 指稱。	• Food and exercise are essential for us to keep good health, because **this** gives us energy and **that** offers us nutrition. 食物和運動是我們保持健康的必要條件，因為運動給我們能量，食物提供我們營養。 Note exercise 距離第二句的位置較近，故以 this 指稱，food 距離第二句的位置較遠，故以 that 指稱。 • On Nick's birthday, he received a dictionary and a laptop as presents; **this** was from his father, and **that** was from his uncle. Nick 在生日時收到一本字典和一台筆記型電腦當作禮物；後者是他爸爸送的，前者是他叔叔送的。 Note this 代替 a laptop (= the latter)，that 代替 a dictionary (= the former)。

Try it! 實力演練

I. 選擇

______ 1. Mom has prepared a chicken pie and a bottle of orange juice; ______ is in the refrigerator, and ______ is in the oven.

(A) this; that (B) that; this (C) these; those (D) those; these

______ 2. There are two iPads on the desk. ______ is my iPad, and that is hers.
(A) These (B) This (C) That (D) Those

______ 3. Look at the stamps. These are my collections, and ______ are Bill's.
(A) these (B) this (C) that (D) those

II. 填入正確的指示代名詞

1. This is Ms. Wang, and ______ are her students.
2. There are some books on the shelf. These are science fictions, and ______ are comic books.
3. Mrs. Andon prepared a cake and a bottle of juice; ______ was for her thirsty son and ______ was for her hungry daughter.

3-2-1 that 跟 those 的特殊用法

指示代名詞 that 與 those 還可以用於代替之前提過的名詞，以避免重複。

用法	範例
用來代替前面提過、同字但不同指示物的名詞，單數用 **that**，複數用 **those**	• The weather in Taichung is usually hotter than **that** in Taipei. 臺中的天氣通常比臺北的炎熱。 Note that = the weather。the weather in Taichung ≠ the weather in Taipei，故不可用 it。 • People from Asia are usually shorter than **those** from Europe. 亞洲人通常比歐洲人矮。 Note those = people。people from Asia ≠ people from Europe，故不可用 they。
that、**those** 與代名詞 **it**、**they** 的比較：和 **that**、**those** 不同，**it** 和 **they** 用於代替相同指示物的名詞	• The weather in Taichung is usually hot, but **it** is cold today. 臺中的天氣通常很熱，但是今天很冷。 Note it = the weather in Taichung，等於前面提過的名詞。 • Taiwanese are often friendly; **they** like to make friends. 臺灣人通常很友善；他們喜歡交朋友。 Note they = Taiwanese，等於前面提過的名詞。

Try it! 實力演練

I. 選擇

______ 1. The tail of a fox is longer than ______ of a rabbit.

(A) it (B) that (C) this (D) those

______ 2. The ears of an elephant are bigger than ______ of a dog.

(A) it (B) that (C) this (D) those

______ 3. The profit of the products in 2017 had increased by 15% compared with ______ in 2015.

(A) it (B) that (C) this (D) those

II. 引導式翻譯 (填入代名詞 that、those、it 或 they)

1. 臺北的生活費比花蓮的生活費高。

The cost of living in Taipei is higher than ______ in Hualien.

2. 這家店的鞋子比那家的便宜。

The shoes in this shop are cheaper than ______ in that shop.

3. 這本小說很有趣。它很暢銷。

The novel is very interesting. ______ sells like hot cakes.

3-3 不定代名詞

1. 不定代名詞用於**沒有特定**的對象，只是概括地指某人、事、物的代名詞。
2. 常用的不定代名詞有：one、other、another、some、any、all、every、each、both、either、neither 等。若其後接名詞，即轉為不定形容詞。
3. 不定代名詞在句中作主詞時，要先確認自身和所指涉者的單複數，以確定動詞變化能符合人稱和數。

3-3-1 one、other、another

1. one

用法	範例
one 的複數是 ones，所有格是 one's，反身代名詞是 oneself	• The Page family is wealthy. Their mansion is a large **one**. Page 家很富有。他們的豪宅很大。 Note one 代替 mansion。 • The salesman brought everyone in the office a sample of the product and some extra **ones** for the manager and the secretary. 推銷員為辦公室的每個人準備產品的樣品，也多準備幾份給經理和秘書。 Note ones 代替 samples of the product。 • To idle away **one's** time amounts to killing **oneself**. 虛度年華等於自殺。
one 可以代替前面的可數名詞，但沒有特定指某一對象	• I need a pencil. Can I borrow **one** from you? 我需要一枝鉛筆。我能跟你借一枝嗎？ Note one = a pencil，任何一枝鉛筆都行，未指定。 • These hats are way too expensive. Show me cheaper ones, please. 這些帽子實在太貴了。請給我看便宜些的。 Note ones = hats，任何便宜的帽子都行，未指定。
one 可用來泛指「人」	• One should keep one's promise. 任何人都應該守信。 • One cannot gain without pains. 不勞則無獲。

注意

比較 one 與 it：one 用來指不特定的對象，而 it 多用來指特定的對象。

• I need a backpack for my field trip. Could you lend me **one**? 我需要一個背包在校外教學時用。你能借我一個嗎？

Note one = a backpack，無特定對象。

• Here is your backpack. Thanks for lending **it** to me. 你的背包在這裡。謝謝你借我。

Note it = the backpack，有特定對象。

學習便利貼

a + N = one，無特定；
the + N = it，有特定。

2. other：表示「其他」，沒有特定對象，複數形為 others。若與冠詞 the 連用，為特定用法。other 的常見搭配用法，整理如下表：

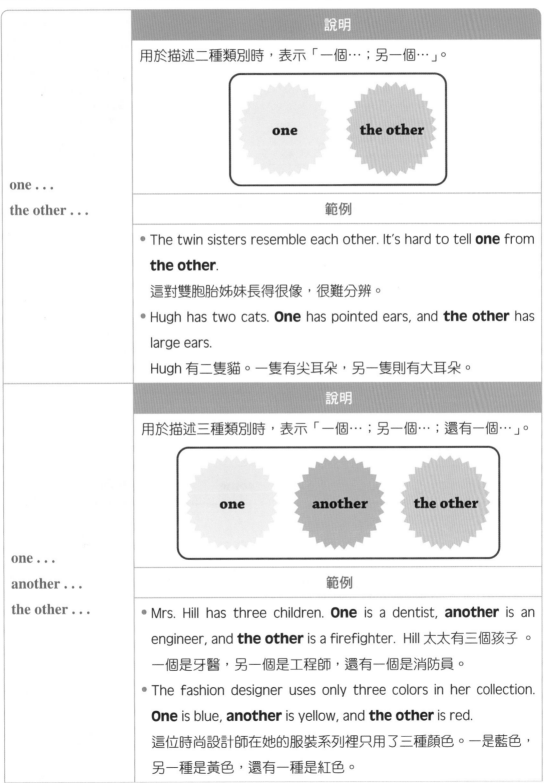

	說明	範例
one . . . the other . . .	用於描述二種類別時，表示「一個…；另一個…」。 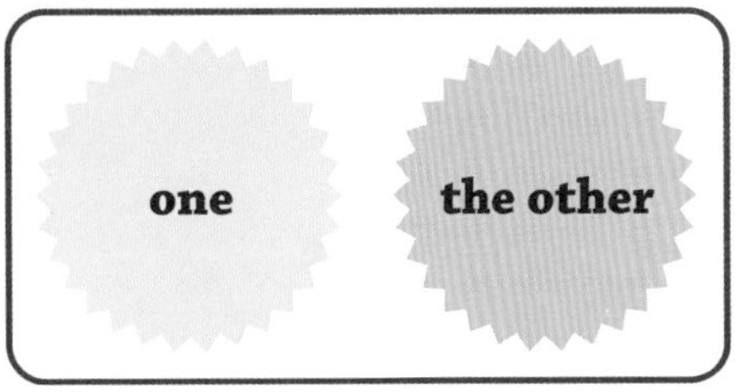	• The twin sisters resemble each other. It's hard to tell **one** from **the other**. 這對雙胞胎姊妹長得很像，很難分辨。 • Hugh has two cats. **One** has pointed ears, and **the other** has large ears. Hugh 有二隻貓。一隻有尖耳朵，另一隻則有大耳朵。
one . . . another . . . the other . . .	用於描述三種類別時，表示「一個…；另一個…；還有一個…」。 	• Mrs. Hill has three children. **One** is a dentist, **another** is an engineer, and **the other** is a firefighter. Hill 太太有三個孩子 。一個是牙醫，另一個是工程師，還有一個是消防員。 • The fashion designer uses only three colors in her collection. **One** is blue, **another** is yellow, and **the other** is red. 這位時尚設計師在她的服裝系列裡只用了三種顏色。一是藍色，另一種是黃色，還有一種是紅色。

<table>
<tr><td rowspan="4">some . . .
others . . .
(still others . . .)</td><td>說明</td></tr>
<tr><td>用於描述未指出範圍的群體裡的二種 (或三種) 類別，表示「有些…；有些… (還有些…)」。
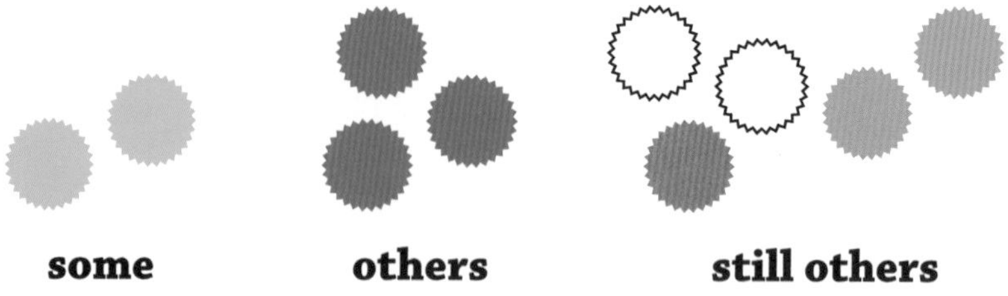
</td></tr>
<tr><td>範例</td></tr>
<tr><td>• Some people like seafood; others dislike it.
有些人喜歡海鮮，有些人不喜歡。
• Some enjoy summer, others like winter, and still others love spring.
有些人享受夏天，有些人喜歡冬天，還有些人則喜愛春天。</td></tr>
<tr><td rowspan="4">some . . .
the others . . .</td><td>說明</td></tr>
<tr><td>用於描述有範圍的群體裡的二種類別，表示「有些…；其他的…」。
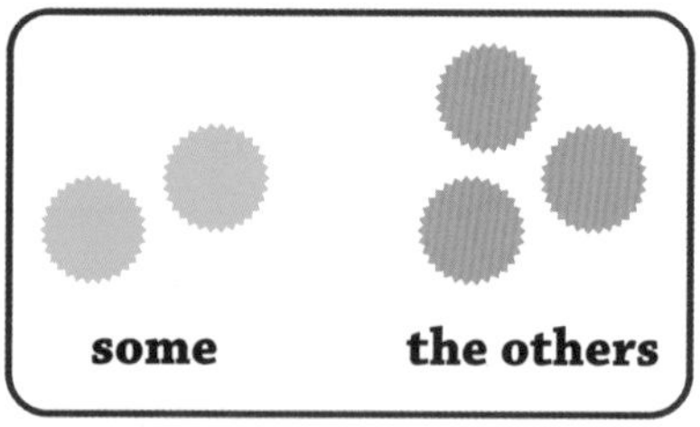
</td></tr>
<tr><td>範例</td></tr>
<tr><td>• Some of the people in this team are experts on marine animals; the others are researchers in the field of animal diseases.
這個團隊的人有些是海洋動物專家，其他是動物疾病領域的研究員。
• Some of my classmates are for the proposal, but the others are against it.
我的同學裡有些贊成這個提議，但是其他的人反對。</td></tr>
</table>

3. another

用法	範例
不定用法，表示「另一個」	• To say is **one** thing, but to do is **another**. 說是一回事，做是另一回事。 • Would you like to have **another** piece of pie? 你要不要再吃一片派？
表示「彼此」，**one another** 用於三者以上，兩者之間用 **each other**	• The Whites love **one another**. White 一家人相親相愛。 • Having no children, the old man and his wife depend on **each other**. 沒有子女，這老人和他的妻子彼此互相依靠。

Try it! 實力演練

I. 在空格中填入 one、it 或 the other

Anna: It's raining! I have no umbrella. Can I use [1]______ of yours?

Judy: No problem. There are two umbrellas over there. Just take [2]______.

Anna: Oh, this red [3]______ is beautiful. And [4]______ looks so familiar. Wait! [5]______ is mine! You borrowed [6]______ from me three months ago, remember?

Judy: Really? I am sorry for not having returned it. Please take [7]______ back.

II. 填入 one、other、another (請做適當變化，每格不限填一字)

1. The man keeps two dogs; ______ is white, and ______ is black.
2. There are three men chasing Wendy; ______ is handsome but poor, ______ is rich but ugly, and ______ is old but rich.
3. Some of my classmates are taking a rest, and ______ are having lunch.

3-3-2 some、any

1. some

用法	範例
表示數或量的「一些」，常用於肯定句	• The soup is hot, but Hank has drunk **some** of it. 湯很燙，但 Hank 喝了一些。 • **Some** of my postcards have been sent out. My friends will receive them soon. 我已經寄出一部份的明信片。我朋友們很快會收到。
表示「請求」或「邀請」時，可用於疑問句	• The potato salad looks delicious. May I have **some**? 這馬鈴薯沙拉看起來真美味。我可以吃一點嗎？ Note 疑問句，表示「請求」。 • I am making coffee. Would you like to have **some**? 我在煮咖啡。你要喝一些嗎？ Note 疑問句，表示「邀請」。

2. any

說明	範例
表示「任何」、「任一」	• Jeremy plays basketball better than **any** of his classmates. Jeremy 比任何同學都會打籃球。 • You can borrow **any** of the books on the shelf. 你可以借架上的任何一本書。
多用於疑問句、否定句	• Do you like **any** of these paintings? 你喜歡這些畫的任何一幅嗎？ • Tiffany didn't meet **any** of her classmates at the party. Tiffany 在派對上沒有遇到任何同學。

注意

1. any 也可作不定形容詞，後面接名詞，表示「任何的」，常用於否定句和疑問句中。用於肯定句時，強調「任何」的意思。
   - Ever since Linda moved, I have never heard **any** news about her.
     自從 Linda 搬家後，我就從未聽過任何關於她的消息。
   - Do you have **any** opinion regarding this proposal? 關於這個提議，你有任何看法嗎？

- If you have **any** question, don't hesitate to ask me.

  如果你有任何問題，不要猶豫，儘管問我。

  Note any 用於肯定句時，強調「任何」的意思。

2. not any + N 相當於 no + N。

- The poor beggar doesn't have **any** money.

  → The poor beggar has no money. 這可憐的乞丐沒有錢。

- Stingy Mike doesn't have **any** friends.

  → Stingy Mike has no friends. 吝嗇鬼 Mike 沒有朋友。

Try it! 實力演練

在空格中填入 some 或 any

Mr. Rex: Honey, I am hungry. I'd like to eat 1______ of the cake you made yesterday.

Mrs. Rex: Oh, we don't have 2______ left. Aren't we going out for dinner later?

Mr. Rex: Yeah, but I am very hungry now. Well, 3______ of the food will do.

Mrs. Rex: Then, how about 4______ of the chocolate? It is the only food I can find for you.

Mr. Rex: All right! Something is better than nothing.

3-3-3 all、each

1. all：不定代名詞 all 表示全部 (三者以上) 的人、事、物。

用法	範例
作主詞表示「人」時，視為複數，接複數動詞	• **All** are waiting for the president's final decision. 大家都在等待總裁的最後決定。 • **All** of my classmates have subscribed to English magazines. 我所有的同學都訂閱英文雜誌。
作主詞表示「事物」時，視為單數，接單數動詞	• **All** is well with us. 我們一切安好。 • **All** the researcher has to do is concentrate on his study. 這研究員必須做的就是專注於他的研究。

❶ 表示「事物」時，可搭配句型：All + S + V + is + V . . .。	• **All** the actor has to do is memorize the lines and prepare for the rehearsal. 這演員必須做的就是背台詞和準備排演。
用於否定句時，表示部分否定	• **All** of the rich men are not happy. 並非所有的富人都快樂。 → Some of the rich men are happy, but the others are not. • The singer didn't answer **all** of the letters from her fans. 這位歌手並沒有回覆所有歌迷的信。 → The singer answered only some of the letters from her fans.

注意

all 也可以作**不定形容詞**，後面接**名詞**，表示「所有的」。

• **All** the students are looking forward to the field trip. 所有的學生都在期待戶外教學。

2. each

用法	範例
表示「各個」，強調個別成員，接單數動詞	• **Each** of the club members has received a warm welcome. 每個俱樂部會員都受到熱烈的歡迎。 • Everyone is unique. **Each** has his or her own style. 每個人都很獨特，有自己的風格。

注意

each 也可以作**不定形容詞**，後面接**名詞**，表示「每個⋯」。

• **Each** applicant for the job has to fill in the form. 每個應徵此工作者都必須填寫表格。

3-3-4 both、either、neither、none

1. both

用法	範例
用於二個對象時，表示「(兩者) 都⋯」，接複數名詞和複數動詞	• On second thought, **both** of the couple changed their minds. 進一步考慮後，這對夫妻都改變了心意。 • **Both** of Pablo's parents encourage him to go abroad for further education. Pablo 的雙親都鼓勵他出國深造。

用於否定句時，表示部分否定	• **Both** of my brothers are not interested in martial arts. 並非我的兩個弟弟都對武術有興趣。 → One of my brothers likes martial arts, but the other doesn't.

注意

both 也可以作**不定形容詞**，後面接**名詞**，表示「兩個…(都)」。

• **Both** novels of this young writer are listed as best-sellers.
這年輕作家的二本小說都被列為暢銷書。

2. either

用法	範例
用於二個對象時，表示「(兩者中的) 任何一個」，沒有特定指示對象，接單數動詞	• The street lights will be mounted on **either** side of the road. 路燈會被設置在路的其中一邊。 • **Either** of my parents will attend my graduation ceremony. 我的爸爸或媽媽會參加我的畢業典禮。
含 either 的否定句可形成全部否定	• We don't trust **either** of them. 我們不信任他們倆。 → We don't trust the two people. • The teacher isn't satisfied with **either** of the reports. 老師不滿意這兩份報告。 → The teacher isn't satisfied with the two reports.

3. neither

用法	範例
描述二個對象，表示「兩者皆否」，表全部否定，接單數動詞	• **Neither** of Mr. and Mrs. Davis is going to attend the fundraising event. Davis 夫婦都不會參加這次的募款活動。 → Mr. Davis isn't going to attend the event, and Mrs. Davis isn't, either. • **Neither** of the invitations was accepted by the famous model. 這兩個邀請都未被這位名模接受。 → Either of the invitations was not accepted by the famous model.

4. none

用法	範例
表示「一點也沒有」，相當於 **not any** 或 **nothing**	• I wanted to have some more cookies, but **none** was left. 我想再吃些餅乾，可是一點也沒剩。 • It's **none** of your business! 你少管閒事！
用於三個或以上的對象時，表示「(三者或三者以上) 沒有任何…」，相當於 **not any** 或 **no one**	• Fortunately, **none** of the porcelain bowls was broken. 幸運的是，沒有瓷碗被打破。 • **None** of these boys can play badminton. 這些男孩中，沒有人會打羽球。
none 可以代替可數名詞，接單、複數動詞皆可；**none** 也可代替不可數名詞，接單數動詞	• **None** of the magazine(s) are/is interesting. 這些雜誌沒有一本是有趣的。 • **None** of the information is reliable. 這些資料沒有一筆是可靠的。

3-3-5 someone、somebody、anyone、anybody、something、anything、nobody、nothing

1. 不定代名詞 some、any、no 可以和 -one、-thing、-body 合併成「**複合不定代名詞**」，如 someone/somebody (某人)、something (某事)、anyone/anybody (任何人)、anything (任何事)、nobody (沒有人)、nothing (沒有事)，均作單數用。
2. 要修飾時，形容詞必須置於複合不定代名詞之後。

• Is Selina expecting **someone** important? Selina 在等某個重要的人嗎？

• I have **something** funny to tell you! 我有好笑的事要告訴你。

• Jerry is a big mouth. Don't tell him **anything** secret.
Jerry 是個大嘴巴。別告訴他任何秘密的事情。

• **Nothing** weird was found in this place. 這地方沒有古怪之處。

Try it! 實力演練

填入正確的不定代名詞

1. 你在派對上有遇到熟面孔嗎？

   Did you meet ______ ______ at the party?

2. 我有些重要的事情要告訴你。

   I have ______ ______ to tell you.

3. Luke 在等某個特別的人嗎？

   Is Luke waiting for ______ ______?

3–4 疑問代名詞

1. who、what、which 兼有疑問詞與代名詞功能，稱為疑問代名詞。
2. 疑問代名詞可作主詞、主詞補語或受詞，有格的變化。

	人			事物	
用法	姓名、身份、關係	職業	選擇	事物	選擇
主格	who	what	which	what	which
受格	whom		which	what	which

1. who、whom

用法	範例
用於詢問人的姓名、身份或關係	• A: **Who** is that basketball player? B: He is Jeremy Lin. A：那位籃球員是誰？ B：他是 Jeremy Lin。 Note 詢問姓名。 • A: **Who** is the man speaking on the stage? B: He is the president of the company. A：在台上講話的男人是誰？ B：他是公司的總裁。 Note 詢問身分。

	• A: **Whom** are these girls talking about? B: They are talking about their idol, a Korean actor. A：這些女孩們在談論誰？ Note 詢問關係。 B：她們在談論她們的偶像，是韓國演員。
疑問句中，疑問代名詞做主詞時，視為第三人稱單數，後面接單數動詞；若做主詞補語，則必須將動詞移至主詞之前，形成疑問句形式	• **Who** wants to go with us? S V Note who 當作主詞，後面加單數動詞。 誰想和我們一起去？ • **Who** can show us how to operate this machine? S V 誰能教我們如何操作這部機器？ • **Who** are those men? V S Note who 當作主詞補語。 那些男子是誰？
當作動詞或介系詞的受詞。當作介系詞的受詞時，可將介系詞移至疑問代名詞之前	• **Whom** did Frank invite? Frank 邀請了誰？ Note whom 為動詞 invite 的受詞。 • **Whom** did the secretary complain about? → About **whom** did the secretary complain? 秘書在抱怨誰？ Note whom 為介系詞 about 的受詞，可將 about 移至 whom 之前。 • **Whom** did Igor buy the gift for? → For **whom** did Igor buy the gift? Igor 買禮物給誰？ Note whom 當作 for 的受詞，可將 for 移至 whom 之前。
口語常用 who 代替 whom，但若疑問代名詞緊接於介系詞後，不可用 who 代替 whom	• **Who(m)** did you play baseball with? → With **whom** did you play baseball? 你和誰打棒球？

2. what

用法	範例
用於詢問事物、職業、身分	• A: **What** do you do for a living? A：你的職業是什麼？ B: I am a street artist. B：我是街頭藝術家。

	• A: **What** is this? A：這是什麼？ B: This is a reflector. B：這是個反射鏡。
當主詞或主詞補語。當主詞時，後接動詞；若當主詞補語，則須將動詞移至主詞之前，形成疑問句形式	• **What** is under the desk? (What = S, is = V) Note what 作主詞，後直接加動詞。 書桌下的東西是什麼？ • **What** happened to Nick last night? (What = S, happened = V) Note what 作主詞，後直接加動詞。 Nick 昨晚發生什麼事了？ • **What** is your favorite food? (is = V, your favorite food = S) Note what 作主詞補語。 你最喜歡的食物是什麼？
動詞或介系詞的受詞	• **What** did Nancy look up on the Internet? Nancy 在網路上搜尋什麼？ Note what 為動詞片語 look up 的受詞。 • **What** did you learn from the documentary film? 你從這部記錄片中學到了什麼？ Note what 為動詞 learn 的受詞。 • **What** does Alexis steep himself in? Alexis 沈浸在什麼事情中？ Note what 為介系詞 in 的受詞。

3. which

用法	範例
疑問代名詞 which 表示「哪個」	• **Which** is right, my answer or his answer? 我和他的答案，哪一個是對的？
當主詞或主詞補語。當主詞時，後接動詞；若當主詞補語，則須將動詞移至主詞之前，形成疑問句形式	• **Which** is more important to you, health or wealth? (Which = S, is = V) 健康和財富對你來說哪個比較重要？ Note which 作主詞，後面直接加動詞。 • **Which** looks better on me, the red dress or the pink one? (Which = S, looks = V) 我穿哪一件洋裝比較好看，紅色或粉色？ Note which 作主詞，後面直接加動詞。 • **Which** is Carol's sister? (is = V, Carol's sister = S) Note which 作主詞補語。 哪一個是 Carol 的妹妹？

	• **Which** is Stuart's smartphone? (V: is; S: Stuart's smartphone) Note which 作主詞補語。 Stuart 的智慧型手機是哪一隻？
動詞或介系詞的受詞	• **Which** does Henry prefer, mocha or cappuccino? Henry 比較喜歡摩卡還是卡布奇諾？ Note which 為動詞 prefer 的受詞。 • **Which** of these theme parks have you visited? 這些主題公園中，你去過哪些？ Note which 為動詞 visit 的受詞。 • **Which** of the animations are you interested in? 這些動畫片中你對哪一部有興趣？ Note which 為介系詞 in 的受詞。 • **Which** is Whitley looking for, a stapler or a paper clip? Whitley 在找什麼，釘書機或迴紋針？ Note which 為介系詞 for 的受詞。

Try it! 實力演練

I. 填入合適的疑問代名詞 (who、whom、what 或 which)

1. ______ ate my cookies? They were here five minutes ago!
2. ______ has made you gain so much weight over the past few weeks?
3. ______ of these purses did Mr. Chen choose for his wife?

II. 依據畫線部份，以疑問代名詞造原問句

1. Helen lent <u>her electronic dictionary</u> to her classmate.

____

2. The boy asked <u>his father</u> about the history of the church.

____

3. <u>The environmental pollution</u> had made the residents suffer from various diseases.

____

Chapter

4 助動詞

助動詞 (auxiliary) 可用來幫助主動詞表示時態、語態、語氣、疑問或否定等。

4-1 助動詞

1. 有些助動詞本身沒有意思，功能在**幫助**主動詞構成時態、語態、語氣、疑問或否定句。
2. 此類的助動詞有 be、do、have 等，可置於句首形成疑問句，加上 not 可形成否定句。

1. be (am, are, is, was, were, been)。由於使用頻率高，故講解時常會被統稱為「be 動詞」。

用法	範例
與現在分詞構成進行式： **be + V-ing**	• [肯定] These athletes **are practicing** hard for the Universiade. 這些運動員正在為世大運努力練習。 • [疑問] **Is** the novelist **looking** for inspiration for her new novel? 這小說家正在為新小說找靈感嗎？ • [否定] Janet **is not making** doughnuts in the kitchen, but cooking noodles. Janet 並非在廚房做甜甜圈，而是煮麵。
與過去分詞構成被動語態： **be + p.p.**	• [肯定] This temple **was built** a hundred years ago. 這座廟建於一百年前。 • [疑問] **Are** the strict laws **enacted** to prevent super-skinny models? 這些嚴格的法律是被制定來防止超瘦模特兒嗎？ • [否定] These books **are not written** in Spanish. 這些書不是用西班牙文寫的。

2. do/does/did

用法	範例
形成疑問句： **do/does/did** 置於句首，後接原形動詞	• **Do** you have the habit of drinking morning coffee? 你有在早上喝咖啡的習慣嗎？ • **Does** Emma enjoy watching Korean dramas? Emma 喜歡看韓劇嗎？ • **Did** the rescue team find the people trapped in the mountains? 搜救隊找到困在山裡的人了嗎？
形成否定句： **do/does/did** 後加上 **not**，再接原形動詞	• These boys **don't** have any interest in extreme sports. 這些男孩對極限運動絲毫不感興趣。 • Timothy has a day off, so he **doesn't** need to get up early today. Timothy 休假一天，所以今天不用早起。 • To Miranda's disappointment, she **didn't** find her lost bike. 讓 Miranda 失望的是，她沒找到遺失的腳踏車。
可以用來代替前面提過的動詞 (片語)，以避免重複	• A: **Do** the residents of this community support this policy? B: Yes, they **do**. Note do = support this policy A：這個社區的居民支持這政策嗎？ B：是的，他們支持。 • A: **Does** Little Johnny enjoy bubble baths? B: Yes, he **does**. Note does = like bubble baths A：小 Johnny 喜歡泡泡浴嗎？ B：是的，他喜歡。
加在肯定句中的原形動詞前，以加強語氣	• We **do** think Ethan is suitable for this position. 我們真的認為 Ethan 很適合這個職位。 • Ellen **does** look elegant in that beautiful dress. Ellen 穿那件漂亮的洋裝看起來很優雅。 • Mr. Robinson **did** realize the importance of health after he got ill. Robinson 先生生病後真的了解健康的重要性。

3. have/has/had

用法	範例
與過去分詞構成完成式：**have + p.p.**	• [肯定] Since Ellen got a new smartphone, she **had been** addicted to it until her parents forbade her overuse of it. 自從 Ellen 拿到新智慧型手機就很沈迷，直到爸媽出面禁止她過度使用。 • [疑問] **Has** this applicant for the scholarship **filled** in the forms? 這個獎學金申請者都填表格了嗎？ • [否定] Mr. and Mrs. Stone **have not sold** their house; they will wait for a good deal. Stone 夫婦還沒賣掉房子；他們要等好價錢。
與「been + 現在分詞」構成完成進行式：**have + been + V-ing**	• [肯定] These players **have been practicing** without taking a rest. 這些球員一直不眠不休地練習。 • [疑問] **Has** this restaurant been receiving customer complaints about their food? 這間餐廳一直收到關於食物的客訴嗎？ • [否定] They **have not been playing** the ukulele. 他們並沒一直在彈烏克麗麗。
與「been + 過去分詞」構成完成式被動語態：**have + been + p.p.**	• [肯定] The car **has been towed** away by the police. 車子已經被警察拖走了。 • [疑問] **Have** the puzzles **been solved**? 謎題被解開了嗎？ • [否定] The burglars **have not been arrested**. They are still at large. 竊賊還沒被逮捕。他們仍然在逃。

Try it! 實力演練

I. 填空 (填入正確的助動詞)

1. Sam ______ listening to music, and his brothers ______ reading books.
2. A: ______ smoking have a bad influence on people's health?
   B: Yes, it ______.
3. All the students ______ finished their tests, so they may leave now.

II. 句子改寫

1. The baby is sleeping soundly in the room. (改疑問句)

____

2. The typhoon caused serious damage to the village. (改否定句)

____

3. The man's speech has moved all the audience. (改疑問句)

____

4-2 情態助動詞

1. 情態助動詞本身具有意義，但不可單獨使用，必須與一般動詞連用。
2. 情態助動詞可以置於句首形成疑問句，加上 not 則形成否定句，後面必須接原形動詞 (VR)。

1. can/could

用法	範例
描述有…能力	• The boy has a talent for music. He **can** play several instruments. 那男孩有音樂的天分。他會彈奏好幾種樂器。 • It is common that people in this country **can** speak three languages. 這國家的人民通常會說三種語言。
表示請求或許可	• **Can** I borrow your iPad? 我可以借你的 iPad 嗎？ • **Can** you turn down the music? 你可以把音樂音量轉小嗎？ • **Could** you give me a hand? 你能幫我個忙嗎？ ❗ could 語氣較 can 委婉。 • You **can** watch the basketball game after you finish your homework. 你寫完功課後可以看籃球賽。
描述可能性	• Too much fast food **can** take a serious toll on your health. 吃太多速食可能有害健康。 • **Can** it be true? 這可能是真的嗎？

2. will/would

用法	範例
表示未來	• Helena **will** celebrate her 20th birthday tomorrow. Helena 明天要慶祝二十歲生日。 • Sophia **will** not go to the movies with us tonight. Sophia 今晚不會和我們去看電影。 • No one ever dreamed that Peter **would** win the game. 大家作夢也沒想到 Peter 會贏得比賽。 • Sean said he **would** show up at the party, but he didn't. Sean 說他會出席這場派對，但他沒有。
表達請求或邀請	• **Will** you close the window, please? 你可以關上窗戶嗎？ • **Would** you do me a favor? 你能幫我一個忙嗎？ ❶ would 語氣較 will 委婉、禮貌。 • **Would** you like to have a cup of coffee? 你要來杯咖啡嗎？

3. should

用法	範例
描述義務、應該做某事	• Derek **should** study harder in order not to fail the exams. Derek 應該要更用功才不會被當。 • You **should** take out the garbage instead of leaving it here. 你應該把垃圾拿出去丟，而不是放在這裡。
表達驚訝	• I can't believe that Patricia **should** break up with her boyfriend. 我不敢相信 Patricia 竟然和男友分手。 • We are surprised that Amy **should** say such words to hurt her parents. 我們很訝異 Amy 竟然會說出這樣的話讓父母傷心。
描述預期或推測	• According to the weather forecast, it **should** be a windy and rainy weekend. 根據氣象預報，這周末預計有強風大雨。 • The show **should** begin in 3 minutes. 表演應於三分鐘後開始。

4. must

用法	範例
描述「必須做某事」，相當於 have to	• The news **must** be announced as soon as possible. 這則消息必須盡快發布。 • The employees **must** do as they are told. 員工們必須照著他們被吩咐的去做。 • They **had to** postpone the game due to the heavy rain. 因豪雨，他們得將比賽延期。 ❶ must 無過去式，過去式用 had to。 • After the factory is closed down, the workers **will have to** find new jobs. 工廠關閉後，工人們將必須另謀高就。 ❶ must 無未來式，未來式用 will have to。
詢問意圖	• A: **Must** I do it right now? A：我現在必須動手做嗎？ B: Yes, you **must**. B：是的，必須。 ❶ 否定回答：No, you don't have/need to. 或者 No, you needn't.。
表達強烈禁止	• You **must** not smoke here. 此處禁止吸煙。 ❶ must 的否定形表示強烈禁止。 • You **must** not leave the door open. 你不可以讓門開著。
表達可能性極高的推測	• Naomi has worked for twelve hours. She **must** be tired. Naomi 已經工作十二小時了。她一定很累。

5. may/might

用法	範例
表達推測	• The cause of this accident **may** never be found. 這件意外的起因可能永遠不會被發現。 • The traffic is heavy. We **might** be late for work. 交通壅塞。我們上班可能遲到。 ❶ might 的可能性比 may 小。
表達請求或許可	• A: **May** I come in? A：我可以進來嗎？ B: Yes, you may. B：可以。 ❶ 否定用 No, you may not.。 • **Might** I borrow your bike? 我可以跟你借腳踏車嗎？ ❶ might 語氣較委婉。
表達祝福	• **May** God bless you! 願上帝保佑你！

Try it! 實力演練

I. 選擇

_____ 1. _____ I borrow your electronic dictionary?
(A) Would (B) May (C) Will (D) Should

_____ 2. _____ you turn on the light for me? I can't see anything!
(A) Might (B) Should (C) Must (D) Could

_____ 3. We are surprised that our principal _____ decide to retire.
(A) may (B) will (C) could (D) should

II. 填空 (根據上下文，填入正確的情態助動詞)

1. It is strange that Betty _____ believe Frank. He is not an honest man.
2. You _____ not talk in class.
3. You _____ get up earlier, so you _____ catch the first train.

4–3 情態助動詞的特殊用法

1. 情態助動詞可以應用在表示推測的句型中。
2. 表示「推測」時，可能性的高低：must > can/may > could/might。

1. 對現在事實的推測：以「助動詞 + 原形動詞」表示。

	說明	意義
肯定	must + V	一定
	can/may + V	可能
	could/might + V	也許

	說明	意義
否定	can't/cannot + V	絕不可能
	may + not + V	可能不會
	could/might + not + V	不太可能

- Judging from the reports, the police **may have** the evidence.
  從報導來看，警方很可能握有證據。 Note 可能性高。

- The boxers have not drunk anything since the competitive game begun. They **must be** very thirsty.
  自從激烈的比賽開始後，二位拳擊手都還沒喝東西。他們現在一定很渴。

學習便利貼
以 must 表示推測時，其否定形為 can't。must not 為強烈禁止之意。

- Jake has been complaining about his work, saying that he **might quit** the job, but I don't think so.
  Jake 一直在抱怨他的工作，說他可能會辭職，但我不這麼認為。 Note 可能性低。
- Steve is a stingy person; he **can't be** willing to donate money to the orphanage. Steve 很吝嗇；他不可能願意捐錢給孤兒院。
- Vicky **cannot be** the jackpot winner. She didn't even buy any lottery ticket.
  Vicky 不可能是頭彩得主。她連一張彩券都沒買。

2. 對過去事實的推測：以「助動詞 + have + p.p.」表示。

	說明	意義
肯定	must + have p.p.	一定
	may + have p.p.	可能
	could/might + have p.p.	也許

	說明	意義
否定	can't/cannot + have p.p.	絕不可能
	may + not + have p.p.	可能不會
	could/might + not + have p.p.	不太可能

- The ground is wet. It **must have rained** just now.
  地上是濕的。剛剛一定下過雨。
- Wesley has dark circles under his eyes; he **may have stayed** up last night.
  Wesley 有黑眼圈；他很可能昨晚熬夜。
- I don't believe what you said. Ted **cannot have been** so rude.
  我不相信你說的。Ted 不可能這麼沒禮貌。
- Mark **cannot have persuaded** his mother into giving him more allowance.
  Mark 不可能說服媽媽多給他點零用錢。

注意

情態助動詞可搭配假設語氣的句型 (would/should/could/might + have + p.p.) 表示「本來會發生或原本該做的事，事實上卻沒有」。

- The speaker **would have arrived** on time, but he was late because of the delayed flight.
  這演講者本來會準時到達，但是因為班機延誤，所以遲到了。

- George and his friends **should have made** an appointment first. The restaurant is full now. George 和他朋友應該先預約的。餐廳現在客滿。
- That was a close call! You **might have been** injured! 真是千鈞一髮！你本來可能受傷的！

Try it! 實力演練

I. 選擇

_____ 1. There are too many spelling mistakes in this report. You _____ more careful while typing it.

(A) must have been (B) may be

(C) should have been (D) might be

_____ 2. Judy _____ where to buy the cheapest shoes since she is a smart shopper.

(A) would know (B) must know

(C) can know (D) may have known

_____ 3. That woman with blue eyes and blonde hair _____ a Taiwanese.

(A) could have been (B) must have been

(C) shouldn't be (D) can't be

II. 翻譯

1. 那些選手剛剛打敗對手。他們現在一定很興奮。

Those players just beat their rivals. They ____________________ thrilled now.

2. 我把袋子放在客廳的角落，但是它不見了。一定有人拿走了。

I left my bag in the corner of the living room, but it's gone now. Someone ____________________ it!

3. Grace 原本可以參加這個比賽，但她扭傷腳了。

Grace ____________________ the tournament, but she sprained her ankle.

Notes

Chapter

5 動詞的時態

時態表示在不同時間點的動作或狀態，須搭配相對應的動詞變化，分為現在式、過去式與未來式。

5-1 動詞時態

1. 依動作發生的**時間**不同，動詞可分為現在、過去和未來三種時態，依動作的**狀態**可分為簡單式、進行式、完成式和完成進行式。
2. 在使用時，動詞必須和主詞與時態相對應。

時間 / 狀態	現在	過去	未來
簡單式	VR/V-s/V-es	V-ed	will + VR
進行式	am/are/is + V-ing	was/were + V-ing	will + be + V-ing
完成式	have/has + p.p.	had + p.p.	will + have + p.p.
完成進行式	have/has + been + V-ing	had + been + V-ing	will + have + been + V-ing

1. 簡單式

- [現在] To protect endangered animals, many people **support** the conservation projects.
  為了保護瀕臨絕種的動物，許多人支持保育計畫。
- [過去] Olivia **participated** in a TED Talk last week and **gained** a new insight into the problems of female education.
  Olivia 上週參加一場 TED 演講，對女性教育問題有了深入的瞭解。
- [未來] Stuart and I **will watch** a musical at National Concert Hall tonight.
  我和 Stuart 今晚要去國家音樂廳欣賞一場音樂劇。

2. 進行式

- [現在] The committee **is having** a serious discussion on this issue.
  委員會正嚴肅地討論這個議題。
- [過去] Ellen **was talking** on the phone when the earthquake happened.
  當地震發生時，Ellen 正在講電話。
- [未來] Fannie and her husband will fly to France today, and they **will be visiting** Paris tomorrow morning.
  Fannie 和丈夫今天將飛往法國，明早將會參觀巴黎。

3. 完成式

- [現在] The Pattersons **have lived** in the countryside since 2000.
  從 2000 年開始，Patterson 一家人就住在鄉下了。
- [過去] Before Charlotte got home, her husband **had had** the dinner ready.
  在 Charlotte 回到家之前，她丈夫已經準備好晚餐。
- [未來] By the end of the year, the government **will have completed** the new exhibition hall. 在年底之前，政府將會完成新的展覽館。

4. 完成進行式

- [現在] Sebastian **has been learning** German for five years.
  Sebastian 已經學五年的德文了。
- [過去] Cinderella **had been working** at the production company before she got married. 在結婚之前，Cinderella 一直都在這家製作公司工作。
- [未來] By next month, my sister **will have been living** in Tainan for ten years. 到下個月，我妹妹就將已經在臺南住十年了。

5-2 簡單式

1. 依據動作發生的**時間**，簡單式分為現在簡單式、過去簡單式、未來簡單式。
2. 現在簡單式表示「現在的事實與狀態」、「格言或真理」或「規律的習慣」。
3. 過去簡單式表示「在過去所發生的事情」。
4. 未來簡單式表示「未來將發生的事情」。

5-2-1 現在簡單式

1. 動詞變化：現在簡單式的動詞必須依照**人稱**及**單複數**加以變化。

主詞 / 動詞	第一人稱單數	第二人稱單數與複數名詞	第三人稱單數
be 動詞	am	are	is
一般動詞	VR	VR	V-s/V-es
助動詞	do	do	does

2. 一般動詞的變化：第三人稱單數變化必須在字尾加上 -s 或 -es。

條件	變化	範例
一般規則	字尾加 -s	• love → loves • appear → appears • explore → explores • control → controls • maintain → maintains
字尾為 -s、-x、-o、-sh、-ch、-z	字尾加 -es	• kiss → kisses • establish → establishes • mix → mixes • reach → reaches • go → goes • buzz → buzzes
字尾為 -y：(1) 子音 + -y	去 y 加 -ies	• study → studies • cry → cries • rely → relies • clarify → clarifies • exemplify → exemplifies
(2) 母音 + -y	字尾加 -s	• play → plays • pray → prays • repay → repays
特殊變化		• have → has

3. 現在簡單式的主要用法，整理如下：

用法	範例
表示現在的事實與狀態	• [事實] Taiwan **is** an island. 臺灣是座島嶼。 • [狀態] It **is** cloudy and windy today. 今天多雲又有風。

表示格言、恆久不變的真理或事實	• [格言] Birds of a feather **flock** together. 【諺】物以類聚。 • [不變事實] The sun **rises** in the east and **sets** in the west. 太陽從東邊升起，西邊落下。
表示規律、持續的日常行為	• Ken **brushes** his teeth before going to bed. Ken 睡前刷牙。 • Ian **prefers** spaghetti to sushi. Ian 喜歡義大利麵勝於壽司。 • **Does** your brother listen to rock'n'roll? 你弟弟聽搖滾樂嗎？
表示習慣性動作，常與頻率副詞或時間副詞連用，如 **always**、**usually**、**sometimes**、**often**、**rarely**、**seldom**、**every day/year** 等	• Oscar is a procrastinator, who **is** often late for work. Oscar 習慣拖延，經常上班遲到。 • My family sometimes **dine** in exotic restaurants. 我家人有時到異國餐廳用餐。 • My neighbor **goes** cycling every weekend. 我鄰居每個週末都去騎自行車。 • Lydia is a phubber. She **spends** much time using her smartphone every day. Lydia 是低頭族。她每天花很多時間玩手機。

Try it! 實力演練

I. 填空 (依提示字填入正確動詞形式)

1. The first class of most students in Taiwan ______ (start) at 8:10 a.m.
2. Maria always ______ (wash) her hands before cooking meals.
3. The young man ______ (rely) much on his parents both mentally and financially.

II. 引導式翻譯

1. Isabella 平均每天花三小時練習打籃球。
   Isabella averagely ______ three hours practicing basketball every day.
2. 這老婦人的視力不好；要開始閱讀前，她都必須戴上眼鏡。
   The old lady ______ poor eyesight; she always ______ to put on her glasses before she ______ to read.
3. A：Carol 搭公車上學嗎？ B：不，她騎腳踏車上學。
   A: ______ Carol go to school by bus? B: No, she ______ by bike.

5-2-2 過去簡單式

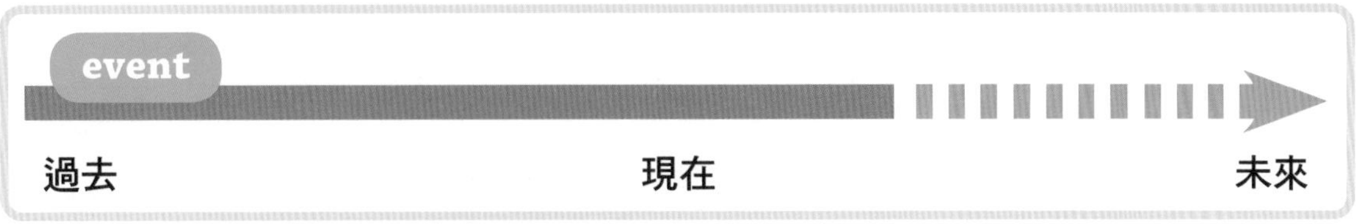

1. 動詞變化：過去簡單式表示過去事實、狀態、習慣與動作，動詞為過去式。

動詞＼人稱	第一人稱	第二人稱	第三人稱
be 動詞	was	were	was
一般動詞	V-ed		
助動詞	did		

2. 過去式動詞的變化

條件	變化	範例	
一般規則	字尾加 -ed	• look → looked • help → helped	• earn → earned • relax → relaxed
字尾為 -e	字尾加 -d	• love → loved • care → cared	• move → moved • memorize → memorized
字尾為 -y： (1) 子音 + -y	字尾去 y，加 -ied	• try → tried • study → studied	• cry → cried • occupy → occupied
(2) 母音 + -y	字尾加 -ed	• pray → prayed	• destroy → destroyed
「短母音 + 單子音」結尾的單音節動詞	重複字尾加 -ed	• stop → stopped • drop → dropped • beg → begged	• shop → shopped • nag → nagged
「短母音 + 單子音」或 [ɝ] 結尾，且重音在最後音節的雙音節動詞	重複字尾加 -ed	• admit → admitted • omit → omitted • transmit → transmitted	• prefer → preferred • transfer → transferred • occur → occurred

字尾為 -c，且發音為 [k]	字尾加 -ked	• picnic → picnic**ked** • panic → panic**ked**
特殊變化(需特別背誦)	不規則變化	• have → had • go → went • do → did • say → said • tell → told • take → took • hear → heard • catch → caught • write → wrote
	和原形動詞一樣	• cut → cut • hit → hit • put → put • hurt → hurt • cost → cost • read → read • spread → spread
	有兩種形式	• learn → learned/learnt • burn → burned/burnt • smell → smelled/smelt

3. 過去簡單式的主要用法，整理如下：

用法	範例
表示「過去的事實、狀態與動作」，常與 **ago**、**just now** (剛剛)、**before**、**yesterday**、**last night/year**、**this morning** 等副詞連用	• [過去事實] A strong typhoon **hit** Taiwan last week. 上週，一個強颱襲臺。 • [過去狀態] Most athletes **were** tired out after the exciting game. 在刺激的比賽後，大部分的運動員都累癱了。 • [過去動作] Celine **turned** down Larry's invitation three days ago. 三天前，Celine 婉拒了 Larry 的邀請。
used to 可以用來表示「過去的習慣」或「以前曾經做的動作或維持的狀態」，後接原形動詞，意為「以前常常」或「以前曾經」	• Before Cynthia got sick, she **used to** practice yoga. Cynthia 生病前，她以前常常練習瑜珈。 • Asher **used to** drink tea in the morning, but now he drinks coffee instead. Asher 以前早上常常喝茶，但是現在改喝咖啡。 • Janet **used to** be a ballet dancer. Janet 以前曾經是芭蕾舞者。

注意

比較下列用法：

1. used to + VR，表示「過去常常…」或「以前曾經」，例如：
   - The naughty boy **used to** play tricks on others. 這頑皮的男孩以前常對別人惡作劇。
   - Shelly **used to** work in Taipei, but now she works in Changhua.
     Shelly 以前在臺北工作，現在則是在彰化。
2. be used to + VR，表示「被用來…」，例如：
   - Clocks **are used to** tell time. 時鐘被用來報時。
   - These old glass jars **are used to** store homemade pickles.
     這些舊玻璃罐被用來保存自製泡菜。
3. be/get used to + V-ing，表示「習慣於…」，例如：
   - Our new neighbor is an American; he **is** not **used to** eating Chinese food.
     我們的新鄰居是美國人；他不習慣吃中國菜。
   - Joe moved to India last month, and he **got used to** living there already.
     Joe 上個月才剛搬到印度，現在已經習慣那邊的生活了。

Try it! 實力演練

填入正確的動詞時態

1. The professor found that there ______ (be) several mistakes in this report.
2. Mr. Parson ______ (get) off work on time every day, because he ______ (have) to pick up his children.
3. Levi ______ (use) to burn the midnight oil, but now he ______ (go) to bed early.
4. The superstar ______ (arrive) at the airport just now.
5. After Eric ______ (put) away his coat, he ______ (sit) down to watch TV.

5-2-3 未來簡單式

未來簡單式由 **will + VR** 構成。

未來簡單式的主要用法，整理如下：

用法	範例
表示未來將發生的動作或狀況，常與表未來的時間副詞連用，如 **tomorrow**、**next week/month**、**in a few days/months**、**the day after tomorrow** 等	• According to the weather forecast, it **will be** sunny tomorrow. 根據氣象預報，明天會是晴天。 • Tonight Cathy **will celebrate** her 17th birthday with her friends. 今晚 Cathy 將會和朋友一起慶祝 17 歲生日。 • Due to maintenance, there **will be** no shuttle bus to the zoo this weekend. 因維修問題，這週末將沒有往動物園的接駁公車。 • Thomas **will graduate** from high school next year. Thomas 明年將從高中畢業。
副詞子句中用現在式代替未來式	• After the manager comes to the office this morning, we **will have** a meeting. 當經理今早到辦公室後，我們將會開會。 ❶ 現在式 comes 代替未來式。 • The children **will clean** up their room before their father returns home this evening. 孩子們會在傍晚爸爸回家前把房間整理乾淨。
動詞如 **come**、**go**、**leave**、**arrive**、**visit** 等，可用進行式來表示未來即將發生的動作	• Hurry up! The train **is leaving** in 10 minutes. → Hurry up! The train **will leave** in 10 minutes. 快點！火車將在十分鐘後出發。 • Uncle Sam **is visiting** us this weekend. → Uncle Sam **will visit** us this weekend. Sam 叔叔這個週末要來拜訪我們。

❶ 注意

要表示「未來的計畫」或「未來的預測」也可用 **be + going to + VR**。

- Kate **is going to finish** her paper this week. Kate 將在這星期完成論文。
- It is cloudy and windy. I think **it is going to rain**. 現在雲多又刮風。我想不久會下雨。

Try it! 實力演練

I. 句子重組

1. go to/will/her hair/a hair salon/Maggie/this Saturday/to dye

____

2. piracy/the government/take action/to fight/will/against

____

II. 選擇

______ 1. The teacher ______ the complicated theory with illustration in the next class.

(A) explains (B) explained (C) will explain (D) has explained

______ 2. According to the weather forecast, there ______ light drizzle tomorrow.

(A) is (B) was (C) are (D) will be

______ 3. As soon as the guest professor ______ at the train station, we will drive him to our university.

(A) will arrive (B) arrives (C) arrived (D) has arrived

5-3 進行式

1. 依據動作發生的**時間**，進行式分為現在進行式、過去進行式、未來進行式。
2. 現在進行式表示「現在正在進行」、「即將發生」或「正在發展或變化」的動作。
3. 過去進行式表示「過去某時刻正在進行的動作」、「過去某動作發生時，正在進行的另一個動作」或「過去時間裡**同時進行**的二個動作」。
4. 未來進行式表示「未來某時間點將會正在進行的動作」、「未來某動作發生時，另一個將正在進行的動作」。

5-3-1 現在進行式

現在進行式是由 **am/are/is + V-ing** 構成，動詞為現在分詞 (V-ing)。

1. 動詞的現在分詞變化

條件	變化	範例
一般規則	字尾加 -ing	• spend → spend**ing** • relax → relax**ing** • deliver → deliver**ing** • perform → perform**ing**
字尾為不發音的 -e	字尾去 e 加 -ing	• drive → driv**ing** • write → writ**ing** • tease → teas**ing** • improve → improv**ing** • manufacture → manufactur**ing**
「短母音 + 子音」結構結尾的單音節動詞	重複字尾加 -ing	• run → run**ning** • shop → shop**ping** • beg → beg**ging** • quit → quit**ting**
結尾是「短母音 + 子音」結構、重音在最後音節的雙音節動詞	重複字尾加 -ing	• begin → begin**ning** • admit → admit**ting** • occur → occur**ring** • transmit → transmit**ting** (傳送)
少數以 -ie 結尾的動詞	字尾去 ie 加 -ying	• die → d**ying** • lie → l**ying** • tie → t**ying**
字尾為 -c，且發音為 [k]	字尾加 -king	• picnic → picnic**king** • panic → panic**king**

2. 現在進行式的主要用法，整理如下：

用法	範例
表示正在進行的動作，常與 **now**、**at this moment** 等字連用	• The salesman **is explaining** how to use the washing machine. 推銷員正在解釋如何使用洗衣機。 • The medical experts **are doing** some research on how to treat lung cancer. 這些醫學專家正在研究如何治療肺癌。
表示即將發生的動作，多用表來去之意的動詞 (如 **come**、**go**、**leave** 等)	• The train **is leaving** in five minutes. 火車五分鐘後就要駛離。 • Adam **is coming** to visit me tomorrow. Adam 明天要來拜訪我。

表示正在發展或變化的動作	• The professor **is writing** a new book about Roman history. 這位教授正在寫一本有關羅馬歷史的新書。
常與 **"Look!"**、**"Listen!"** 連用，表示現在正在發生的動作	• Look! The bus **is coming**! 瞧！公車來了！ • Listen! A bird **is chirping**! 聽！鳥兒在歌唱！
表示「逐漸…，越來越…」，動詞多用 **get**、**become**、**turn** 等	• As summer approaches, the weather **is getting** hotter and hotter. 隨著夏天接近，天氣越來越熱了。 • Alice **is becoming** mature. Alice 漸漸變得成熟了。 • The maple leaves **are turning** red. 楓葉逐漸轉紅。

注意

1. 感官動詞 (see 、 smell) 或表示下列意義的字通常不用進行式 ， 如 「心理狀態」 (know 、 understand)、「擁有」(have、belong、own)、「喜惡」(like、love、hate)、「存在」(exist)、「需求」(need、want、lack)、「記憶」(remember、forget)。
   - [O] The smart girl **knows** how to solve the riddle.
     [X] The smart girl is knowing how to solve the riddle.
     這聰明的女孩知道如何解這個謎語。
   - [O] Some people **like** to read tabloid newspapers.
     [X] Some people are liking to read tabloid newspapers.
     有些人喜歡讀通俗小報。
2. 上述的 have、see 有其他意思時，可以用進行式。
   - Hank is having dinner with his family.
     Hank 正在和家人共進晚餐。 Note have 表示「吃」。
   - Mr. Trump is seeing an important client.
     Trump 先生正在和一個重要的客戶會面。 Note see 表示「會面」。

Try it! 實力演練

I. 填空 (依提示字填入正確動詞形式，不限填一字)

1. Look! Some doves ______________________ (fly) toward us!
2. It's sunny today. Many people ______________________ (lie) on the grass to enjoy the sunshine and breeze.

3. Jasper and his wife ______________ (shop) for groceries in the supermarket right now.

II. 選擇

_____ 1. My classmates _____ baseball on the field now.

(A) play (B) plays (C) are playing (D) is playing

_____ 2. The bus _____ in ten minutes.

(A) comes (B) is coming (C) has come (D) came

_____ 3. Penelope _____ steak for dinner right now. She _____ steak very much.

(A) has; likes (B) has; liking

(C) is having; is liking (D) is having; likes

5-3-2 過去進行式

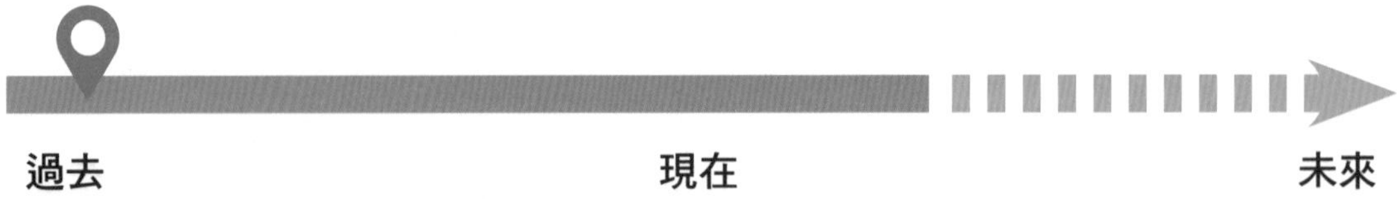

過去進行式由 **was/were + V-ing** 構成。

過去進行式的主要用法，整理如下：

說明	範例
表示過去某時刻正在進行的動作 ❶ 在此用法中，會明確指出過去動作發生的時間。	• At 6 p.m. yesterday, Samantha **was watching** a clip from the new Leonardo DiCaprio movie. 昨晚六點時，Samantha 正在看 Leonardo DiCaprio 新電影的短片。 • I **was having** a picnic with my family at noon yesterday. 昨天中午，我正和家人一起野餐。
表示過去某一動作發生時，正在進行的另一個動作	• When the clock struck nine, Toby **was listening** to the radio. 當九點鐘響時，Toby 正在聽廣播。 • I **was taking** a shower when the phone rang. 電話響時，我正在洗澡。 ❶ 突發的動作使用過去簡單式，正在進行的動作用過去進行式。

表示在過去時間裡同時進行的二個動作，常與連接詞 **while**、**when** 連用	• While Cathy **was doing** her homework, her brother **was watching** TV. 當 Cathy 正在做功課時，她弟弟正在看電視。 • Fred **was brushing** his teeth while his wife **was drying** her hair. 當 Fred 在刷牙時，他老婆正在吹乾頭髮。 ❶ 二個動作都使用過去進行式，表示在過去時間裡同時進行。

Try it! 實力演練

I. 填空 (依提示字填入正確動詞形式，不限填一字)

1. The students ______________________ (take) a math test at 9:10 this morning.
2. When Lewis woke up at 11 this noon, his mother ______________________ (cook) lunch.
3. Wendy ______________________ (use) the computer when her boss stepped into the office.

II. 選擇

_____ 1. Derek _____ on the phone when his father came home.
(A) talked (B) is talking (C) had talked (D) was talking

_____ 2. While the teacher _____ the complicated theory, some students _____ comic books.
(A) was explaining; were reading (B) explained; had read
(C) is explaining; read (D) was explaining; read

5-3-3 未來進行式

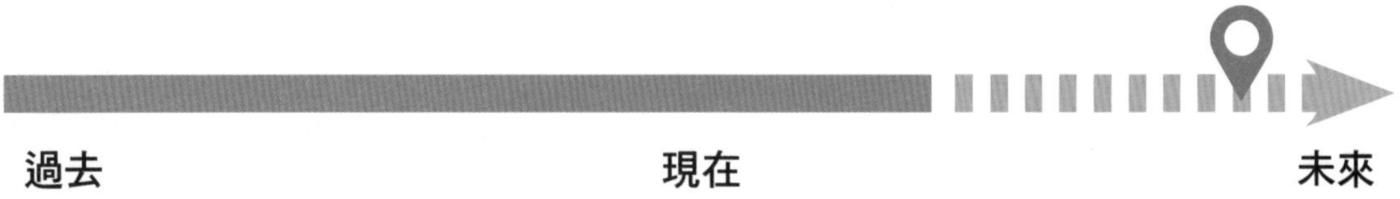

未來進行式由 **will + be + V-ing** 構成。

未來進行式的主要用法，整理如下：

用法	範例
表示未來某一時間點將會正在進行的動作	• Gabriel **will be having** a romantic dinner with his girlfriend at 7 tomorrow. Gabriel 明天晚上七點會和女朋友共享浪漫的晚餐。 • The manager **will be hosting** a meeting at three this afternoon. 今天下午三點，經理會來主持會議。 ❶ 在此用法中，會明確指出未來動作將發生的時間。
表示未來某一動作發生時，另一個將會正在進行的動作	• Richard **will be doing** his homework when his parents come home tonight. 當 Richard 的父母今晚回家時，他將會在寫作業。 • The children **will be playing** in the garden when the guests come. 當客人來時，孩子們將會在花園裡玩。 ❶ 副詞子句中用現在式時態代替未來式。

Try it! 實力演練

I. 填空 (依提示字填入正確動詞形式，不限填一字)

1. Mrs. Johnson probably ______________________ (bake) a cake when you pay her a visit tomorrow.
2. The committee members ______________________ (discuss) this proposal in the meeting at 2 p.m. tomorrow.
3. The girls ______________________ (sing) karaoke when we ______________________ (meet) them tonight.

II. 句子改寫 (依提示將下列各句改為未來進行式)

1. Sarah will bathe her baby tonight. (at eight o'clock)

____

2. Caroline will watch a soccer game this evening. (at six o'clock)

____

3. The students will read the poems on their textbooks. (when their teacher comes)

____

5-4 完成式

1. 依據動作發生的**時間**，完成式分為現在完成式、過去完成式、未來完成式。
2. 現在完成式表示「從過去到現在為止，已經或剛完成或尚未完成的動作」、「從過去某時間點開始並持續到現在的動作」或「從過去到目前為止的經驗」。
3. 過去完成式表示「過去某時已經完成的動作」、「在過去某時之前就已經持續的動作或狀態」或「過去的經驗」。
4. 未來完成式表示「未來某時間點或某一動作之前將已經完成的動作」。

5-4-1 現在完成式

現在完成式由 **have/has + p.p.** 構成。

現在完成式的主要用法，整理如下：

說明	範例
表示「從過去到現在為止已經或剛完成或尚未完成的動作」，常與 **already**、**just**、**yet** 等字連用	• The couple **has** already **paid** off their loan. 這對夫婦已經付清貸款。 • These athletes **have** just **finished** their warm-ups. 這些運動員剛剛做完暖身運動。 • The search party **has** not **found** the missing boy yet. 搜索隊還沒找到那個失蹤的男孩。
表示「從過去某一時間點開始一直持續的動作」，可以和下列用法連用： **a. for +** 一段時間 **b. lately**、**recently**	• The carnival **has lasted** for two days. 這個嘉年華會已經持續兩天了。 • Angela **has been** busy with her report recently, so she hasn't spent time with her friends. Angela 最近忙著做報告，所以沒找朋友。

c. since + 過去時間 / 過去式子句	• Since last year, no one **has heard** from Liam. 從去年起就沒人有 Liam 的消息。 • Jake **has lived** in Hualien since he was five. 從五歲起，Jake 就一直住在花蓮。
表示「從過去到目前為止的經驗」，常與 **ever**、**never** 等字連用	• Miriam is the most beautiful girl that I **have** ever **seen**. Miriam 是我見過最美的女孩。 • "**Have** you ever **been to** London?" 你曾去過倫敦嗎？ "No, I **have** never **been to** London." 不，我從沒去過倫敦。

注意

have been to 與 have gone to 的意義不同。have been to 表示「曾經去過某地」，談論時，人已離開那個地點，可用於第一、二、三人稱；have gone to 表示「已經去某地」，談論對象仍然在那個地點，故只用於第三人稱。

• Jessica **has been to** Barcelona, and I have been there, too.
Jessica 曾去過巴塞隆納，我也去過。 Note 表示經驗，可用於第一、二、三人稱。

• Luke **has gone to** Barcelona.
Luke 已經去巴塞隆納了。 Note 表示已經去，只用於第三人稱。

Try it! 實力演練

I. 選擇

______ 1. The chef ______ to prepare the big meal, so the guests may have to wait for some time.
(A) is begun (B) has just begun (C) beginning (D) has begins

______ 2. The woman ______ in bed with flu for two days.
(A) has been (B) is (C) was (D) is being

______ 3. Since Jason ______ 10, he ______ a fan of the singer Lady Gaga.
(A) has been; was (B) is; was (C) was; was (D) was; has been

II. 引導式翻譯

1. 最近天氣很熱。
The weather ______ ______ scorching hot recently.

2. 你曾去過冰島嗎？

______ you ever ______ to Iceland?

3. A: 你知道 Harry 在哪嗎？我試著聯絡他，但是找不到他。

B: 我聽說他已經去泰國了。

A: Do you know where Harry is? I tried to contact him, but I still can't find him.

B: I heard that he ______ ______ ______ Thailand.

5-4-2 過去完成式

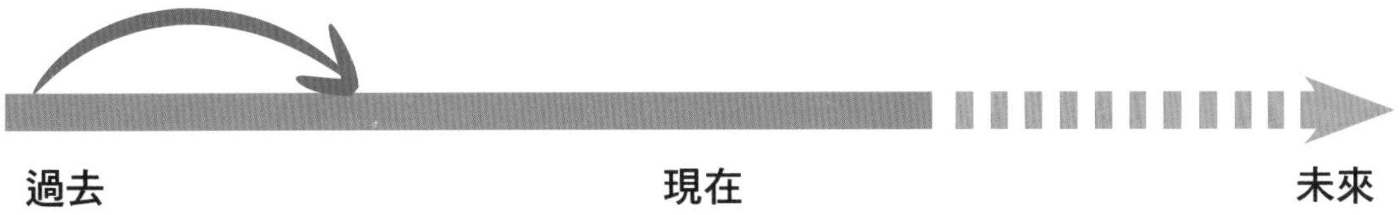

過去完成式由 **had + p.p.** 構成。

過去完成式的主要用法，整理如下：

說明	範例
表示過去某個時間點已經完成的動作	• The workers **had finished** their work, so they began their lunch. 工人們已經做完工作，所以開始吃午餐。 • After the Wangs moved to Mexico for a year, they **had got** used to the food there. 王家人搬去墨西哥一年後，他們就習慣當地的食物了。
表示在過去某個時間點之前就已經持續的動作或狀態	• When Jeff received his master's degree, he **had studied** in the UK for 5 years. 當 Jeff 拿到碩士學位，他已經在英國讀五年書了。 • When Lucy came home, her child **had slept**. 當 Lucy 回到家時，她的小孩已經睡了。
表示過去的經驗	• Susanne **had** never **seen** koalas before she traveled to Australia. 在去澳洲旅行前，Susanne 從沒看過無尾熊。
用來表示兩個過去動作的先後關係；先完成的動作用過去完成式，後完成的用過去簡單式	• When we hurried to the stadium, the game **had** just **begun**. 當我們趕去體育場時，比賽剛剛開始。 • When the police arrived at the bank, the robbers **had escaped**. 當警察趕到銀行時，搶匪已經跑了。 • Nora noticed that someone **had broken** into her house. Nora 注意到有人闖進她家。

學習便利貼

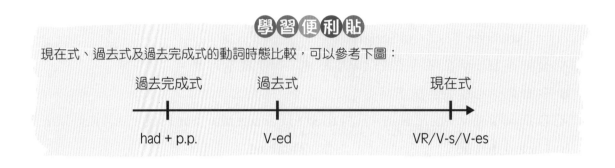

現在式、過去式及過去完成式的動詞時態比較，可以參考下圖：

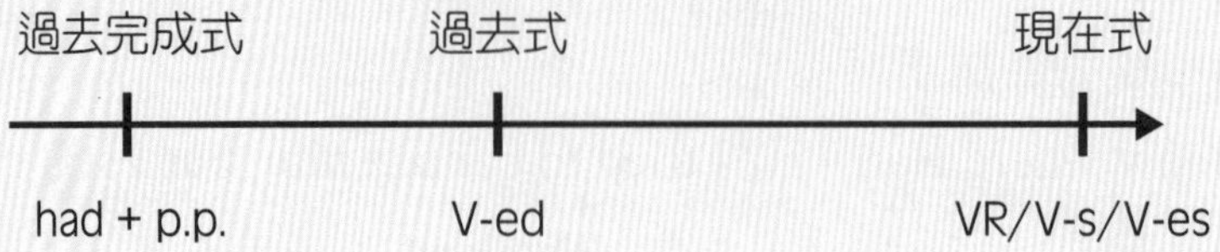

Try it! 實力演練

I. 填空 (依提示字填入正確動詞形式，不限填一字)

1. Those workers ____________________ (finish) their work at five, so they packed up and went home.
2. Nobody knew what ____________________ (happen) earlier that day.
3. Mark ____________________ (find) the book that he ____________________ (lose) last week.

II. 填空 (根據上下文情境，填入正確動詞形式，不限填一字)

Kevin 1. ____________________ (invite) his girlfriend to a fancy restaurant last Saturday. When he was going to pay the bill, he 2. ____________________ (find) that he 3. ____________________ (forget) to put some money in his wallet before he 4. ____________________ (leave) home that morning. Although he 5. ____________________ (feel) so embarrassed, he 6. ____________________ (have) no choice but to borrow money from his girlfriend!

5-4-3 未來完成式

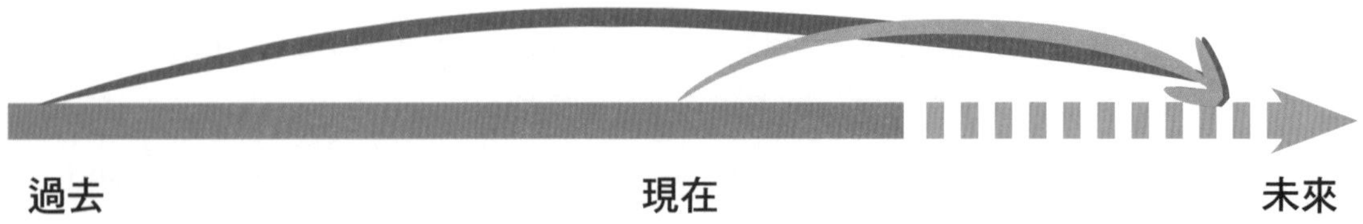

未來完成式由 **will + have + p.p.** 構成。

未來完成式的主要用法，整理如下：

用法	範例
表示「未來某時間點或某一動作之前將已經完成的動作」	• The researchers **will have finished** the project at the end of the year. 研究人員在年底前將已經完成這項計畫。 • Lavender **will have saved** enough money before she begins her trip. 在出發旅行前，Lavender 將已經存夠錢。
常與「by + 時間點」或「by the time + 未來動作」連用	• By next summer, the young singer **will have released** his first album. 在明年夏天前，這年輕歌手將已經發行他的首張專輯。 • By the time his wife returns, Alex **will have prepared** a surprise for her. 在老婆回來之前，Alex 將會為她準備一個驚喜。 ❗ 副詞子句用現在式代替未來式。

Try it! 實力演練

I. 填空 (依提示字填入正確動詞形式，不限填一字)

1. 下週三之前，Becky 將已經看完兩本小說。

   By next Wednesday, Becky ______________ (read) two novels.

2. 當 Eli 從西班牙回來時，他的西班牙文將會有所進步。

   By the time Eli ______________ (come) back from Spain, his Spanish ______________ (be) improved.

3. 在 Hiddleston 夫婦回來前，孩子們將已經整理好房間。

   By the time Mr. and Mrs. Hiddleston ______________ (get) home, their children ______________ (tidy) up their rooms.

II. 選擇

______ 1. By the end of the year, the bridge ______.

(A) will have been built　　(B) will build

(C) is built　　(D) will be building

______ 2. By 10 this morning, the union members ______ to a conclusion.

(A) will be coming　(B) will come　(C) are coming　(D) will have come

______ 3. By the time my uncle ______, we ______ our dinner.

(A) arrived; will finish (B) arrives; will have finished
(C) will arrive; finished (D) is arriving; are finishing

5-5 完成進行式

1. 依據動作發生的**時間**，完成進行式分為現在完成進行式、過去完成進行式、未來完成進行式。
2. 現在完成進行式表示「從過去某個時間開始，持續到現在的狀態，或仍然在進行的動作」。
3. 過去完成進行式表示「動作或狀態從過去某個時間開始，且持續到過去某個時間點停止」。
4. 未來完成進行式表示「動作或狀態會持續到未來某個時間，且會繼續進行」。

完成式與完成進行式的比較：

完成式	完成進行式
強調動作的完成	強調動作的持續性
• Jessica **has watched** TV all night. Jessica 已經看一整晚的電視了。 Note 表示 Jessica 已經看了一整晚的電視，強調動作的完成。 • Eddie **had done** his assignment before his mother came home. 在媽媽回家前，Eddie 已經寫完作業了。 Note 強調 Eddie 已經寫完作業，表示動作的完成。	• Jessica **has been watching** TV for three hours. Jessica 已經持續看三個小時的電視了。 Note 表示 Jessica 一直在看電視，已經持續三小時了，並強調動作仍在進行。 • Eddie **had been doing** his assignment before his mother came home. 在媽媽回家前，Eddie 一直在寫作業。 Note 強調 Eddie 一直在寫作業，表示動作仍在進行。

5-5-1 現在完成進行式

現在完成進行式是由 **have/has + been + V-ing** 構成。表示「從過去某一個時間開始，持續到現在的狀態或仍在進行的動作」，強調動作的**持續性**，常與 for 或 since 引導的時間副詞片語或子句連用。

- I **have been learning** English since I was ten.
  我從十歲就開始學英文了。
- The baby **has been crying** for ten minutes.
  這嬰兒已經哭十分鐘了。
- Sarah **has been playing** the piano since four o'clock.
  Sarah 從四點就一直在彈鋼琴。
- The boys **have been reading** comic books for two hours.
  這些男孩已經看二個小時的漫畫了。

Try it! 實力演練

句子改寫 (將下列句子合併或改寫成現在完成進行式)

1. { Andrew started to play video games after he updated his Facebook status.
   Andrew is still playing video games now. (since)

   ____

2. The artist is painting. (for five hours)

   ____

3. Mia is working in the bakery across the street. (since she moved to this town)

   ____

5-5-2 過去完成進行式

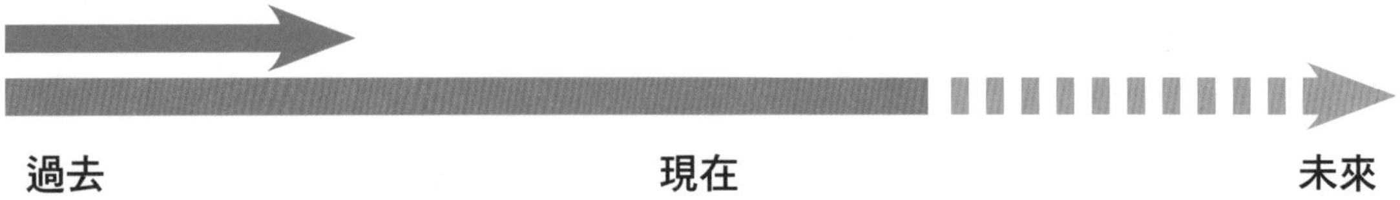

過去完成進行式是由 **had + been + V-ing** 構成，表示「動作或狀態從過去某個時間開始，且持續到過去某個時間點停止」。

- We **had been waiting** for the bus for twenty minutes before it came.
  在公車來之前，我們已經等二十分鐘了。
- These basketball players **had been practicing** for an hour before the coach came.
  在教練來之前，這些籃球選手已經練習一個小時了。
- Mr. Smith **had been taking** care of his children the whole day before his wife got home.
  在他太太回到家之前，Smith 先生已經照顧孩子一整天了。
- Belle **had been staying** in the hospital for two days after she had an operation on her leg.
  在 Belle 動腿部手術後，她已經住院兩天了。

Try it! 實力演練

引導式翻譯

1. 在看到路標之前，我們已經走 15 分鐘的路了。
   We ______ ______ ______ for fifteen minutes before we saw the road sign.
2. 在找到有人幫忙之前，Kim 一直試著修漏水的水龍頭。
   Kim ______ ______ ______ to fix the leaky faucet before she got someone to help.
3. 在我們抵達祖父母家前，爸爸已經開好幾個小時的車了。
   Father ______ ______ ______ for hours before we arrived at Grandparents' house.

5-5-3 未來完成進行式

未來完成進行式是由 **will + have + been + V-ing** 構成，表示「動作或狀態會持續到未來某一時間，且會繼續進行」，強調**動作的持續性**。

- By September, Lydia **will have been learning** ballet for a year.
  在九月之前，Lydia 將已經學芭蕾滿一年了。
- By the end of the month, Ron **will have been living** here for ten years.
  在這個月底之前，Ron 就在這裡住十年了。
- The workers **will have been doing** their work for two hours when their boss comes.
  當老闆來時，這些工人將已經工作兩小時了。
- Before the superstar arrives, her fans **will have been waiting** at the airport for three hours.
  在這位巨星到達之前，她的影迷將已經在機場等三小時了。

Try it! 實力演練

引導式翻譯

1. 當 Taylor 老師的學生今年畢業時，她將已經在這間學校教七年書了。
   When Mrs. Taylor's students graduate this year, she ____________________ at this school for seven years.
2. 在這個星期天之前，雨將已經持續下兩個禮拜了。
   By this Sunday, it ____________________ for two weeks.
3. 在這些馬拉松選手抵達終點之前，他們將已經跑一個小時了。
   Before the marathon runners reach the finish line, they ____________________ for an hour.

Notes

Chapter

6 主動語態與被動語態

語態表示主詞與動詞之間的關係，分為主動語態與被動語態。

6–1 主動語態與被動語態

1. 語態能表達出主語和述語的關係，分為**主動語態**和**被動語態**。
2. 主動語態表示「主詞是執行動作者」，被動語態表示「主詞是接受動作者」。

主動語態改為被動語態時，要將受詞改為新主詞，動詞形式改為 **be 動詞 + p.p. (過去分詞) (+ by 動作執行者)**。

[主動語態] A (S) + V + B (O).

[被動語態] B (新 S) + **be p.p.** + (**by** + A).

例句：

[主動語態] Leonardo da Vinci painted the Mona Lisa.

[被動語態] The Mona Lisa **was painted** **by** Leonardo da Vinci.

達文西畫了蒙娜麗莎的肖像。

用法	範例
要強調動作的接受者	• Karen decorated the living room yesterday. Karen 昨天佈置了客廳。 → The living room **was decorated** by Karen yesterday. • Benjamin uploaded several video clips to YouTube. Benjamin 上傳好幾部影片到 YouTube 上。 → Several video clips **were uploaded** to YouTube by Benjamin.

當動作的執行者不明確或不必提出時，可以省略「by + 執行者」	• Someone broke the window. 有人打破窗戶。 → The window **was broken**. • Some workers repaired the road. 有些工人修理道路。 → The road **was repaired** (by some workers).
做客觀的說明時	• It was reported that many houses **were destroyed** by the mudslide. 據報導，許多房子被土石流摧毀。

注意

動詞片語如 put off、take care of、look after 等，在被動語態中視為一體，不省略介系詞。

- The deadline of this paper was **put off**. 這篇論文的繳交期限延後了。
- The children are **taken care of** by their grandmother. 孩子們由祖母照顧。

6-2 簡單式的被動語態

簡單式的被動語態形式為 **be 動詞 + p.p. (過去分詞)**，表示「動作被執行」，可分為現在式的被動語態、過去式的被動語態與未來式的被動語態。

現在式的被動語態

am/are/is + p.p.

- Dad steams some stuffed buns every morning. 爸爸每天早上都會蒸一些包子。
  → Some stuffed buns **are steamed** by Dad every morning.
  每天早上，一些包子都會被爸爸蒸。
- According to scientists, many facts support this theory.
  根據科學家，許多事實證實了這理論。
  → According to scientists, this theory **is supported** by many facts.
  根據科學家，這個理論被許多事實證實。

過去式的被動語態

was/were + p.p.

- Eric soothed his headache by taking some medicine. Eric 吃藥，緩解了頭痛。
  → Eric's headache **was soothed**. Eric 的頭痛被緩解。

- The government founded this university fifty years ago.
政府於 50 年前建立這所大學。
→ This university **was founded** fifty years ago by the government.
這所大學被政府在 50 年前建立。

未來式的被動語態

will + be + p.p.

- The mayor will build a museum in this city.
市長將會在這個城市蓋一座博物館。
→ A museum **will be built** in this city (by the mayor).
一座博物館將被建在這城市裡。
- The farmer will spread organic fertilizer on his land. 農夫將在農地上灑有機農藥。
→ Organic fertilizer **will be spread** on the farmer's land.
有機農藥將被撒在這農夫的農地上。

Try it! 實力演練

I. 填空 (依提示字填入正確動詞形式，不限填一字)

1. The musical The Phantom of the Opera ____________ (perform) from Monday to Saturday in Her Majesty's Theater in London.
2. The broken CD player ____________ (fix) by my brother yesterday.
3. A concert ____________ (hold) in the newly built auditorium next Saturday.

II. 句子改寫 (將下列句子改寫成被動語態)

1. They canceled the baseball game because of the heavy rain.

____

2. The technology company will introduce their new products at the trade fair tomorrow.

____

6-3 進行式的被動語態

進行式的被動語態形式為 **be 動詞 + being + p.p.**，表示「動作正在被執行」，分為現在式的被動語態與過去式的被動語態。注意，be 動詞必須隨主詞變化。

現在進行式的被動語態

am/are/is + being + p.p.

• The television station is broadcasting the president's farewell address.
電視臺正在播出總統的卸任演說。
→ The president's farewell address **is being broadcast** (by the television station).
總統的卸任演說正在被 (電視臺) 播出。

• The committee members are discussing this issue in the meeting.
委員正在會議中討論這個議題。
→ This issue **is being discussed** (by the committee members) in the meeting.
這個議題正在會議中被 (委員) 討論。

過去進行式的被動語態

was/were + being + p.p.

• The police were interrogating some suspects at eight last night.
昨晚八點警察正在審問一些嫌疑犯。
→ Some suspects **were being interrogated** (by the police) at eight last night.
昨晚八點，一些嫌疑犯正被 (警察) 審問。

• The chef and his assistants were preparing a wedding feast.
主廚和助手們正在準備婚宴。
→ A wedding feast **was being prepared** (by the chef and his assistants).
婚宴正被 (主廚與助手) 準備。

Try it! 實力演練

I. 填空 (依提示字填入正確動詞形式，不限填一字)

1. The soup ________________ (heat) up on the stove now.
2. The journalist reported that the incident ________________ (still/investigate) by the police, and they hadn't found any clues.

II. 句子改寫 (將下列句子改寫成被動語態)

1. The workers are building the new concert hall in the city center.

____

2. The engineer was updating the software when the phone rang.

____

6-4 完成式的被動語態

完成式的被動語態形式為 **have + been + p.p.**，表示「已經被完成的動作」，分為現在完成式的被動語態、過去完成式的被動語態與未來完成式的被動語態。

現在完成式的被動語態

have + been + p.p.

- Michael Phelps has broken several world records.
  Michael Phelps 已打破許多世界紀錄。
  → Several world records **have been broken** by Michael Phelps.
  許多世界紀錄已被 Michael Phelps 打破。
- The ambulance has sent the injured man to the hospital.
  救護車已將傷者送醫。
  → The injured man **has been sent** to the hospital.
  傷者已經被送去醫院。

過去完成式的被動語態

had + been + p.p.

- Before Joseph submitted his composition, he had revised it several times.
  在 Joseph 交作文前，他已經修改好幾次了。
  → Joseph's composition **had been revised** several times before he submitted it. 在交作文前，Joseph 已經改寫好幾次了。
- The guard had taken the drunken man to the police station.
  警衛已經把這醉漢帶到警察局。
  → The drunken man **had been taken** to the police station (by the guard).
  這醉漢已被 (警衛) 帶到警察局。

未來完成式的被動語態

will + have + been + p.p.

- Alison will have completed the project by next Friday.
  在下週五之前，Alison 將會已經完成這個計畫。
  → The project **will have been completed** (by Alison) by next Friday.
  這個計畫在於下週五前就會被完成。
- The best-selling author will have finished her sixth novel by this October.
  在十月之前，該暢銷作者將會完成第六本小說。
  → The best-selling author's sixth novel **will have been finished** by this October. 該暢銷作家的第六本小說，10 月前就會被完成。

Try it! 實力演練

I. 填空 (依提示字填入正確動詞形式，不限填一字)

1. Don't worry. The problem ________________________ (have solved).
2. The robber ________________________ (had caught) by the police.
3. By Friday, the package ________________________ (will have delivered) to Mr. Huang.

II. 句子改寫 (將下列句子改寫成完成被動語態)

1. The boy had sharpened all of his pencils before he went to bed.

____

2. Jack has painted his house white.

____

3. By this May, this kind-hearted lady will have donated a million dollars.

____

6-5 助動詞、使役動詞與感官動詞的被動語態

1. 助動詞搭配被動語態的用法

助動詞 **+ be + p.p.**

- The students should turn in their assignments today.
  學生們應該要在今天交作業。
  → The students' assignments **should be turned in** today.
  學生們的作業應該在今天繳交。
- You can find the answers to these questions in this book.
  你可以在這本書裡找到這些問題的答案。
  → The answers to these questions **can be found** in this book.
  這些問題的答案可以在這本書裡被找到。

2. 使役動詞 make 的被動語態用法

be + made + to V

使役動詞 let、have、make 中，只有 make 可改為被動結構，並必須將其後接續的動詞改為不定詞 to V。

- Ms. Trunchbull made the boys sweep the floor.
  Trunchbull 老師要男孩們掃地。
  → The boys **were made to** sweep the floor (by Ms. Trunchbull).
  男孩們被 (Trunchbull 老師) 叫去掃地。

- The manager made his employees receive regular job training.
  經理讓員工接受定期的工作訓練。
  → The employees in this company **were made to** receive regular job training (by the manager).
  這間公司的員工被 (經理) 要求接受定期工作訓練。

3. 感官動詞的被動用法

be + 感官動詞 p.p. + to V

- We heard a girl singing in the room. 我們聽到有個女孩在房間唱歌。
  → A girl **was heard to** sing in the room. 有個女孩被聽到在房間裡唱歌。
- We saw several old men do tai chi in the park.
  我們看到很多老人在公園打太極拳。
  → Several old men **were seen to** do tai chi in the park.
  很多老人被看到在公園打太極拳。

Try it! 實力演練

I. 填空 (依提示字填入正確動詞形式，不限填一字)

1. An invitation card ________________ (must send) to Mr. Yang today.
2. The man ________________ (make/move) the heavy box.
3. The naughty child ________________ (see/play) a trick on the little girl this morning.

II. 句子改寫 (將下列句子改寫成被動語態)

1. The police made the suspect tell the truth.

____

2. Many people saw the runner fall in the race.

____

Chapter

7 動名詞與不定詞

7-1 動名詞

1. 動名詞的形式為 V-ing，是由動詞轉變而來的名詞，**本身具有動詞的意義，但其特性和用法都屬於名詞**，可以當作主詞、受詞或補語。
2. 一動名詞視為一名詞，作主詞時，動名詞個數會影響其後動詞的單複數變化。

用法	範例
當主詞	• **Jogging** benefits people's health. 慢跑有益健康。 Note 一個動名詞視為一個名詞，作主詞時，動詞用單數形。 • **Mastering a foreign language** requires much practice. 精通外語需要許多練習。 • **Listening to heavy metal** and **reading comic books** are Eddie's favorite pastimes. 聽重金屬樂和看漫畫是 Eddie 最喜歡的消遣。 Note 二個動名詞視為二個名詞，作主詞時，動詞用複數形。 • **Exercising** and **eating less** help people lose weight. 運動和少吃幫助減重。
當動詞或介系詞的受詞	• Many students enjoy **surfing the Internet**. 很多學生喜歡上網。 Note 動名詞 surfing the Internet 當動詞 enjoy 的受詞。 • Can you imagine **living without TV**? 你能想像沒有電視的生活嗎？ • The two talkative people kept on **gossiping** until it got dark. 這兩個多話的人一直聊八卦到天黑。 Note 動名詞 gossiping 當介系詞 on 的受詞。 • As soon as the fire broke out, the little girl thought of **calling** 911. 火災一發生，小女孩就想到打電話給消防隊。

當主詞補語	• Seeing is **believing**.【諺】眼見為憑。 Note 本句有二個動名詞：seeing 當主詞，believing 當主詞補語。 • What the children like the most is **visiting theme parks**. 孩子們最喜歡的就是到主題樂園玩。 Note 動名詞 visiting theme parks 當主詞 what . . . most 的補語。 • What Nora likes to do is **having afternoon teas with her friends**. Nora 喜歡做的事就是和朋友一起喝下午茶。
否定形式： **no/not/never +** 動名詞 **(V-ing)**	• No **littering** is allowed here. 此處禁止丟垃圾。 • Johnson apologized to his best friend for not **being able to attend her wedding**. Johnson 因為無法參加好友婚禮而向她道歉。 • I am sorry for not **having replied earlier**. 抱歉沒早點回信。 • Persistence means never **giving up**. 堅持意味著永不放棄。

注意

1. 有些及物動詞後常接動名詞，必須牢記。如 finish、avoid、imagine、keep、mind、enjoy、practice、quit、consider、postpone、delay 等。
   - Smart people avoid **making** the same mistake over and over again.
     聰明的人避免重蹈覆轍。
   - Have you ever imagined **having** a robot which can do everything for you?
     你曾想像過能有一個機器人為你做所有的事情嗎？
   - Do you mind **turning** down the volume? 你介意把音量轉小嗎？
   - The doctor advised Ralph to quit **smoking** and **drinking**. 醫生建議 Ralph 要戒除煙酒。
2. 有些動詞片語中的 to 當介系詞用，後面接動詞時，必須變成動名詞。如 object to (反對)、look forward to (期待)、pay attention to (注意)、be/get used to (習慣於…)、be accustomed to (習慣於…)、be devoted to (致力於…)、be dedicated to (致力於…)、be opposed to (反對)、in addition to (除了)、when it comes to (當提到…)、the key to (…的關鍵)。
   - Lavender looks forward to **hearing** from her pen pal. Lavender 期待她筆友的消息。
   - In addition to **swimming**, Annie is good at playing badminton.
     除了游泳，Annie 還擅長打羽球。
   - My father is used to **taking** a walk after dinner. 我爸爸習慣在晚餐後去散步。
   - Dr. King was devoted to **promoting** human rights. 金恩博士致力於促進人權。

Try it! 實力演練

I. 選擇

______ 1. ______ in the heavy snow is challenging.

(A) Drive (B) Drives (C) Driving (D) Driven

______ 2. One of Fred's hobbies is ______ stamps.

(A) collect (B) collects (C) collected (D) collecting

______ 3. Choose the correct sentence.

(A) The old woman is used to take a nap every afternoon.

(B) Nancy is considering applying for this job.

(C) The girls are talking about go shopping later.

(D) When it comes to paint, this talented boy is second to none.

II. 填空 (將提示字改為正確動詞形式)

1. My brother's pastime is ______ (play) the video games.
2. No ______ (swim) is allowed in this lake.
3. Do you mind ______ (turn) down the volume of the CD player?

7–2 不定詞 (to V)

1. 不定詞的形式為 to V，概念與動名詞相同，具有動詞的意義，但有名詞、形容詞與副詞的功能。
2. 不定詞當作名詞時可以當主詞、受詞或補語。一個不定詞視為一個名詞，作主詞時，不定詞的**個數**會影響其後動詞的單複數變化。
3. 有些動詞後固定接不定詞，必須牢記。常見的此類動詞有 ask、want、intend、decide、promise、need、expect、order、demand、request、advise、allow、cause、refuse 等。

1. 作名詞

用法	範例
當主詞	• **To see** is to believe. 【諺】眼見為憑。 Note 一個不定詞視為一個名詞，作單數主詞，動詞用單數形。 • **To build a skyscraper overnight** is impossible. 要一夕之間建造摩天大樓是不可能的。 • **To get up early** and **to go to bed early** are difficult for the lazy man. 早起和早睡對這懶人而言都很困難。 Note 二個不定詞視為二個名詞，作複數主詞，動詞用複數形。 • **To take care of children** and **to educate them** require much love and patience. 照顧小孩和教育小孩需要很多愛與耐心。
當動詞的受詞	• Anita likes **to play tennis with her friends**. Anita 喜歡和朋友打網球。 Note 不定詞當動詞 like 的受詞。 • The mean salesman intended **to sell a fake watch to me**. 這壞心的銷售員想賣假錶給我。 • Plucking up the courage, Daniel decided **to propose to Fannie**. 鼓起勇氣後，Daniel 決定向 Fannie 求婚。 • Don't be angry. Kim didn't mean **to offend you**. 別生氣。Kim 不是有意冒犯你。
當主詞補語	• To see is **to believe**. 【諺】眼見為憑。 • This traffic rule is **to ensure the safety of the pedestrians**. 這項交通規則是要確保行人的安全。 • Sean's plan is **to save five thousand dollars every month**. Sean 的計畫是要一個月存五千元。 • What Gary expects is **to meet his girlfriend this weekend**. Gary 期待的事情就是這週末和他的女朋友見面。
當受詞補語	• The rising temperatures caused icebergs **to melt**. 上升的溫度讓冰山融化。 • The doctor advised the obese woman **to cut down on fatty foods**. 醫生建議這肥胖的女人減少油膩的食物。

否定形： **not/never + to V**	• Elaine's boss warned her not **to be late again**. Elaine 的老闆警告她不要再遲到。 • Tom promised never **to stand his friends up again**. Tom 答應不會再放朋友們鴿子。 • Ms. Honey asks her students not **to cheat on the exam**. Honey 老師要學生們考試不能作弊。 • The father wants his child never **to lie again**. 這父親要孩子別再說謊。

注意

當不定詞片語較長時，可用虛主詞 it 或虛受詞 it 代替不定詞，將其移到句尾，以避免句子「頭重腳輕」的情形。常用的句型為：

1. **It is + adj. + to V . . .**：主詞是不定詞時，可以用虛主詞 it 代替，並將不定詞移到句尾。
   - To cry over spilt milk is useless.

     → It is useless **to cry over spilt milk**. 【諺】覆水難收。
   - To go whitewater rafting is exciting.

     → It is exciting **to go whitewater rafting**. 泛舟很刺激。
2. **S + Vt + it + N/adj. + to V**：受詞是不定詞時，可以用 it 代替，並將不定詞移到句尾。
   - Scientists make it possible **to travel to space**. 科學家讓太空旅行變成可能。
   - The shy boy found it difficult **to deliver a speech in public**.

     這害羞的男孩發現公開演講不是易事。

2. 作形容詞

用法	範例
修飾名詞與代名詞	• Asher complains that he has much homework **to do**. Asher 抱怨有很多作業要做。 • Ellen's husband is very considerate; she has nothing **to complain** about him. Ellen 的丈夫很體貼；她對他無可抱怨。
be + to V 用於表示安排、預定、義務等	• The laser show **is to kick off** at 7 o'clock. 雷射表演預定在七點開始。 • This department store **is to hold annual sales** next week. 這間百貨預定在下週舉行週年拍賣。

3. 作副詞，用於修飾動詞、形容詞與副詞。常見用法整理如下：

表示目的	**說明** a. 不定詞形成的短語可放句首或動詞片語後，描述「做某事的目的」。 b. in order to + V 也可用來表示「目的」。表示否定時，使用 in order not to V 或 so as not to V。 **範例** • **To increase her vocabulary**, Pauline decides to memorize twenty words every day. → In order to increase her vocabulary, . . . 為了增加字彙量，Pauline 決定每天背二十個單字。 • Ed contacted the manufacturer **to get more information about their products**. Ed 聯絡製造商，以得到產品的更多資訊。 • The girl laughed **to express her joy**. 女孩用笑來表達她的喜悅。 • The Korean superstar waved his hand **to greet his fans**. 這名韓國巨星向他的歌迷揮手問候。 • The man set off the alarm clock **in order not to** sleep late. → The man set off the alarm clock **so as not to** sleep late. 這男人設定鬧鐘，為了不要起得太晚。
表示情緒、反應	**說明** 置於形容詞後：**be + adj. + to V** 的結構可描述「對於某事件的情緒或反應」。所用的 adj. 須為表示情緒或感受的字詞，如 surprised、shocked、happy、sad、excited、amazed、proud 等。 **範例** • Megan is surprised **to know** that her children made a birthday cake for her. Megan 對於孩子們做了生日蛋糕給她感到驚訝。 Note 不定詞修飾 surprised，表示原因。 • This poor couple was shocked **to learn** that there were five babies on the way. 這對貧窮的夫婦很震驚得知他們懷了五胞胎。 Note 不定詞修飾 shocked，表示原因。

表示判斷、評論	**說明** **be + adj. + to V** 的結構還可描述「對於某事件的判斷、評論、態度」。常用的形容詞有：willing、right、careful、certain 等。 **範例** • Rita is willing **to serve** as a social worker. Rita 願意擔任社工。 Note 修飾 willing。 • The best-selling author is sure **to attend** the fund-raising party tonight. 這暢銷作家確定會參加今晚的募款餐會。
表示結果	**說明** a. to V 可表示做某事後，發現意外或失望的結果，意為「結果卻⋯」。 b. 在此用法中，常使用 **only to V** 的結構。 **範例** • The student went to the library, **only to find** that it was closed. 學生去圖書館，結果卻發現它沒開。 • The old lady hurried to the station, **only to see** that the train just left. 老婦人趕到火車站，結果卻看到火車剛剛離開。
修飾整句	**說明** 以「獨立不定詞片語」的形式呈現，通常置於句首，若置於句中、句尾，必須用逗號與句子其他部分隔開。 **範例** • Harry was late for the meeting. He was stuck in traffic. **To make matters worse**, his car broke down. Harry 趕不上開會了。他被困在車陣中。更糟的是，他的車拋錨了。 • Elle is arrogant and self-centered, **to tell the truth**. No wonder she has few friends. 老實說，Elle 自負又以自我為中心。難怪她很少朋友。
其他常用句型	**說明** a. be + adj. + enough + to V (夠⋯而能～) b. be + too + adj. + to V V + too + adv. + to V (太⋯而不能～)

	範例
	• Zoe is tall enough **to join** the professional basketball team. Zoe 夠高，可以參加職業籃球隊。Note 修飾 enough。 • The dress is too small for Lily **to wear**. 這件洋裝太小，Lily 不能穿。Note 修飾 too。 • One is never too old **to learn**. 【諺】活到老，學到老。 • It is never too late **to mend**. 【諺】亡羊補牢，猶未晚矣。

Try it! 實力演練

I. 選擇

______ 1. ______ a red light is against traffic rules. (複選)

(A) Running (B) To run (C) Run (D) Ran

______ 2. Linda dressed up ______ that she took the party as a formal event.

(A) shows (B) showed (C) show (D) to show

______ 3. It is refreshing ______ iced tea on a hot summer day.

(A) to drink (B) drinks (C) drank (D) drunk

II. 填空 (依提示字填入正確動詞形式，不限填一字)

1. The TED speaker's intention is ________________ (raise) people's awareness about the situation of endangered species.
2. Kate makes it a rule ________________ (do) yoga every day.

7-3 動名詞與不定詞的比較

有些動詞後面接動名詞與不定詞時，分別有**不同**的意義，這類動詞有：remember、forget、stop、regret 等。

1. remember 的用法比較

句型	意思	重點
remember + to V	記得要去做	未做，但記得要做
remember + V-ing	記得做了	已做，且記得做過

學習便利貼

將 to V 的 to 記為「去」，要「去」做即是**還未做**。這樣就能容易記得動名詞 V-ing 表示「已做」。forget 和 regret 也可運用此祕訣！

- Isabella remembered **to turn** off the light.
  Isabella 記得要關燈。Note 未關，但記得。
- Grandfather remembered **turning** off the gas.
  爺爺記得他已經關瓦斯了。Note 已關，且記得。

2. forget 的用法比較

句型	意思	重點
forget + to V	忘記去做	未做，且忘記要做
forget + V-ing	忘記做了	已做，但忘記做過

- The secretary was so busy that she forgot **to make** copies of the important document.
  秘書太忙了，以致於忘記要影印重要文件。Note 未印，且忘記要印。
- Antony forgot **attaching** his recent photograph to his application form for the job.
  Antony 忘記他已在求職表中貼近照。Note 已貼，但忘記有貼。

3. stop 的用法比較

句型	意思	重點
stop + V-ing	停止…	停止正在做的事
stop + to V	停止…去～	停止 (某動作) 去做…

學習便利貼

將動名詞 V-ing 記為進行式的 V-ing，表示進行，故 stop + V-ing 記為停止正在進行的動作。將不定詞 to V 的 to 記為「去」做，故 stop + to V 表示「停止 (某動作) 去做 (另一事)」。

- As soon as the bell rang, the students stopped **writing**. 鐘聲一響，學生們就停止寫字。
- The workers stopped **to have lunch** at twelve o'clock.
  十二點時，工人們停下來吃午餐。

4. regret 的用法比較

句型	意思	重點
regret + to V	遺憾要去…	對將要做的事情感到遺憾
regret + V-ing	後悔已做…	對已做的事情感到後悔

- I regret **to inform** you that you are fired. 我很遺憾要告訴你，你被解聘了。
- Mandy regretted **purchasing** that expensive watch.
  Mandy 後悔買了那個昂貴的手錶。

Try it! 實力演練

I. 選擇

_____ 1. To save energy, Felix always _____ off the computer after using it.

(A) remembers turning (B) remembers to turn

(C) forgets turning (D) forgets to turn

_____ 2. The teacher regretted _____ Lisa that she failed the exam.

(A) tells (B) told (C) has told (D) to tell

_____ 3. Choose the **wrong** sentence.

(A) The lady never forgets to pay her credit card bills.

(B) Mia asked her husband to remember locking the door before going to bed.

(C) It seems that those noisy children never stop talking!

(D) Ray regretted telling May the truth, which had made her unhappy.

II. 填空 (依提示字填入正確動詞形式，不限填一字)

1. Allen has replied to all the emails from his clients, and he remembers it.
   → Allen remembers _____________ (reply) to all the emails from his clients.
2. Naomi had borrowed an umbrella from her neighbor, but she forgot about it.
   → Naomi forgot _____________ (return) the umbrella to her neighbor.
3. As soon as the teacher entered the classroom, the students stopped _____________ (talk).

Chapter

8 形容詞與副詞

形容詞主要用於修飾**名詞**，副詞主要用於修飾**動詞**，兩者都有原級、比較級與最高級用法。

8-1 形容詞

1. 形容詞的修飾可分為限定用法與敘述用法。在限定用法中，形容詞置於**名詞前**，修飾名詞；在敘述用法中，形容詞置於**連綴動詞後**，作為主詞補語。
2. 形容詞可分為代名形容詞、數量形容詞與性狀形容詞。

8-1-1 代名形容詞

指由代名詞轉換而成的形容詞，包括所有形容詞、指示形容詞、疑問形容詞和關係形容詞。

1. 所有形容詞

即人稱代名詞的所有格，表示名詞的所屬，置於名詞之前，不可與冠詞 (a、an、the) 或指示形容詞 (this、that、these、those) 連用。

人稱代名詞	I	you	he	she	it	we	you	they
所有形容詞	my	your	his	her	its	our	your	their

- This is **my** sister and that is **his** brother. 這是我的妹妹，而那是他的弟弟。
- **Our** house is situated in the downtown area, and **their** house is located in the uptown area. 我們的房子位於鬧區，而他們的房子位於住宅區。
- [O] **Her** T-shirt is trendy. 她的 T 恤很潮。

  [X] Her the T-shirt is trendy. Note 所有形容詞不可與冠詞連用。

- [O] **Your** suggestion is helpful. 你的建議很有幫助。

  [X] Your this suggestion is helpful. Note 所有形容詞不可與指示形容詞連用。

2. 指示形容詞

a. 用於指示特定的人、事、物，置於名詞之前，不可與所有形容詞 (my、your、his 等) 或冠詞 (a、an、the) 連用。

b. 指示代名詞 this、that、these、those 後方接名詞時，即成指示形容詞。

- **This** kids' stool was invented by a five-year-old girl.

  這個童椅凳是由一個五歲女孩發明的。

- **These** students are looking forward to their field trip.

  這些學生正期待著校外教學。

- [O] **Those** handbags were gone. 那些手提包不見了。

  [X] Those their handbags were gone. Note 指示形容詞不可與所有形容詞連用。

3. 不定形容詞

無特定指示某人或某物的形容詞，置於名詞之前，常用的有：every、each、both、all、some、certain、any、another、other、either、neither。

- Alex took **some** medicine to soothe his headache. Alex 吃了一些藥舒緩頭痛。
- Here are two pencils. You can use **either** one.

  這裡有兩枝筆。你可以使用其中一枝。

- This program is sponsored by the company and **other** organizations.

  這個計畫由這家公司與其他機構所資助。

4. 疑問形容詞

a. 即 what、which、whose，兼有疑問詞與形容詞的功能，置於名詞之前。

b. 疑問形容詞可以置於句首，形成疑問句或引導名詞子句。

- **What** time is it? 現在幾點了？
- **Which** book is for beginners? 哪一本書是給初學者看的？
- Do you know **what** time it is? 你知道現在幾點了？

  Note 疑問形容詞引導名詞子句。

- I wonder **whose** bicycle is in front of the house.

  我想知道誰的腳踏車停在屋前。

Try it! 實力演練

I. 選擇

______ 1. Janet just bought a second-hand car. ______ car is a real bargain.
(A) It (B) Her (C) My (D) His

______ 2. ______ the twin brothers are interested in baseball. They always play together on Sundays.
(A) Either (B) Both (C) Any (D) All

______ 3. ______ diamond ring is lost?
(A) Whose (B) Who (C) Where (D) When

II. 引導式翻譯

1. 你可以把車停在路的任何一邊。
You can park your car on ______ side of the road.

2. 如果你還口渴，再喝一杯水吧。
If you are still thirsty, have ______ glass of water.

8-1-2 數量形容詞

數量形容詞可以用來表示「數」、「量」或「程度」，主要分為數詞和不定數量形容詞，通常置於名詞之前。

1. 數詞：包括基數詞和序數詞。

	說明	範例
基數詞	表示數目	one、two、three、four、five、ten、twenty、dozen、hundred、thousand 等
序數詞	表示順序	first、second、third、fourth、fifth、tenth、twentieth、thirtieth、fortieth 等

2. 不定數量形容詞：用來表示約略的數、量或程度。

	說明	範例
表數者	修飾可數名詞	many、few、a few、a lot of、some、several 等
表量者	修飾不可數名詞	much、little、a little、a lot of、some 等
表程度者	修飾可數或不可數名詞	a lot of、all、any、enough、no、some 等

注意

a lot of (= lots of = a large number of) + 可數名詞

a lot of (= lots of = a large amount of = a great deal of) + 不可數名詞

	意思	用法	範例
a few	[肯定] 一些	+ 可數名詞	• **A few** boys are playing baseball on the field. 一些男孩在運動場上打棒球。
few	[否定] 幾乎沒有		• Sally is a person of **few** words. Sally 沉默寡言。
a little	[肯定] 一些	+ 不可數名詞	• Don't worry. We still have **a little** money. 別擔心。我們還有點錢。
little	[否定] 幾乎沒有		• The boy is seriously ill. There seems to be **little** hope of recovery. 這男孩病情嚴重。復原希望渺茫。

Try it! 實力演練

I. 填空 (依提示在空格中填入正確的基數詞或序數詞)

1. Jill's family is composed of ______ (six) persons; she is the ______ (two) daughter.
2. Running fast, Oscar won the ______ (one) prize in the race.

II. 請圈選正確的數量形容詞

1. The famous director has directed (many/much) blockbusters (賣座電影).
2. This report is written very carefully, so only (few/a few) mistakes are found.
3. The machine broke down, so only (little/a little) work has been done up to now.

8-1-3 性狀形容詞

描述性質、尺寸、形狀、新舊、顏色等的形容詞，大多有比較級和最高級變化：
(1) 敘述形容詞，如 good、tall、deep、tough、foolish、talkative、silent、prosperous 等。
(2) 物質形容詞，如 wood、gold、silver、iron、stone、leather 等。
(3) 專有形容詞，如 Taiwanese、French、American、British、Greek 等。

構成

性狀形容詞除了原有的形容詞類外，還可由改變名詞或動詞字尾、動名詞與分詞轉化而來。請見以下說明：

1. 基本字：不須由其他詞類衍生而來。

例如：a **short** boy (一個矮的男孩)、a **hot** day (炎熱的一天)、a **cold** drink (一杯冷飲)、a **poor** man (一個窮人)、a **thick** dictionary (一本厚厚的字典)、a **modern** city (一個現代化的城市)、an **expensive** restaurant (一間昂貴的餐廳) 等。

2. 衍生字：由名詞或動詞的字尾做變化，或加上形容詞字尾而形成。

形容詞字尾	範例
-y	sleepy、rainy、sunny、guilty、thirsty、lucky、mighty、noisy、furry、gossipy 等
-ly	friendly、weekly、monthly、lovely、deadly、costly、earthly、manly、womanly 等
-ful	useful、helpful、hopeful、careful、colorful、meaningful、delightful、thankful、peaceful、skillful、harmful 等
-less	useless、helpless、hopeless、careless、meaningless、homeless、harmless 等
-ive	active、creative、attractive、expressive、impressive、reflective、infective 等
-ish	childish、boyish、girlish、foolish、selfish 等
-like	childlike、gentlemanlike、ladylike、manlike、godlike 等

-ic	basic、classic、automatic、ironic、heroic、poetic、genetic、economic、optimistic、fantastic 等
-al	historical、practical、magical、central、national、continual、industrial 等
-ous	furious、courageous、dangerous、humorous、poisonous、mountainous、victorious、ambitious、continuous 等
-ent、-ant	dependent、consistent、different、violent、pleasant、important、significant 等
-able、-ible	acceptable、comfortable、profitable、changeable、dependable、desirable、knowledgeable、accessible、sensible、edible 等
-some	tiresome、troublesome、awesome、lonesome 等

3. 分詞作形容詞：置於名詞之前修飾 (請參見 CH12)。

分詞	意義	範例
現在分詞 (V-ing)	表示「主動」或「正在進行」	a **sinking** ship (下沈中的船)、**falling** leaves (飄落的葉子)、the **rising** sun (正在升起的太陽)、a **sleeping** baby (沉睡的嬰兒)、a **flying** bird (飛鳥) 等
過去分詞 (p.p)	表示「被動」或「已經完成」	a **sunken** ship (沈船)、**fallen** leaves (已落下的葉子)、a **lost** necklace (被遺失的項鍊)、a **stolen** wallet (被偷的皮夾)、a **broken** cup (被打破的杯子) 等

4. 由表示「情緒」的動詞衍生成分詞而來。

過去分詞形表示「感到…的」，通常以**人**當主詞；現在分詞表示「令人感到…的」，通常以**事物**當主詞 (請參見 CH12)。

- Jessica is **surprised** that Susanne broke up with her boyfriend.
  Jessica 很驚訝 Susanne 和男友分手。
- It is **surprising** that Susanne broke up with her boyfriend.
  Susanne 和男友分手的消息令人感到驚訝。
- David is **interested** in the movie starring Jim Carrey.
  David 對金凱瑞主演的這部電影有興趣。
- It is **interesting** to watch the movie starring Jim Carrey.
  看這部金凱瑞主演的電影很有趣。

Try it! 實力演練

I. 選擇

______ 1. No one has seen Nora's ______. She has been looking for it. (選錯)

(A) lost bicycle (B) stolen purse (C) breaking bottle (D) missing dog

______ 2. Choose the **wrong** sentence.

(A) The courage mountaineer didn't cry when she got lost in the mountain.

(B) The teacher used to give his students a weekly test in class.

(C) The treasure hunter found many gold coins in an ancient sunken ship.

(D) The man felt so helpless. He couldn't find anyone to solve his problem.

II. 填空 (將提示字改為形容詞)

1. Our class will go camping tomorrow. Everyone is praying for a ______ (sun) day.
2. Amy is a ______ (create) artist. Her paintings are very ______ (color) and full of imaginary figures.
3. What Peter said is ______ (meaning); it didn't make sense at all.

8-1-4 形容詞的位置

1. 置於名詞之前

在限定用法中，形容詞置於所修飾的名詞前，做前位修飾，以描述該名詞的狀態或特質。

- The host and the guests of the talk show talked about many **social** problems.
  這談話節目的主持人和來賓談論了許多社會問題。
- The **sunken** ship was not found until last year. 直到去年，這艘沈船才被發現。
- All the kids listened to the **interesting** story attentively.
  所有孩子都聚精會神地聽那個有趣的故事。

2. 置於連綴動詞之後

在敘述用法中，形容詞置於連綴動詞 (be、seem、become、look 等) 之後，作主詞補語。有些形容詞只有敘述用法，沒有限定用法，不可置於名詞之前，如

awake、asleep、afraid、ashamed、aware、alike、alone、alive 等。

- The artist is **popular** among young people. 該藝術家很受年輕人歡迎。
- It is getting **warm**. 天氣越來越暖了。
- The dancer seems **satisfied** with his performance.
  這舞者似乎滿意自己的表現。
- The twin brothers look **alike**, so most people have difficulty telling one from the other. 這對雙胞胎兄弟很像，大多數的人很難分辨他們。

3. 多種形容詞並列時的順序

多個不同類的形容詞同時修飾一個名詞時，常按一定的順序排列，通常意義較具體或與名詞關係密切的形容詞要靠近名詞。排列順序如下：

代名形容詞	不定形容詞	all、both、some、few 等
	指示、所有形容詞	this、that、these、those、my、your 等
數量形容詞	序數	first、second、third 等
	基數	one、two、three 等
性狀形容詞	狀態	good、bad、hungry、cheap 等
	尺度、形狀	little、big、small、long、tall 等
	新舊、溫度	new、old、cold、hot 等
	顏色	red、blue、black、green 等
	分詞、專有形容詞	sunken、newly-built、American、Japanese 等
	物質形容詞	gold、silver、wood、stone 等

- Mr. Wang bought **new black sneakers** for his two sons.
  王先生買新的黑色運動鞋給他的兩個兒子。
- **The first three chapters** of **this book** are about an **exciting adventure** of a **young sailor**. 這本書的前三章是關於一個年輕水手驚險刺激的冒險之旅。

4. 置於複合不定代名詞之後

修飾複合不定代名詞 (some-/any-/no-/every-) 的形容詞要放在其後，做後位修飾。複合不定代名詞有 something、someone、anything、anyone、nothing、nobody、everything、everyone 等。

- Something **strange** happened last night.
  昨晚發生怪事。
- Henry seldom talks about anything **meaningful**.
  Henry 很少說些有意義的事情。
- Tina would like to give her hand-made gift to someone **special**.
  Tina 想把親手做的禮物送給某個特別的人。

Try it! 實力演練

I. 句子重組

1. bought/my/a/dress/pink/beautiful/mother/me

____

2. movie/makes/the/boring/long/the audience/sleepy

____

II. 挑錯 (選出錯誤的選項，並加以改正)

1. Global warming (A) requires public close attention (B) to prevent it from getting worse (C).

答：(______), ______________________

2. Stalked by a old strange man, (A) the frightened girl (B) ran to the police station (C) for protection.

答：(______), ______________________

3. In order to comfort his depressed son, (A) Mr. Wilson said positive something (B) to make him look on the bright side of life (C).

答：(______), ______________________

8-2 副詞

1. 副詞大多用於修飾動詞，表示時間、地方、情態、程度、頻率等。
2. 大多數的副詞可由形容詞字尾加變化而成。

- The exhausted man **unconsciously** added sugar to the corn soup.
  這疲累的男人不自覺地把糖加到玉米湯裡。 Note 副詞 unconsciously 修飾動詞 added。
- The children are playing **happily** in the park.
  孩子們正在公園裡開心地玩耍。 Note 副詞 happily 修飾動詞 are playing。
- With the gentle breeze blowing, Grandfather sat by the window **comfortably**.
  在微風的吹拂下，爺爺舒服地坐在窗邊。 Note 副詞 comfortably 修飾動詞 sat。
- This intelligent man deals with things **systematically**.
  這個聰明的男人很有系統地做事。
- The patient was released from the hospital two days ago and has not **fully** recovered from his illness yet. 這個病人兩天前剛出院，還沒完全恢復。
- Mia was such an eloquent speaker that everyone **truly** believed what she said.
  Mia 是位非常有說服力的講者，以致於每個人完全相信她說的話。

1. 構成規則：

形容詞類別	副詞構成法	範例
一般規則	字尾加 -ly	cold**ly**、hopeful**ly**、quiet**ly**、anxious**ly**、quick**ly**、attentive**ly**、humorous**ly**、efficient**ly**、frequent**ly** 等
-y 結尾	字尾去 y 改成 -ily	eas**ily**、laz**ily**、happ**ily**、heav**ily**、nois**ily**、bus**ily**、angr**ily** 等
-le 結尾	字尾去 e 加 -ly	possib**ly**、gent**ly**、comfortab**ly**、humb**ly**、simp**ly**、subt**ly** 等
-ic 結尾	字尾加 -ally	historic**ally**、ironic**ally**、scientific**ally**、basic**ally**、systematic**ally** 等
-ll 結尾	字尾加 -y	full**y**、dull**y** 等
-ue 結尾	字尾去 e 加 -ly	tru**ly**、du**ly** 等

注意

1. 有些副詞與形容詞同形，如 early、late、fast、hard、far 等。
   - If Edison finishes his homework **early**, he can go to the movie with his friend.
     如果 Edison 早點做完功課，他就可以和朋友去看電影。
   - Michael studies **hard** in the hope that he can enter a good university.
     Michael 用功讀書，希望能進入好大學。
2. 形容詞 good 的副詞為 well。
   - The actress performed so **well** that all the audience burst into applause.
     這名女演員表演精湛，以致於所有觀眾熱烈鼓掌。
3. -ly 結尾的字，不一定都是副詞，有些是屬於形容詞，如 friendly、lively、lonely、deadly、lovely、daily、weekly、monthly、yearly、timely 等。

2. 副詞的種類與用法

種類	說明	用法	範例
時間副詞	表示動作發生的時間	常置於句末，加強語氣時可置於句首。	now, then, before, ago, today, yesterday, etc.
	範例	• The museum is closed **today**. The guests will have to visit it **tomorrow**. 博物館今天休館。來賓必須明日再來參觀。 • **Yesterday**, Willis went to a musical. Willis 昨天去看一齣音樂劇。	
地方副詞	表示動作發生的地點	常置於所修飾的動詞後，前面不加介系詞。	here, there, nearby, everywhere, etc.
	範例	• The Jackson decided to buy the house because there is a park **nearby**. Jackson 一家決定買下這棟房子，因為附近有公園。	
情態副詞	表示動作的狀態或性質	常置於所修飾的動詞後，字尾是 -ly 者可置動詞之前。	slowly, sadly, quickly, eagerly, easily, well, etc.
	範例	• The ballet dancer danced **elegantly**. 這名芭蕾舞者優雅地跳舞。 • The clerk spoke **slowly** so the foreign customer could understand her. 店員慢慢地說明，好讓這名外籍顧客能理解。	

<table>
<tr><td rowspan="2">頻率副詞</td><th colspan="2">說明</th><th>用法</th><th>範例</th></tr>
<tr><td colspan="2">表示動作發生的頻率</td><td>置於 be 動詞後、一般動詞前、或助動詞與一般動詞之間。</td><td>always, often, usually, sometimes, seldom, frequently, etc.</td></tr>
<tr><td></td><td>範例</td><td colspan="3">• Abigail is often late for work.
Abigail 常常上班遲到。
• Emma usually goes to the gym to exercise.
Emma 通常去健身房運動。
• Drivers should always follow traffic rules to avoid accidents.
汽車駕駛應該總是遵守交通規則才能避免意外。</td></tr>
<tr><td rowspan="3">程度副詞</td><th colspan="2">說明</th><th>用法</th><th>範例</th></tr>
<tr><td colspan="2">表示動作發生的程度</td><td>常置於被修飾的形容詞或副詞之前，但 enough 須置於形容詞或副詞之後。</td><td>very, really, much, enough, too, quite, only, a bit, etc.</td></tr>
<tr><td>範例</td><td colspan="3">• Aaron is really excited about the concert tonight.
Aaron 對今晚的演唱會真的很興奮。
• Emily isn't mature enough to handle such a difficult problem.
Emily 不夠成熟，無法處理如此困難的問題。</td></tr>
</table>

注意

有些情態副詞可置於句首，用於修飾整句話，表示整句的情況、結果或強調，如 surprisingly、fortunately、unfortunately、luckily、unluckily、undoubtedly、interestingly、obviously、suddenly。

- **Surprisingly**, the typhoon has done such damage to this village.
  令人驚訝地，這個颱風對這個村莊竟然造成如此的損害。
- **Obviously**, the manager doesn't support this proposal.
  明顯地，經理不支持這個提議。
- **Suddenly**, a cat jumped from the window into the kitchen to eat the fish.
  突然地，有隻貓從窗戶跳進來廚房吃魚。

Try it! 實力演練

I. 將下列形容詞改為副詞

形容詞	副詞	形容詞	副詞
sudden	1.	true	2.
patient	3.	possible	4.
natural	5.	scientific	6.

II. 句子重組

1. always/Patricia/work/doing/delays/her

____

2. the exam result/are/waiting/the students/nervously/for

____

8-3 比較句型

形容詞和副詞的比較句型可以分為原級、比較級和最高級。兩者之間的比較用**原級比較**或**比較級**，三者或三者以上之間的比較用**最高級**。

8-3-1 原級比較

表示兩個被比較的對象有相同的特質或特性：

肯定句型	A + be + as + adj./adv. + as + B	A 像 B 一樣…
範例	• Kevin is **as heavy as** his brother. Kevin 跟他哥哥一樣重。 • These workers are **as busy as** bees. 這些工人非常忙碌。 • Jack drives **as carefully as** his father. Jack 開車跟他爸爸一樣小心。 • The athlete runs **as fast as** a leopard. 這運動員跑得像豹一樣快。	

否定句型	A + be + not + as/so + adj. + as + B A + 助動詞 + not + V + as/so + adv. + as + B	A 不像 B 一樣⋯
範例	• Amy is **not so organized as** her sister. Amy 不像她姊姊那樣有條理。 • Lisa **doesn't** play badminton **so well as** her brother. Lisa 不像她弟弟一樣會打羽球。	

學習便利貼

原級比較的句型有些固定的搭配用法，可以讓描述更生動，如：

- as busy as a bee 非常忙碌
- as sly as a fox 非常狡猾
- as stubborn as a mule 非常固執
- as light as a feather 輕如鴻毛
- as easy as pie/ABC 易如反掌
- as proud as a peacock 非常驕傲
- as brave as a lion 勇猛如獅
- as poor as a church mouse 一貧如洗
- as cool as a cucumber 極為冷靜
- as blind as a bat 有眼無珠

注意

有些原級比較的句型擁有其它意義，例如：as well as (也；和)、as soon as (一⋯就⋯)、as long as (只要⋯)。

- Isabella invited her colleagues **as well as** her friends to her wedding.
  Isabella 邀請同事和朋友參加婚禮。
- Give me a call **as soon as** you get home. 到家打通電話給我。
- You can speak English fluently **as long as** you practice often.
  只要你多練習，你就能說一口流利的英文。

Try it! 實力演練

I. 引導式翻譯

1. 姚明看起來像巨人一樣高。
   Yao Ming looks ______ ______ ______ a giant.
2. Parker 唱歌像張學友一樣好聽。
   Parker sings ______ ______ ______ Jacky Cheung.

II. 句子改寫 (以原級比較的句型改寫以下各句組)

1. This watch is NT$30000. That necklace is also NT$30000.

   This watch is ____

2. Caden works diligently. Sean works diligently, too.

   Caden works ____

3. Carol studies English hard. Carol's brother also studies English hard.

   Carol's brother studies ____

8-3-2 級的構成

1. 形容詞比較級和最高級的構成可分為規則與不規則變化。

規則變化：

	形容詞類別	變化	原級	比較級	最高級
單音節或雙音節	一般規則	比較級 字尾 + -er 最高級 字尾 + -est	low deep quiet strict	lower deeper quieter stricter	lowest deepest quietest strictest
	-e 結尾	比較級 字尾 + -r 最高級 字尾 + -st	large wise close brave	larger wiser closer braver	largest wisest closest bravest
	-y 結尾	比較級 去 y + -ier 最高級 去 y + -iest	dry heavy wealthy	drier heavier wealthier	driest heaviest wealthiest
	單音節，結尾為「短母音 + 子音」者	比較級 重複字尾 + -er 最高級 重複字尾 + -est	hot big fat thin	hotter bigger fatter thinner	hottest biggest fattest thinnest

雙音節或多音節	大多數的雙音節、多音節形容詞前面加 **more/less** 形成比較級，加 **most/least** 形成最高級	比較級 more + adj. (較…) 最高級 most + adj. (最…)	useful	**more** useful	**most** useful
			patient	**more** patient	**most** patient
			difficult	**more** difficult	**most** difficult
			efficient	**more** efficient	**most** efficient
		比較級 less + adj. (較不…) 最高級 least + adj. (最不…)	active	**less** active	**least** active
			delicious	**less** delicious	**least** delicious
			expensive	**less** expensive	**least** expensive
			exciting	**less** exciting	**least** exciting
部分雙音節	某些雙音節形容詞變化與單音節相同，字尾為 **-y** 的雙音節形容詞多屬於此類		clever	clever**er**	clever**est**
			cruel	cruel**er**	cruel**est**
			simple	simpl**er**	simpl**est**
			narrow	narrow**er**	narrow**est**
			busy	bus**ier**	bus**iest**
			early	earl**ier**	earl**iest**
			happy	happ**ier**	happ**iest**
			pretty	prett**ier**	prett**iest**

不規則變化：

原級	比較級	最高級
good/well	better	best
bad/ill	worse	worst
many/much	more	most
little	less	least
late	later	latest
far (遠的)	farther/further	farthest/furthest

2. 副詞比較級和最高級的構成亦分為規則與不規則變化。

規則變化：

說明	原級	比較級	最高級
單音節和少數雙音節的副詞字尾加 **-er** 形成比較級，加 **-est** 形成最高級	fast hard near high	fast**er** hard**er** near**er** high**er**	fast**est** hard**est** near**est** high**est**
大多數雙音節或多音節副詞前加 **more** 形成比較級，加 **most** 形成最高級	firmly easily quickly beautifully	**more** firmly **more** easily **more** quickly **more** beautifully	**most** firmly **most** easily **most** quickly **most** beautifully

不規則變化：

原級	比較級	最高級
well (好地)	better	best
badly/ill (壞地)	worse	worst
much (很，非常)	more	most
little (少地)	less	least
late (遲地，晚地)	later	latest
far (遠地)	farther (距離較遠地)/ further (更進一步地)	farthest (最遠地)/ furthest (最大程度地)

Try it! 實力演練

I. 填空 (在空格中填入下列各形容詞的比較級與最高級變化)

原級	比較級	原級	最高級
fierce	1.	cautious	4.
healthy	2.	slim	5.
good	3.	bad	6.

II. 填空 (在空格中填入下列各副詞的比較級與最高級變化)

原級	比較級	原級	最高級
hard	1.	well	4.
early	2.	badly	5.
much	3.	skillfully	6.

8-3-3 比較級的句型

1. A 比 B… (優等比較)

A + {連綴動詞 / V} + 比較級 + than + B

- The weather in London is **colder than** that in Taipei. 倫敦的天氣比臺北冷。
- The paella tastes **more delicious than** the spaghetti.
  這西班牙海鮮飯嚐起來比這義大利麵可口。
- Ben studies **harder than** his brother. Ben 比他哥哥用功。
- Ken works **more industriously** than his colleagues. Ken 比同事們更努力工作。

2. A 不比 B… (劣等比較)

A + 連綴動詞 + less adj. + than B

A + V + less adv. + than + B

- Victoria is **less independent than** her sister. Victoria 比她妹妹不獨立。
- The new employee seems **less ambitious than** his colleagues.
  這新員工似乎比他同事更沒企圖心。
- Rachel takes this matter **less seriously than** her friends.
  對於此事，Rachel 比她的朋友們更不以為意。
- Trains travel **less rapidly than** high speed rails. 火車比高鐵慢。

注意

比較級可用 much、even、a lot、far、a little 等詞修飾。

- A lion runs **much** faster than a deer. 獅子跑得比鹿快。
- This poor man is **even** more generous than that rich man. 這個窮人比那個富人更為慷慨。

3. 兩者之中比較…

S + be + the + 比較級 **+ of the two . . .**

- The boy is **the heavier of the two**.
  這男孩是兩人當中比較胖的。
- The steak is **the tastier of the two dishes**.
  牛排是這兩道菜之中比較美味的。

注意

下列形容詞為特殊用法，本身已有比較之意，不另做變化並與介系詞 to 連用：superior to (優於…)、inferior to (劣於…)、senior to (較…資深)、junior to (較…資淺) 等。

- Due to collaboration and discipline, this football team is **superior to** its rivals.
  由於團隊合作和紀律，這個足球隊比對手好多了。
- Unfortunately, the company's new smartphone are **inferior to** its previous ones.
  很遺憾地，該公司的新款智慧型手機比舊款來得差。

Try it! 實力演練

I. 引導式翻譯

1. 我認為草莓比蘋果更加好吃。
   I think strawberries taste ______ ______ ______ apples.
2. Issac 比 Claire 聰明 (intelligent)，但是他工作比她沒效率 (efficiently)。
   Issac is ______ ______ ______ Claire, but he works ______ ______ ______ she.

II. 句子改寫

1. Teresa is good at cooking, but her sister isn't.
   (1) When it comes to cooking, Teresa is ______ than her sister.
   (2) When it comes to cooking, Teresa is ______ to her sister.
   (3) When it comes to cooking, Teresa's sister is ______ than she.
2. The white box is light, and the black one is heavy. (. . . of the two)
   The white box ____.

8-3-4 最高級的句型

1. (在某範圍中) 最…的 (優等比較)

S + 連綴動詞 + 最高級 (+ 單數 N)
S + V + 最高級
} + { **of all** / **of/among + the** + 數字 / **in** + 某群體/範圍 }

- This novel is **the most interesting** of all. 這本小說是所有小說中最有趣的。
- Hank is the **most handsome** of the three. Hank 是這三個人中最帥的。
- MRT is **the most convenient** means of transportation in this city.
  捷運是這城市中最便利的交通方式。
- The young man performs **the best** in the talent show.
  在這才藝秀中，這年輕人表演得最好。

2. (在某範圍中) 最不…的 (劣等比較)

S + 連綴動詞 + **the least adj.** (+ 單數 N)
S + V + **the least adv.**
} + { **of all** / **of/among + the** + 數字 / **in** + 某群體 / 範圍 }

- This city is **the least polluted** of all. 這個城市是所有城市中污染最少的。
- Mr. Wood worked **the least diligently** in this office.
  在這辦公室，Wood 先生工作最不勤勞。

3. 用原級的形式表示最高級的概念

No other + 名詞 + { 連綴動詞 + **as/so + adj.** / **V + as/so + adv.** } + **as . . .**

- In the zoo, **no other** animals are **as large as** the elephant.
  在這個動物園裡，大象是最大的動物。
- **No other** city in the UK is **as prosperous as** London.
  在英國，倫敦是最繁榮的城市。
- **No other** student in my class sings **so well as** Greg.
  在我的班上，Greg 歌唱得最好。

注意

no other 後面可接單數或複數名詞，動詞需隨主詞的單複數作變化。

4. 用比較級的形式表示最高級的概念

S + {連綴動詞 / V} + 比較級 + **than** + **any other** + 單數 **N . . .**

- Ms. Brown is **richer than any other** person in this club.
  Brown 太太是這個俱樂部裡最有錢的人。
- Taipei 101 is **taller than any other** building in Taiwan.
  臺北 101 是臺灣最高的建築物。
- Louis studies **harder than any other** student in his class. Louis 是班上最用功的學生。

注意

最高級前面要加 the，可用 almost、by far、much、nearly、practically 等字詞來修飾。

- Teresa is nearly **the tallest** girl that I have ever seen。
  Teresa 幾乎是我見過最高的女孩。
- Your suggestion is by far **the most practical**. 你的建議是最實際的。

Try it! 實力演練

I. 選擇

_____ 1. Victor is the _____ of these children.
(A) smart (B) smarter (C) smartest (D) most smart

_____ 2. Sarah drives the _____ among her friends.
(A) slowest (B) slower (C) slowlier (D) most slowly

_____ 3. No other girl in the class looks _____ Eleanor. She is by far the prettiest.
(A) prettier as (B) prettier than (C) as prettier as (D) as pretty as

II. 句子改寫

1. This type of car is the most expensive in this car company. (No other . . .)

____

2. Shawn speaks English the most fluently in this department.

(1) (No other . . .) ______________________________

(2) (. . . than any other . . .) ______________________________

8-4 延伸句型與用法

以下討論其他與形容詞和副詞相關的用法及句型。

1. 其他用法

the + adj. = 複數名詞

敘述形容詞與定冠詞 the 連用時，可表示某一類人事物的複數，如 the rich = the rich people、the poor = the poor people、the young = the young people。

- **The rich** are not always happy. 富人未必總是快樂。
- **The young** should take care of **the old**.
  年輕人應該照顧老年人。

of + 抽象名詞 = adj.

of + great + 抽象名詞 = very + adj.

of + no + 抽象名詞 = not + adj.

例：of use = useful、of great significance = very significant、
　　of no importance = unimportant。

- This trade company is looking for a man **of ability** for this position.
  這間貿易公司正在找能幹的人擔任這個職位。 Note = an able man。
- Thanks for your information; it is **of great value**.
  感謝你提供的訊息，它很有價值。 Note = very valuable。

with (+ great) + 抽象名詞 = (very +) adv.

with + no + 抽象名詞 = without + 抽象名詞

例：with patience = patiently、with delight = delightedly。

- The teacher listened to the student **with patience**.
  這老師很有耐心地聽學生說話。 Note = patiently。
- The old man told his story to his grandchildren **with delight**.
  這老人開心地向孫兒們說著他的故事。 Note = delightedly。

2. 比較級的延伸句型

as + { adj. (+ N) / adv. } + as possible → as + { adj. (+ N) / adv. } + as one can

表示：盡可能…

- To catch the robbers, the police drove **as fast as possible**.
  → To catch the robbers, the police drove **as fast as they could**.
  為了抓到搶匪，警察盡可能地開快車。
- The patient drank **as much water as possible**.
  → The patient drank **as much water as she could**.
  這個病人盡可能地喝很多水。

比較級 **+ and +** 比較級

adj.-er and adj.-er

adv.-er and adv.-er

more and more adj./adv.

表示：越來越…

- The workers decided to call it a day as it got **darker and darker**.
  工人們決定休息，因為天色越來越黑了。
- Due to his successful investment strategy, Mr. Wormwood becomes **richer and richer**. 由於成功的投資策略，Wormwood 先生變得越來越有錢。
- With the wind blowing, the kite flies **higher and higher**.
  隨著風吹，風箏越飛越高。
- As he grows older, Kenny becomes **more and more mature**.
  隨著年紀增長，Ken 變得越來越成熟。
- Alice walked **faster and faster**. Alice 走得越來越快。

The + 比較級 **(+ S + V), the +** 比較級 **(S + V) . . .**

表示：越…就越…

- **The sooner** (it is), **the better** (it is). 越快越好。
- **The more** Zoe makes, **the more** she spends. Zoe 賺得越多，就花得越多。
- **The more** you eat, **the heavier** you will become. 你吃得越多，就變得越胖。

3. 搭配「倍數詞」比較

A + { **be** 動詞 / **V** } + 倍數詞 + **as** + { **adj. (+ N)** / **adv.** } + **as** + **B**

倍數詞 + 原級比較：A 是 B 的…倍

- Eddie's room is **half as large as** his brother's.
  Eddie 的房間是他哥哥的一半大。
- Sally reads **three times as many books as** I.
  Sally 讀的書是我讀的三倍多。
- It is surprising that the sandals are **three times as expensive as** the sneakers.
  驚人的是，這雙涼鞋是那雙運動鞋的三倍貴。

A + { **be** 動詞 / **V** } + 倍數詞 + 比較級 + **than** + **B**

倍數詞 + 比較級：A 是 B 的…倍

- Diana's hair is **two times longer than** mine. Diana 的頭髮是我的兩倍長。
  → Diana's hair is **twice as long as** mine.
  Note half 與 twice 需搭配 as . . . as 的句型。
- The laptop is **three times more expensive than** the smartphone.
  這台筆電是那支手機的三倍貴。

A + { **be** 動詞 / **V** } + 倍數詞 + **the** + **N** + **of** + **B**

倍數詞 + 名詞：A 是 B 的…倍

在此句型中常用的名詞有 ： size 、 length 、 width 、 height 、 depth 、 weight 、 number、sum、amount、age、price 等。

- The little boy is **half the age of** his brother.
  這小男孩的年紀是他哥哥的一半大。
- The sumo wrestler is **five times the weight of** that young lady.
  這相撲選手的體重是那位年輕女士的五倍。
- This skyscraper is **several times the height of** that building.
  這棟摩天大樓是那棟建築的好幾倍高。

Try it! 實力演練

I. 選擇

______ 1. After the big earthquake, the homeless ______ in need of help.

(A) are (B) is (C) be (D) will

______ 2. Anne is a teacher ______ patience, who teaches her students ______ patience.

(A) at; about (B) with; of (C) of; with (D) for; under

______ 3. To pass the exam, Jessica studies ______.

(A) as hard as possibly (B) as hard as she can

(B) as hardly as possible (D) as hard as she does

II. 翻譯

1. 王太太在百貨公司待得越久就買越多。

____

2. 這個湖是那座游泳池的三倍大。

____

Notes

Chapter

9 連接詞

連接詞用於連接單字與單字、片語與片語或子句與子句，可以分為**對等連接詞**、**相關連接詞**、**從屬連接詞**與**準連接詞**。

9-1 對等連接詞

對等連接詞如 and、but、or 用來連接**文法結構相等**的單字、片語、子句或句子。

連接詞	用法	範例
and **(和；而且)**	連接前後意思高度相關、語意連續的字詞、片語、子句或句子。	• Air **and** water are necessary for living creatures. 空氣和水對生物是必要的。Note 連接名詞。 • Lydia left the room **and** locked the door. Lydia 離開房間，鎖上門。Note 連接動詞片語。 • It started to rain, **and** many people opened their umbrellas. 開始下雨了，人們都撐起傘。Note 連接句子。
but **(但是)**	連接前後意思相反或對比的字詞、片語、子句或句子。	• I am not a student, **but** my brother is. 我不是學生，但我弟弟是。Note 連接句子，表相反。 • This grapefruit tastes sour **but** sweet. 這葡萄柚嚐起來酸酸的，但又甜甜的。 Note 連接形容詞，表對比。 • Allen explained very hard, **but** no one believed him. Allen 努力解釋，但是沒人相信他。Note 連接句子，表對比。
or **(或者)**	連接有選擇性的字詞、片語、子句或句子。	• Which color do you like, pink **or** purple? 你喜歡哪一個顏色，粉紅色或紫色？Note 連接名詞。 • Are you for the policy **or** are you against it? 你贊成或反對這個新政策？Note 連接句子。

Try it! 實力演練

I. 填空 (填入正確的對等連接詞 and、but、or)

1. The girl turned on the light _____ started to read.
2. Ken got up early, _____ he still missed the bus.
3. Which subject do you like, English _____ math?

II. 句子合併

1. { My father bought a bicycle for me. / My father also bought a smartphone for me. } (以對等連接詞連接名詞)

→ ______________________________

2. { The patient took the medicine. / The patient felt better after that. } (以對等連接詞連接動詞片語)

→ ______________________________

3. { Does Jake like coffee? / Does Jake like tea? } (以 Which . . . , . . . or . . . 的句型合併)

→ ______________________________

9-2 相關連接詞

1. 一起出現並有特定意義的連接詞組稱為相關連接詞。
2. either A or B、neither A nor B 與 not only A but also B 連接二個主詞時，動詞須配合最接近主詞變化。因多用於直述句，故記為「與 B 一致」。

相關連接詞	連接主詞時的動詞形式	範例
either A or B (不是 A 就是 B)	與 B 一致	• Chloé will cook **either** noodles **or** rice for dinner. Chloé 不是煮麵就是煮飯當晚餐。 • **Either** you **or** I am wrong. 不是你就是我錯。 • **Either** Lia **or** her classmates have to write the experiment report. 不是 Lia 就是她同學們得寫實驗報告。

neither A nor B (不是 A 也不是 B)	與 B 一致	• The student is interested in **neither** history **nor** geography. 這學生對歷史或地理都沒興趣。 • **Neither** Michael **nor** his teammates are going to practice volleyball tomorrow. Michael 和他隊友們明天都不打算練習排球。 • **Neither** Sebastian **nor** his parents have been to Canada. Sebastian 和他爸媽都沒去過加拿大。
not only A but also B (不只 A 而且 B)	與 B 一致	• Naomi is **not only** smart **but also** beautiful. Naomi 不只很聰明也很漂亮。 • **Not only** Peter **but also** his friends are crazy about online games. 不只 Peter 還有他的朋友們都熱衷於線上遊戲。 • **Not only** my parents **but also** my sister always gets up early. 不只我父母還有我的妹妹總是早起。
both A and B (A 和 B 兩者都)	複數	• Joe invited **both** Nancy **and** her boyfriend to his party. Joe 邀請 Nancy 和她男友參加派對。 • **Both** the government **and** experts are optimistic about this policy. 政府和專家對於這個政策都抱持樂觀的態度。 • **Both** Mr. **and** Mrs. Piaget like jogging. Piaget 夫婦都喜歡慢跑。
A as well as B (A 和 B 都…)	與 A 一致	• Davis bought jeans **as well as** socks in the store. Davis 在店裡買了牛仔褲和短襪。 • Raymond **as well as** I is curious about what this relationship expert says about gender differences. Raymond 和我對這位二性專家提到的性別差異很好奇。 • The players **as well as** the coach are excited about their winning the championship. 選手們和教練都對贏得冠軍很興奮。

Try it! 實力演練

I. 選擇

______ 1. Both Hugh's brother and sister ______ to volunteer work.

(A) is devoted (B) are devoted

(C) devotes themselves (D) are devoted themselves

______ 2. ______ Samuel ______ his girlfriend can attend Eric's wedding. They are both busy.

(A) Both; and (B) Either; or

(C) Neither; nor (D) Not only; but also

______ 3. ______ are interested in this crossword game. They all want to know how to solve it.

(A) Either Zack or his classmates

(B) Neither Zack nor his classmates

(C) Zack as well as his classmates

(D) Not only Zack but also his classmates

II. 句子合併

1. { Sweaters are necessary in winter. / Scarves are necessary in winter. } (Both . . . and . . . .)

→ ____

2. { You have to clean the room. / Otherwise, your sister has to do it. } (Either . . . or . . . .)

→ ____

3. { Yolanda speaks English. / Yolanda speaks Japanese, too. } (. . . not only . . . but also . . . .)

→ ____

9-3 從屬連接詞

從屬連接詞可以用來引導表示「時間」、「原因」、「結果」、「讓步」、「條件」、「目的」、「狀態」、「對比」等意思的副詞子句，此時又稱作**從屬子句**。

類型	例字	範例
結果	so (所以)	• It is raining heavily, **so** the game is postponed. 雨下得很大，所以比賽延期。
	so . . . that、such . . . that (如此…以致…)	• The patient is **so** weak **that** she totally loses her appetite. 這病患如此虛弱，以致於完全失去胃口。 → so + adj./adv. + that • Katie is **such** a smart girl **that** she learns everything very quickly. Katie 如此聰明，所以學每件事都很快。 → such (+ adj.) + N + that
讓步	although、though (雖然)、even if、even though (即使)	• **Although**/**Though** Carl keeps silent, he knows what happened. 雖然 Carl 保持沈默，他知道發生了什麼事。 • **Even though** Fiona won the game, she was not proud at all. 即使 Fiona 贏得比賽，她一點也不傲慢。
條件	if (如果)、as long as (只要)	• **If** any problem arises, we'll try our best to solve it. 如果有任何問題，我們會盡力解決。 • **As long as** you devote yourself to the work, you can make it. 只要你專心於這份工作，你就能成功。
狀態	as if、as though (彷彿)	• Lucy looks **as if**/**as though** she saw a ghost. Lucy 看起來彷彿見鬼了。 • The young man talks **as if**/**as though** he were a doctor. 這年輕人說起話來彷彿他是醫生。
目的	so that、in order that (以便…)	• Eat less sweets **so that** you can lose weight. 少吃點甜食就能減肥。 • Diana went to bed early **in order that** she could get up early. Diana 早睡以便能早起。

時間	when、as、while (當)	• **When** Ryan comes tonight, he will help decorate the house. 當 Ryan 今晚來時，他會幫忙佈置房子。 • **As** my sister was listening to the radio, she heard some strange noise. 當我姊姊正在聽廣播時，她聽到怪聲。 • **While** Darren was taking a shower, the doorbell rang. 當 Darren 在洗澡時，門鈴響了。
	before (在…之前)	• **Before** Rex explained, his friends misunderstood him. 在 Rex 解釋之前，他的朋友誤會他了。
	after (在…之後)	• **After** Audrey graduated from high school, she took a gap year to travel and work. 在 Audrey 高中畢業後，她利用空檔年去旅行和工作。
	since (自從)	• **Since** Eleanor was a child, she has been passionate about science. Eleanor 從小就熱衷於科學。
	as soon as (一…就…)	• **As soon as** my brother got home, he turned on the TV. 我弟弟一回家就打開電視。
	until、till (直到)	• Stuart played football with his classmates **until**/**till** it got dark. Stuart 和朋友踢足球直到天黑。
原因	because、as (因為)	• The manager flew into a fury **because** the salespeople failed to hit their sales targets. 經理勃然大怒，因為業務員未能達到銷售目標。 • Richard caught a cold **as** he didn't wear warm clothing. Richard 因為沒穿禦寒衣物而感冒了。
	since、now that (既然)	• **Since** it's so late, you had better go to bed. 既然這麼晚了，你最好去睡了 • **Now that** you have a day off, you can take a good rest. 既然你放假一天，你可以好好休息。
對比	while、whereas (而)	• Alex likes soccer, **while** his brother likes baseball. Alex 喜歡足球，而他弟弟喜歡棒球。 • My brother's room is big, **whereas** mine is small. 我哥哥的房間很大，而我的很小。

Try it! 實力演練

I. 選擇

_____ 1. Wendy heard a loud scream _____ she was walking on the street.
(A) because (B) while (C) before (D) after

_____ 2. _____ you know what to do, you may start your project.
(A) As if (B) Even if (C) Now that (D) So that

_____ 3. The baby didn't stop crying _____ his mother held him in her arms.
(A) since (B) while (C) if (D) until

II. 句子合併

1. { The guest took off her shoes. / She entered the house. } (. . . before . . .)
→ ____________________

2. { The soccer team lost the game. / They were not discouraged at all. } (Although . . .)
→ ____________________

3. { You show friendliness. / You can make friends easily. } (As long as . . .)
→ ____________________

9-4 準連接詞

1. 準連接詞又稱為副詞連接詞，屬於轉折語，本身是副詞，卻可以將兩個獨立子句的意思串連起來，使其成為有意義、有關聯的句子。
2. 注意，準連接詞**並非連接詞**，其用法屬於副詞，故其前面必須使用句號 (.)、分號 (;) 或連接詞 (and)，後面要加逗點，以分隔兩個句子。

依情境與用法，將準連接詞整理如下：

<table>
<tr><th>情境</th><th colspan="2">準連接詞</th><th>用法</th></tr>
<tr><td rowspan="2">此外</td><td colspan="2">besides、moreover、furthermore, what's more、in addition、additionally 等</td><td>表示額外提及與主題相關的事情</td></tr>
<tr><td>範例</td><td colspan="2">• This composition is poorly written; besides, it has many spelling mistakes.
→ This composition is poorly written. Besides, it has many spelling mistakes.
這篇作文寫得欠佳；此外，它還有很多拼字錯誤。
• Music can entertain people; moreover, it can relax people's minds.
→ Music can entertain people. Moreover, it can relax people's minds.
音樂可以娛樂大眾；此外，它可以讓人們放鬆心情。</td></tr>
<tr><td rowspan="2">然而</td><td colspan="2">however、yet、still、nevertheless 等</td><td>表示語氣轉折或前後文意相反</td></tr>
<tr><td>範例</td><td colspan="2">• Jaden promised to help; however, he changed his mind at the last minute.
→ Jaden promised to help. However, he changed his mind at the last minute.
Jaden 答應要幫忙，但卻在最後一刻改變心意。
• The worker was tired out; nevertheless, he had to finish painting this room.
→ The worker was tired out. Nevertheless, he had to finish painting this room. 這工人很疲倦，然而他必須把房間粉刷完。</td></tr>
<tr><td rowspan="2">因此</td><td colspan="2">therefore、thus、hence、as a result、as a consequence、consequently、accordingly 等</td><td>表示結論或結果</td></tr>
<tr><td>範例</td><td colspan="2">• Tim has worn out his shoes; therefore, he has to buy a new pair.
Tim 把鞋子穿壞了，因此，他必須買雙新的。
• The salesman worked very hard. Thus, he got a promotion.
這業務員很努力工作。因此，他獲得升遷。</td></tr>
<tr><td rowspan="2">否則</td><td colspan="2">otherwise、or</td><td>表示若 A 沒發生，會導致 B 發生</td></tr>
<tr><td>範例</td><td colspan="2">• Before going to another country, we have to learn their customs; otherwise, we may offend the locals.
在到其他國家前，我們必須學習他們的習俗；否則，我們可能會冒犯當地人。</td></tr>
<tr><td rowspan="2">相反地</td><td colspan="2">instead、on the contrary 等</td><td>表示相反的情況</td></tr>
<tr><td>範例</td><td colspan="2">• Colton didn't go to school. Instead, he went to the Internet café.
Colton 沒去學校。相反地，他去網咖。</td></tr>
</table>

舉例	for example、for instance 等	列舉情形
	範例 • The manager tried hard to promote this product. **For example**, he used commercials to make his product known to customers. 這個經理努力促銷這個產品。例如，他利用廣告讓顧客們注意到這個產品。	
同樣地	likewise、similarly、in the same way 等	表示兩件事有相同的情形
	範例 • Many e-mail users are annoyed with junk mail. **Likewise**, many companies are troubled with this problem. 許多 E-mail 用戶覺得垃圾郵件令人困擾。同樣地，許多公司也為此同感困擾。	
換句話說	namely、in other words、that is、that is to say 等	用另一種說法來闡述前面提及的事情
	範例 • Amelia is generous; **that is**, she is willing to help others with all she can. Amelia 很大方；也就是說，她願意盡所能去幫助他人。 • Mr. Anderson is always punctual. **In other words**, he is never late. Anderson 先生總是很準時。換句話說，他從不遲到。	

Try it! 實力演練

I. 選擇

_____ 1. Some people believe in aliens; _____, others don't.

(A) moreover (B) thus (C) however (D) otherwise

_____ 2. Google is a successful company. It encourages creativity; _____, it stresses the importance of cooperation.

(A) besides (B) hence (C) yet (D) instead

_____ 3. The pop singer's voice cracked during her performance; _____, she felt extremely embarrassed.

(A) namely (B) therefore (C) nevertheless (D) for example

II. 句子合併

1. { Frank wrote a love letter to Sandra. / Frank sang a love song to her. } (. . . moreover . . .)

→ ______________________________

2. The teacher has explained the theory several times. / The students still can't understand the theory. (. . . however . . .)

→ ______________________________

3. Dry your wet hair. / If you don't do so, you will catch a cold. (. . . otherwise . . .)

→ ______________________________

9-5 延伸句型

以下討論其他與連接詞相關的應用句型。

1. 不是…而是…

not . . . but . . .

連接的字詞、片語或子句必須有相同的文法結構。

- The girl wearing boots is **not** my sister **but** my friend.
  這位穿靴子的女孩不是我的妹妹，而是我的朋友。
- Marcelo does**n't** come from Spain **but** from Brazil.
  Marcelo 不是來自西班牙而是巴西。

2. …，那麼…就會…

祈使句，**and + S + will/can + V . . .**

- Go to bed early, **and** you can get up early.
  你早睡就能早起。
- Hurry up, **and** you can catch the train.
  動作快點，那麼你就能趕上火車。
  (請參見 CH15)

3. …，否則…就會…

祈使句，**or + S + will/can + V . . .**

- Get up early, **or** you will be late. 早點起床，否則你會遲到。
- Hurry up, **or** you will miss the train. 動作快點，否則你會錯過火車。

Try it! 實力演練

I. 翻譯

1. 這孩子並非無禮，而是好奇。

   The child is ______ impolite ______ curious.

2. 把書本放回書架上，否則你的房間就會看起來很雜亂。

   Put your books back on the shelves, ______ your room will look messy.

3. 你可以問問王先生的意見，你就會知道該怎麼做。

   You can ask for Mr. Wang's advice, ______ you will know what to do.

II. 句子合併

1. { Put on your coat. / You will catch a cold. } (以連接詞 and 或 or 合併句子)

   → ____

2. { Have some more cake. / You won't feel hungry. } (以連接詞 and 或 or 合併句子)

   → ____

3. { Doris is not afraid of cockroaches. / Doris is afraid of dogs. } (以 not . . . but . . . 合併句子)

   → ____

Notes

Chapter

10 關係詞

本單元將討論關係詞的用法。關係詞可用於引導形容詞子句修飾名詞，用法可分為**關係代名詞**與**關係副詞**。

10-1 關係代名詞

1. 關係代名詞 (以下稱為關代) 具有代名詞與連接詞功能，用來引導形容詞子句，置於名詞後修飾；被修飾的名詞稱為**先行詞**。
2. 關係詞引導的子句又可稱「關係子句」，以下統一稱為**形容詞子句**。
3. 關係代名詞的格由其在形容詞子句中的功能決定。若當形容詞子句的主詞，關代用主格；若當形容詞子句中動詞或介系詞的受詞，則關代用受格。
4. 當前面有**介系詞**或**逗號**時，關代不可為 that。

1. 關係代名詞與先行詞的對應整理如下：

	人		動物 / 事物		人 + 動物 / 事物
主格	who	that	which	that	that
受格	whom	that	which	that	that
所有格	whose		of which/whose		×

2. 用關係代名詞合併二個句子的步驟如下：

Step 1 先找出兩句相同的名詞，其中一個當成先行詞。

Step 2 根據先行詞，使用適當的關代引導形容詞子句。

Step 3 將形容詞子句緊接於所修飾的先行詞之後。

- The automobile manufacturer recalled many cars.
  These cars had engine problems.

Step 1 找出兩句相同的名詞 cars。

Step 2 依先行詞，使用關代 which 引導形容詞子句 had engine problems。

Step 3 將形容詞子句 which had engine problems 接於所修飾的先行詞 cars 之後。

→ The automobile manufacturer recalled many cars（先行詞） **which** had engine problems（形容詞子句）. 這家汽車製造商召回許多有引擎問題的車輛。

10-1-1 關係代名詞當主詞的用法

> 句型：**who/which/that + V**
>
> 形容詞子句中，關係代名詞可以代替先行詞當作主詞，其後接動詞。

- My classmate is a moviegoer.
  My classmate knows a lot about films.

  → My classmate（先行詞） **who** knows a lot about films（形容詞子句） is a moviegoer.

  我那位對電影瞭解很多的同學是個電影迷。

  Note 先行詞為人 (my classmate)，故關代用 who，在形容詞子句中當主詞。

- The man is the new manager of this company.
  The man is speaking German.

  → The man **that** is speaking German is the new manager of this company.

  那個正在說德文的人是這間公司的新任經理。Note 關代 that 當主詞。

- Tanya's boyfriend bought her a watch **which** was made in Switzerland.

  Tanya 的男友買了瑞士製的錶給她。

  Note 先行詞為物 (the watch)，故關代用 which。

- The little girl and her dog **that** were running on the beach were enjoying the sunshine. 小女孩和她的狗在沙灘上奔跑，享受著陽光。

  Note 先行詞為人與物 (the little girl and her dog)，故關代用 that。

Try it! 實力演練

I. 填空

1. The cook ______ has won the cooking competition is Kim's uncle.

2. The building ______ is designed by a famous architect looks magnificent.
3. The artist and her paintings ______ are known to the public have attracted much attention.

II. 句子合併 (以適當的關係代名詞合併下列句子)

1. The tourist is looking for the train station.
   The tourist has a map in her hand.
   → ____________________

2. The words are blurred.
   The words are written with a pencil.
   → ____________________

10-1-2 關係代名詞當受詞的用法

句型：**whom/which/that + S + V**

形容詞子句中，關係代名詞可以代替先行詞當作受詞，其後為「主詞 + 動詞」的結構。

- We are talking about the pop singer.
  Ann likes the pop singer.
  → We are talking about the pop singer (先行詞) **whom** Ann likes (形容詞子句).
  我們正在談論 Ann 喜歡的流行歌手。
  Note 先行詞為人 (the pop singer)，且在形容詞子句中關代是 like 的受詞，故用 whom。
- Julio came across a friend.
  Julio hadn't seen this friend for ages.
  → Julio came across a friend **whom** he hadn't seen for ages.
  Julio 遇到他一個很久沒見面的朋友。
  Note 關代 whom 當 seen 的受詞。
- Allen lost the wallet **which** his father bought for him. Allen 弄丟了爸爸買給他的皮夾。
  Note 關代 which 作 bought 的受詞。

學習便利貼

判斷關代為主格或受格的方法：由基本句子結構是 S + V 的概念判斷。
(1) 結構為**關代 + V** 時，關代為主格。
(2) 結構為**關代 + S + V** 時，關代為受格。

- The woman was looking for her son and her cat **that** we just saw on the street.
  那個女人正在找她的兒子和貓，我們剛剛在街上看見他們。
  Note 先行詞為人 + 物 (the woman's son and her cat)，故關代用 that，作 saw 的受詞。

補充用法整理如下：

用法	補充
關係代名詞可作動詞的受詞	關係代名詞當作受詞時，可以省略。
範例	• To the club members' disappointment, the guest speaker (**whom**) they have invited will not come. 讓俱樂部成員失望的是，他們邀請的客座演講者不會來。 • The boy (**that**) the police saved was too frightened to say anything. 警察拯救出來的小男孩嚇到說不出話來。 • The sashimi (**which**) Ivan and his family ate was not fresh. Ivan 和家人吃的生魚片不新鮮。
關係代名詞可作介系詞的受詞	1. 介系詞可置於子句的**句尾**，此時可**省略**當受詞的關係代名詞。 2. 當介系詞移到關係代名詞前，不可省略關係代名詞，且不可用 **that**。
範例	• There stands the boy (**whom/that**) Kelly has a crush **on**. → There stands the boy **on whom** Kelly has a crush. Kelly 喜歡的男孩站在那裡。 • Oliver's brother is the only person **on whom** he can depend. Oliver 的哥哥是他唯一可依靠的人。

Try it! 實力演練

I. 填空

1. The patient ______ the nurse is looking after looks very ill.
2. The math question ______ the teacher asked was too difficult for the student.
3. The fashion designer about ______ the women are talking is very famous.

II. 句子合併

1. { The cyclist was sent to the hospital. / The careless driver hit the cyclist. } (用關代連接)

→ ______________________________

2. { The stray dog was adopted.
The animal rescue team saved the stray dog. } (省略關代)

→ ______________________________

3. { The science fiction appeals to young readers.
Sharon is talking about the science fiction. } (將介系詞移到關代之前)

→ ______________________________

10-1-3 關係代名詞當所有格的用法

句型：**whose + N + V**

關係代名詞在形容詞子句中可以當所有格。在此用法中，不論先行詞為人、動物或事物，關係代名詞的所有格一律用 **whose**；先行詞是**事物**時，whose 可與 **of which** 做代換。

• { These people have no places to go.
These people's houses were burned down. }

→ These people **whose** houses were burned down have no places to go.

這些房子被燒毀的人無處可去。

Note 先行詞為人 (these people)，關代替換所有格 (these people's)，故用 whose。

學習便利貼

先行詞為事物時，其關係詞的所有格可用以下方式表示，但第一種結構比較常見。

(1) 先行詞 + whose + N

(2) 先行詞 + of + which + N

• { The old man looks like Santa Claus.
The old man's beard is white. }

→ The old man **whose** beard is white looks like Santa Claus.

那白鬍子老人看起來像耶誕老人。

Note 先行詞為人 (the old man)，關代替換所有格 (the old man's)，故用 whose。

• { The house belongs to Mr. and Mrs. Hiddleston.
The roof of the house is red. }

→ The house **whose** roof is red belongs to Mr. and Mrs. Hiddleston.

→ The house **of which** the roof is red belongs to Mr. and Mrs. Hiddleston.

那個屋頂是紅色的房子屬於 Hiddleston 夫婦。

Try it! 實力演練

I. 引導式翻譯

1. 那些會員卡 (membership card) 失效的人不得進入俱樂部。

   Those people ______ ______ ______ are invalid are not allowed to enter the club.

2. 那輛輪胎 (tire) 是新品的自行車被偷了。

   The bicycle ______ ______ ______ were new was stolen.

II. 句子合併

1. { The earthquake victim's leg was bleeding. / The earthquake victim was saved by the rescue team. } (whose)

   → ______________________________

2. { Donald will work in a Canadian company. / The logo of the company is a maple leaf. } (whose)

   → ______________________________

10-2 關係代名詞的限定與非限定用法

依據先行詞的特性與形容詞子句的功用，關係代名詞引導的形容詞子句可分為限定用法與非限定用法。

限定及非限定用法的比較如下：

	限定用法	非限定用法
意義	先行詞**不夠明確**或有**多個對象**時，必須以形容詞子句來做限定，稱為限定用法。	1. 當先行詞為**唯一的**、**明確的對象**或**專有名詞**時，因先行詞很明確，不需形容詞子句來做限定，而是以形容詞子句做**補充說明**，此用法稱為非限定用法。 2. 此用法中，省略非限定子句不影響句意。
說明	關係代名詞之前不加逗點。	關係代名詞之前**必須**加**逗點**，故在非限定用法中，不可用 that 當關代。

範例		
範例	• Mrs. Robinson often talks about her son **who** is a college student. Robinson 太太常聊到她讀大學的兒子。 Note Robinson 太太的兒子不僅一人，以形容詞子句限定所談論的是上大學的那位。 • We just met Bobby's uncle **who** got married last month. 我們剛剛遇到 Bobby 上個月結婚的叔叔。 Note Bobby 的叔叔不只一人，必須以形容詞子句限定所談論的是上個月結婚的叔叔。	• This is Jason's sister, **who** studies in college. 這是 Jason 的姊姊，她在讀大學。 Note Jason 只有一個姊姊，以形容詞子句**補充說明**她在就讀大學；因為對象明確，形容詞子句的部分當作補充說明，即使去掉也不影響句意。 • Sara's uncle, **who** works as an engineer, will move to Japan next year. Sara 當工程師的叔叔明年將搬去日本。 Note Sara 只有一個叔叔，是唯一對象，形容詞子句補充說明他是工程師。

注意

在非限定用法中，which 尚有當**主詞**指前面整句的用法。在此用法中必須**加逗號**，且不可用 that。

• Alley devotes herself to helping stray dogs**, which** is very kind of her.

Alley 致力於幫助流浪狗，真是好心。

Note which 指前面整件事，須加逗號。

Try it! 實力演練

I. 選擇

______ 1. My mother ______ likes to go jogging in the morning.

(A) who always gets up early (B) , who always gets up early,

(C) that always gets up early (D) , that always gets up early,

______ 2. In the novel, Frankenstein ______ had created an ugly and horrible monster.

(A) , was a scientist, (B) who was a scientist

(C) , which was a scientist, (D) , who was a scientist,

______ 3. The superstar drove under the influence ______ irritated the public.

(A) , which (B) which (C) , that (D) that

II. 句子改寫

1. Greg has three aunts. One of his aunts lives in Los Angeles, and she will come to visit his family next week.
   Greg's aunt ______________________________ is coming to pay a visit to his family next week.
2. Fiona has only one watch. It was made in Switzerland and it was from her mother.
   Fiona's watch ______________________________ was from her mother.
3. Paris is the capital of France. It is known for perfumes and cosmetics.
   Paris ______________________________ is famous for perfumes and cosmetics.

10-3 關係代名詞 that 的用法

在下列情境條件中，關係代名詞必須用 that：
(1) 先行詞是「**人＋動物／事物**」。
(2) 當有**最高級**、**the only**、**the very**、**the same**、**all**、**any**、**序數**修飾先行詞時。
(3) 疑問詞是 **who**、**which** 時，避免重複。

使用 that 的情境條件，整理如下：

情境條件	範例
先行詞為「人＋動物／事物」	• The old lady and her dog **that** are walking in the park are enjoying the fresh air. 正在公園裡散步的老太太和狗正在享受新鮮空氣。
有最高級修飾先行詞	• Sarah is the most beautiful girl **that** Ben has ever seen. Sarah 是 Ben 見過最美的女孩。
有 all、any、the only、the very、the same 修飾詞	• Sarah is the only girl **that** Ben loves. Sarah 是 Ben 唯一愛的女孩。 • Sarah is the very girl **that** Ben wants to spend his lifetime with. Sarah 正是 Ben 想一起度過一生的女孩。

有序數修飾先行詞時	• Sarah was the first girl **that** attracted Ben's attention. Sarah 是第一個吸引 Ben 注意的女孩。
疑問句是 who 或 which	• Who is the girl **that** is standing at the door? 那個站在門邊的女孩是誰？ • Which is the right answer **that** the teacher mentioned? 那一個是老師提到的正確解答？

注意

在下列情形中，關係代名詞不可用 **that**：

1. 關係代名詞前有介系詞時。

• [O] The pianist **about whom** they were talking came from Britain.
[X] The pianist about that they were talking came from Britain.
他們談論的鋼琴家來自英國。

• [O] The summer resort **about which** my friends talk sounds great.
[X] The summer resort about that my friends talk sounds great.
我朋友們談論的避暑聖地聽起來很棒。

2. 關係代名詞前有逗點時。

• [O] Taipei**, which** is the largest city in Taiwan, is highly populated.
[X] Taipei, that is the largest city in Taiwan, is highly populated.
臺北是臺灣最大的城市，人口眾多。

Try it! 實力演練

I. 選擇

______ 1. In Greek mythology, Helen was the very girl ______ the prince of Trojan loved.
(A) which (B) who (C) that (D) whose

______ 2. Columbus is said to be the first person ______ discovered America.
(A) that (B) who (C) whose (D) whom

______ 3. This is the most expensive scarf ______ Judy has ever bought.
(A) which (B) , whom (C) that (D) , that

II. 句子改寫

1. { Claire was the second person.
   Claire objected the proposal.

Claire was the second person ______________________________

2. { Mr. Ford and his two cats live in a house with a beautiful garden.
   They welcome their neighbors and share the garden with them.

Mr. Ford and his two cats ______________________________

3. No one can solve this problem except Charles.

Charles is the only person ______________________________

10-4 關係副詞

1. 關係副詞兼有**連接詞**與**副詞**的功能，相當於「介系詞 + 關係代名詞」，使用的介系詞必須搭配先行詞變化。
2. 關係副詞有 when (表時間)、where (表地方)、why (表原因)。

1. 關係副詞與相對應之「介系詞 + 關係代名詞」一覽表

說明＼先行詞	關係副詞	介系詞 + 關係代名詞	
表時間	when	at/in/on	which
表地方	where	at/in/on	which
表原因	why	for	which

2. 用關係副詞合併二個句子的步驟如下：

Step 1 先找出兩句相同的名詞，當成先行詞。

Step 2 將另一句「介系詞 + 該先行詞」的部分換成關係副詞，引導形容詞子句。

Step 3 將形容詞子句緊接於所修飾的先行詞之後。

• { The local government will build a new park.
  People can relax and exercise **in** the park.

Step 1 先找出兩句相同的名詞 park，當成先行詞。

Step 2 將另一句有「介系詞 + 該先行詞」的部分 (in the park) 取代成關係副詞 where，引導形容詞子句。

Step 3 將形容詞子句緊接於所修飾的先行詞之後。

→ The local government will build a new park (先行詞) **where** people can relax and exercise. (形容詞子句)

當地政府將建造新公園讓人們可以在那兒放鬆和運動。

- This is the day **when** Harry met Sally.

  → This is the day **on which** Harry met Sally.

  這就是 Harry 遇見 Sally 的那一天。

  Note 由先行詞 day 決定使用介系詞 on。

- This is the restaurant **where** Harry met Sally.

  → This is the restaurant **in which** Harry met Sally.

  這就是 Harry 遇見 Sally 的餐廳。

- This is the reason **why** Harry fell in love with Sally.

  → This is the reason **for which** Harry fell in love with Sally.

  這就是 Harry 愛上 Sally 的原因。

3. 關係副詞與關係代名詞的比較：

關係副詞	關係代名詞
關係副詞 + 完整的子句 (因關係副詞不影響子句的句型結構)	關係代名詞 + 不完整的子句 (因關係代名詞代替形容詞子句中的主詞或受詞，故接不完整的子句)
• Anita will sell the house **where** she has been living for 10 years. Anita 將會賣掉她已經住十年的房子。 Note 關係副詞 where 不影響句型結構，其後接完整的子句。	• Anita will sell the house **which** is located in the downtown area. Anita 將會賣掉她位在鬧區的房子。 Note 關係代名詞 which 代替形容詞子句的主詞，故其後接不完整的子句。

Try it! 實力演練

I. 選擇（複選）

______ 1. Before winter approaches, migratory birds make long flights to warmer regions ______ they can easily find food.

(A) which (B) in which (C) where (D) when

______ 2. These old men can't forget the day ______ the war broke out.

(A) on which (B) at which (C) how (D) when

______ 3. The boy can't give any reason ______ he was late for school.

(A) why (B) for which (C) where (D) in which

II. 句子合併

1. { Many people like to go camping in spring.
   The weather is comfortable in spring.

→（以關係副詞合併）________________________________

→（以介系詞 + 關代合併）________________________________

2. { Philip is looking for a quiet room.
   Philip can take a nap in that room.

→（以關係副詞合併）________________________________

→（以介系詞 + 關代合併）________________________________

Chapter

11 疑問句

疑問句可分為直接問句，間接問句與附加問句三種類型。

11-1 直接問句

直接問句的基本結構為動詞在主詞之前，即 **Be + S + SC?** 或 **Aux. + S + V . . . ?**，可由移動直述句中的 be 動詞 、 情態助動詞 (如 can 、 will) 或加入助動詞 (do 、does、did) 而形成。

形成直接問句的方法整理如下：

種類	說明
be 動詞	(1) 將直述句的 be 動詞移到主詞前。 (2) 以 Yes/No 回答問句。 範例 • [問] **Is** Catherine addicted to smartphones? Catherine 有沉迷於智慧型手機嗎？ [答] **Yes,** she is. 是的，她有。 • [問] **Are** these people waiting in line for the new ramen restaurant? 這些人在排隊要在新開的拉麵店用餐嗎？ [答] **No,** they are not. 不，他們不是。
情態助動詞	(1) 將直述句的情態助動詞移到主詞前。 (2) 以 Yes/No 回答問句。 範例 • [問] **Can** Mr. Rogers speak several languages? Rogers 先生會說多國語言嗎？ [答] **Yes,** he can. 是的，他會。 • [問] **Will** the committee members make the final decision this afternoon? 委員會今天下午會做出最後決定嗎？ [答] **No,** they will not. 不，他們不會。

一般動詞	(1) 在句首加上 do、does 或 did，原本句中的一般動詞須使用原形。 (2) 以 Yes/No 回答問句。 範例 • [問] **Does** Daisy **collect** stamps? Daisy 有收集郵票嗎？ [答] **Yes,** she does. 是的，她有。 • [問] **Do** these girls **like** fish and chips? 這些女孩們喜歡炸魚薯條嗎？ [答] **No,** they don't. 不，她們不喜歡。
疑問詞 **(wh-/how)**	(1) 疑問詞置於句首，並將句子改為疑問句結構：**wh- + be/aux. + S . . .**。 (2) 不以 Yes/No 回答問句。 範例 • [問] **Who** is the girl dressed in yellow? 那位穿黃衣服的女孩是誰？ [答] She is my neighbor. 她是我的鄰居。 • [問] **Where** did you go with Benjamin? 你和 Benjamin 去哪裡？ [答] We went to the bookstore. 我們去書局。 • [問] **How** old is Chloé's brother? Chloé 的弟弟幾歲？ [答] He is ten. 他十歲。

Try it! 實力演練

I. 句子改寫

1. Everyone in the room was surprised at the news. (Was . . . ?)

____

2. The patient should change his diet. (Should . . . ?)

____

3. Adam gets up early every morning. (Does . . . ?)

____

II. 造句 (請依畫線部分造原問句)

1. My uncle and his family will leave for San Francisco tonight.

____

2. Nancy ate fried rice and chicken soup for lunch.

____

11-2 間接問句

1. 當疑問詞 (wh-/how) 引導的疑問句出現在句子中間而非句首時，必須改為間接問句，使用**直述句**「wh- + S + be/V/ 情態助動詞」的結構。
2. 在間接問句中，不可使用疑問句結構，也不使用構成疑問句的一般助動詞 do/does/did。

形成間接問句的方法整理如下：

種類	說明
be 動詞	句型：**. . . wh- + S + be . . .** 範例 • Who is the man wearing a tall hat? → Nobody knows **who** the man wearing a tall hat is. (who = wh-；the man wearing a tall hat = S；is = V) 沒人知道戴高帽子的男人是誰。
情態助動詞	句型：**. . . wh- + S + 情態助動詞 + V . . .** 範例 • When will the exam results be announced? → We wonder **when** the exam results will be announced. (when = wh-；the exam results = S；will be announced = V) 我們想知道考試結果何時會公佈。
一般動詞	句型：**. . . wh- + S + V** 將含一般動詞的問句改成間接問句時，須去掉 do/does/did。注意間接問句中一般動詞的時態與單複數變化。 範例 • Where do birds rest after it gets dark? → The kids want to know **where** birds rest after it gets dark. (where = wh-；birds = S；rest = V) 孩子們想知道天黑後鳥兒們在哪歇息。 Note 間接問句中去掉 do。 • How did the magician play the trick? → Tell me **how** the magician played the trick. (how = how；the magician = S；played = V) 告訴我魔術師怎麼變出戲法。 Note 間接問句去掉 did，動詞改成 played。

疑問詞當主詞	句型：**. . . wh- + be/V** 若疑問詞兼作**主詞**時，句型結構已為 S + V，不須再做變化。	
	範例	• Who has the ticket to the soccer game? → I am not sure **who** has the ticket to the soccer game. (who: wh-; has: V) 我不確定誰有足球比賽的票。 • What is inside the box? → Show us **what** is inside the box. 讓我們看盒子裡有什麼東西。 (what: wh-; is: V)
if/whether 引導的間接問句	句型：**if/whether + S + be/V** 「不含疑問詞的問句」或「答句為 Yes/No 的問句」，在改寫成為間接問句時，以 if/whether 來引導。	
	範例	• Is Jennifer a vegetarian? → We need to know **if** Jennifer is a vegetarian. 我們需要知道 Jennifer 是不是吃素。 • Did Lucy go to school by bus? → Frank asked Lucy **whether** she went to school by bus. Frank 問 Lucy 是不是搭公車上學。

注意

將直接問句改為間接問句時，其句末的標點符號視新句子為直述句或疑問句的結構決定。

- [直] **Was Derek late** for school yesterday?

  [間] I wonder **if Derek was late** for school yesterday.

  我想知道 Derek 是否昨天上學遲到。 Note 新句子為**直述句**，句末使用句號。

  [間] Do you know **if Derek was late** for school yesterday?

  你知道 Derek 昨天上學有否遲到嗎？ Note 新句子為**疑問句**，句末使用問號。

Try it! 實力演練

I. 句子合併

1. Can you join us?
   Let me know it.

   → ______________________________

2. { What did Richard buy for his wife for their anniversary?
We are curious about it.

→ ______________________________

II. 句子改寫

1. Where does Cathy's foreign friend come from?

Let me guess ______________________________

2. When was the sit-in protest finished?

The police want to know ______________________________

3. What have you been doing lately?

Can you tell me ______________________________

11-3 附加問句

1. 附加在句子之後，用於向對方確認意見或尋求認同的問句，稱為附加問句。
2. 附加問句的主詞必須用代名詞。

1. 附加問句的主要用法，統整如下：

用法	範例
用於向對方確認意見或尋求認同	• The new teacher is very humorous, **isn't she**? 新老師很幽默，不是嗎？ • This book is worth reading, **isn't it**? 這本書值得一讀，不是嗎？
肯定句的附加問句用否定形式；否定句的附加問句用肯定形式	• The talented young man is optimistic about his future, **isn't** he? 這有天分的年輕人對未來很樂觀，不是嗎？ Note 口訣：前肯後否。 • The singer doesn't eat spicy food, **does** he? 這歌手不吃辣的食物，對吧？ Note 口訣：前否後肯。
附加問句使用否定形式時，必須用縮寫形	• Alex will apply for this job, **won't he**? Alex 會申請這工作，不是嗎？ • The designer is a creative person, **isn't she**? 這位設計師是個有創意的人，不是嗎？

附加問句的動詞必須依敘述句的動詞決定 (請參照下表)	• The boy is bilingual, **isn't** he? 這男孩會說兩種語言，不是嗎？ • Technology improves our lives, **doesn't** it? 科技改善我們的生活，不是嗎？ • The skillful mechanic can solve any mechanical problems, **can't** she? 這厲害的技師能解決任何機械的問題，不是嗎？ • The child had a hamburger for breakfast, **didn't** he? 這孩子早餐吃漢堡，不是嗎？ ❶ 敘述句中的 had 是一般動詞，表示「吃」，附加問句用一般助動詞 did。 • Mr. and Mrs. Raymond have been to Germany, **haven't** they? Raymond 夫婦曾經去過德國，不是嗎？ ❶ 敘述句中的 have 是助動詞，附加問句也用助動詞 have。

2. 敘述句與附加問句的動詞對照

	敘述句	附加問句
動詞	be 動詞	be 動詞
	一般動詞	do/does/did
	can, will, should . . .	can, will, should . . .
	助動詞 have/has/had	助動詞 have/has/had

❶ 注意

其他形式的附加問句

1. 若敘述句是 **There + be . . .** 的句型，則附加問句的句型為 **be + there**。例如：
   - **There** wasn't much snow last year, was **there**? 去年沒下很多雪，是嗎？
   - **There** are numerous visitors to Disneyland every year, aren't **there**?
     每年有許多遊客到迪士尼，不是嗎？
2. 敘述句中若有否定含意的字詞時，視為否定句，因此附加問句使用肯定句結構。常見的否定字有：seldom、rarely、hardly、never、nothing、nobody 等。
   - Terry **seldom** exercises in the gym, **does he**? Terry 很少去健身房運動，不是嗎？
   - These police officers have **never** seen such a cunning thief, **have they**?
     這些警察從來沒遇過這樣狡猾的小偷，不是嗎？

Try it! 實力演練

I. 選擇

______ 1. Grandmother will visit us next week, ______?

(A) will not Grandmother (B) will Grandmother not

(C) won't she (D) will she not

______ 2. The stain on the dress has not been removed, ______?

(A) has it (B) will it (C) does it (D) is it

______ 3. There will be a flea market next weekend, ______?

(A) will there (B) be there (C) will it (D) won't there

II. 在空格中填入正確的動詞 / 主詞

1. English is not difficult to learn, ______________________ it?
2. Allen had too much food for dinner, ______________________ he?
3. Peter and his family have moved to Hualien, ______________________?
4. There is nothing wrong with this proposal, ______________________?

Notes

Chapter 12 分詞

12-1 分詞

1. 分詞是由動詞變化而來，分為**現在分詞**與**過去分詞**。在規則動詞變化下，現在分詞的形式為 V-ing，過去分詞的形式為 -ed 或 -en 結尾。
2. 分詞可以當作**形容詞**修飾名詞或作主詞補語。

1. 作形容詞用 (請參見 CH8)

(1) 置於名詞前做修飾用

a. 現在分詞表示「主動」與「進行」。

b. 過去分詞表示「被動」與「完成」。

例：a **developing** country (開發中國家)、a **developed** country (已開發國家)、a **crying** child (哭泣的孩子)、a **moving** car (正移動的車) 等。

(2) 由表「情緒」的動詞衍生

a. 現在分詞 V-ing 表示「令人…」，通常修飾**事物名詞**，或以**事物名詞**當主詞。

b. 過去分詞 p.p. 表示「感到…」，以**人**當主詞，其後若有受詞，必須搭配特定的介系詞。

- The actress refused to answer **embarrassing** questions.
  這女演員拒絕回答令人尷尬的問題。
  Note 現在分詞 embarrassing 修飾 questions。
- Mr. Lawrence was **embarrassed** about his son's naughty behavior.
  Lawrence 先生對他兒子的頑皮行為感到很尷尬。
  Note 過去分詞 embarrassed 修飾 Mr. Lawrence。
- The spread of the disease is **astonishing**. 這疾病的散播令人驚訝。

- Scientists were **surprised** at the reproduction of HeLa cells.
  科學家對於海拉細胞的繁殖很驚訝。

(3) 以下列舉較常見動詞之分詞變化與用法：

動詞	分詞變化	範例
bore (使厭煩)	bored (+ with)	• We are **bored** with this story. 我們對這故事感到厭煩了。
	boring	• This story is **boring**. 這故事令人感到無聊。
embarrass (使尷尬)	embarrassed (+ about)	• Danny is **embarrassed** about the situation. Danny 對這狀況感到尷尬。
	embarrassing	• This situation is **embarrassing**. 這是令人尷尬的情況。
excite (使興奮)	excited (+ about)	• People feel **excited** about the news. 人們對這則新聞感到很興奮。
	exciting	• This news is **exciting**. 這則新聞令人激動。
disappoint (使沮喪)	disappointed (+ at/about)	• The tennis player and her coach feel **disappointed** at/about the result. 這網球選手和她的教練對結果感到失望。
	disappointing	• The result is **disappointing**. 這個結果令人失望。
interest (使感興趣)	interested (+ in)	• The boys are **interested** in board games. 這些男孩們對桌遊感到有興趣。
	interesting	• These board games are **interesting**. 這些桌遊很有趣。
satisfy (使滿意)	satisfied (+ with)	• Mia's parents are **satisfied** with her grades. Mia 的父母對她的成績感到滿意。
	satisfying	• Mia's grades are **satisfying**. Mia 的成績令人滿意。

surprise (使驚訝)	surprised (+ at/by)	• The audience are **surprised** at/by the magician's tricks. 觀眾對魔術師的戲法感到驚奇。
	surprising	• The magician's tricks are **surprising**. 魔術師的戲法令人驚奇。

2. 作補語：分詞可以當主詞補語或受詞補語

(1) 當主詞補語

a. 置於連綴動詞後。

b. 置於 **come**、**go**、**sit**、**stand**、**lie** 之後，表示另一個同時發生的動作。

• This idea sounds **interesting**. 這主意聽起來很有趣。

• The students look **bored** with this exhibition.
學生們看起來對這場展覽感到厭倦。

• Oscar's parents seem **surprised** at his decision.
Oscar 的父母似乎對他的決定感到驚訝。

• The girl came **running**. 這女孩跑過來。

• The lazy man lay on the bed **watching** TV.
這懶惰的男人躺在床上看電視。

(2) 當受詞補語

a. 在某些動詞或句型後的受詞會需要受詞補語 (OC) 使句意完整。

b. 當受詞與受詞補語為**主動**意義時，使用**現在分詞**；當受詞與受詞補語為**被動**意義時，使用**過去分詞**。

• I heard the girls **talking** about the newly-opened department store.
我聽到女孩們談論新開幕的百貨公司。

Note 受詞 the girls 與 talk 是主動關係，故受詞補語使用現在分詞形 talking。

• Ashley was surprised to find her pearl necklace **stolen**.
Ashley 很驚訝發現她的珍珠項鍊被偷了。

Note 受詞 her pearl necklace 與 steal 是被動關係，故受詞補語使用過去分詞形 stolen。

c. 可用分詞當受詞補語的動詞或句型：

感官動詞	see、watch、notice、look at、hear、listen to	+ 受詞 +	受詞補語 (V-ing/p.p.)
特殊動詞	keep、leave、find、catch		
表附帶狀況	with		

- Tara enjoys listening to her nightingale **singing** every day.
  Tara 喜歡每天聽夜鶯唱歌。 Note 夜鶯唱歌屬於主動動作，用 V-ing。
- The lady saw a little boy **chased** by a fierce dog and saved him.
  這女士看到一個小男孩被一隻凶猛的狗追，並救了他。
  Note 小男孩被狗追屬於被動，故用 p.p.。
- To keep warm, Zac left the fire **burning** in the fireplace.
  為了保暖，Zac 讓火在壁爐裡繼續燃燒。 Note 火燃燒屬於主動，用 V-ing。
- The mother is watching TV with her baby **sleeping** in her arms.
  這個媽媽懷裡抱著睡著的孩子在看電視。
  Note 孩子睡覺屬於主動，用 V-ing。
- The man is taking a rest on the sofa with his sleeves **rolled up**.
  這男人捲起袖子，在沙發上休息。 Note 袖子捲起屬於被動，用 p.p.。

! 注意

1. 當使役動詞 have、get 後接被動意義的受詞補語時，使用過去分詞，句型為 **have/get + O + p.p.**，意為「使…被…」。
   - The owner of the house had it completely **refurbished**. 屋主將房子全部整修。
   - Luke got his salary **saved** in the bank. Luke 把他的薪水都存在銀行裡。
2. let 接過去分詞時，必須接 **be + p.p.**。
   - The secret agent can't let her traces **be found**. 祕密探員的行蹤不能被發現。

Try it! 實力演練

I. 選擇

______ 1. If you are thirsty, you can drink the ______ water in the bottle.

(A) boiling (B) boiled (C) boil (D) to boil

______ 2. Having said something ______ to his friend makes Jason ______.

(A) embarrassing; embarrassing (B) embarrassed; embarrassing

(C) embarrassing; embarrassed (D) embarrassed; embarrassed

______ 3. Choose the correct sentence.

(A) While walking on the street, I saw a man hitting by a car.

(B) The reckless driver was caught speeded.

(C) Patricia was taking a shower with the windows closing.

(D) The lady had her apartment redecorated.

II. 填入正確的分詞形式

1. I suggest that you read this ______ (interest) novel; I am sure you will feel ______ (interest) in the plot and characters.
2. As the saying goes, there is no use crying over ______ (spill) milk.
3. The detective had all the important files ______ (store) in his computer.

12-2 分詞片語

以關係代名詞當主詞的形容詞子句 (關係子句) 可以簡化成分詞片語，置於名詞之後，用於修飾名詞。

當形容詞子句簡化為分詞片語時，有以下幾個步驟：

Step 1 省略關係代名詞，若有 be 動詞，通常一併省略。

Step 2 將動詞改分詞。形容詞子句的動詞有**主動**或**進行**的意義時，改為現在分詞 (V-ing)，形容詞子句的動詞有**被動**或**已完成**的意義時，改為過去分詞 (p.p.)。

以下分成幾種情況來說明：

N + {who / which / that} + V → N + V-ing (主動)

形容詞子句的動詞為主動意義時，省略關代，並將動詞改為 V-ing。

- The man who exercises every day looks healthy and energetic.
  → The man **exercising** every day looks healthy and energetic.
  那個每天運動的男人看起來健康又有活力。
- Tiffany introduced to the club members the man that wore a tuxedo.
  → Tiffany introduced to the club members the man **wearing** a tuxedo.
  Tiffany 為俱樂部會員介紹那個穿燕尾服的男人。
  Note exercise 與 wear 均為主動的動作，使用現在分詞形。

N + {who / which / that} + be + V-ing → N + V-ing (進行)

形容詞子句的動詞表進行之意時，省略關代與 be 動詞，並保留動詞的 V-ing 形。

- The speaker who is delivering a speech wins popularity with youngsters.
  → The speaker **delivering** a speech wins popularity with youngsters.
  那位正在演講的演說者受到青少年的歡迎。
- David has a crush on the girl that is performing on the stage.
  → David has a crush on the girl **performing** on the stage.
  David 迷戀那位在舞台上表演的女孩。

Note 在例句中，deliver a speech 和 perform 都是正在進行的動作，使用現在分詞。

N + {who / which / that} + be + p.p. → N + p.p. (被動／完成)

形容詞子句的動詞表被動或完成之意時，省略關代與 be 動詞，保留 p.p.。

- The watch which was made in Switzerland cost a fortune.
  → The watch **made** in Switzerland cost a fortune.
  這只在瑞士製造的手錶價值不菲。
- This is the architecture that was designed by Gaudi.
  → This is the architecture **designed** by Gaudi. 這是高第設計的建築。

Note 由於物品是被製作或設計建造出來的，在例句中，make 與 design 均屬於被動的意義，故使用過去分詞。

$N + \begin{Bmatrix} \text{who} \\ \text{which} \\ \text{that} \end{Bmatrix} + \text{have} + \text{p.p.} \rightarrow N + \text{having} + \text{p.p.}$ **(完成式)**

形容詞子句有完成式時，省略關代，將 have 改為 having。

• The customers <u>who have purchased</u> this faulty hairdryer can ask for a refund.

→ The customers **having purchased** faulty hairdryer can ask for a refund.
已經購買這款有瑕疵吹風機的顧客可以要求退貨。

• The best-selling author will hold a book signing event for people <u>that have bought</u> his novels.

→ The best-selling author will hold a book signing event for people **having bought** his novels. 這個暢銷作家將會為購買他小說的讀者舉辦簽書會。

Note 將完成式動詞改為分詞時，只需將 have/has/had 改為 having。

$N + \begin{Bmatrix} \text{who} \\ \text{which} \\ \text{that} \end{Bmatrix} + \begin{Bmatrix} \text{have} \\ \text{has} \\ \text{had} \end{Bmatrix} + \text{been} + \text{p.p.} \rightarrow N + \text{having} + \text{been} + \text{p.p.}$ **(完成被動)**

形容詞子句有完成被動式時，省略關代，將 have 改為 having。

• The cake <u>which had been kept</u> for Dad was gone.

→ The cake **having been kept** for Dad was gone. 留給爸爸的蛋糕不見了。

• The principal rejected the proposal <u>which had been put forward</u> by Mr. Huang.

→ The principal rejected the proposal **having been put forward** by Mr. Huang.
校長拒絕了黃老師提出的建議。

Note 將完成式動詞改為分詞時，只需將 have/has/had 改為 having。

! 注意

非限定用法的關係子句 (請參見 CH10) 改成分詞片語時，必須保留逗號。

• Paris<u>, which has many fantastic parks and historical buildings,</u> attracts numerous tourists every year.

→ Paris**, having many fantastic parks and historical buildings,** attracts numerous tourists every year. 巴黎有許多很讚的公園和歷史建築，每年吸引許多遊客。

• Pandora's only son, who has finished his college education, plans to pursue a master's degree in Australia.

→ Pandora's only son, **having finished his college education,** plans to pursue a master's degree in Australia. Pandora 的獨生子已經完成大學學業，計畫到澳洲讀碩士。

Try it! 實力演練

I. 選擇 (複選)

_____ 1. This club welcomes people _____ Jazz music.

(A) enjoy (B) enjoyed (C) enjoying (D) who enjoy

_____ 2. This is a new film _____ by Ang Lee.

(A) has directed (B) directing

(C) that is directed (D) directed

_____ 3. The man _____ all his savings in the stock market is now on the verge of bankruptcy.

(A) who has invested (B) had invested

(C) having invested (D) having been invested

II. 句子改寫

1. Cherry's son is a spoiled child, who always has his own way.

(將畫線部分改為分詞片語)

____

2. Sebastian works in a computer company which is set up by Bill Gates.

(將畫線部分改為分詞片語)

____

3. { On the baseball field, there are many baseball players.
These baseball players are practicing for the upcoming game.

(1) (以關係詞改寫) ______________________________

(2) (改為分詞片語) ______________________________

12-3 分詞構句

分詞構句由**對等子句**或**從屬子句**簡化而來，可以表示時間、原因、理由、條件或附帶狀態等。

分詞構句的改寫方式與句型如下：

1. 由對等子句簡化而來：用於對等子句前後的主詞相同時。

Step 1 省略連接詞 and，加上逗點。

Step 2 若後句有主詞須省略；若有 be 動詞，一般也會將其省略。

Step 3 將後句的動詞改為分詞：

(1) 表示**主動**或**進行**意義的動詞改為現在分詞 (V-ing)；

(2) 表示**被動**或**完成**意義的動詞，一般將 be 刪去，只保留過去分詞 (p.p.)。

以下分成幾種情況來說明：

$S + V_1$ and $V_2 \rightarrow S + V_1, V_2$-ing

$S + V_1$ and be V_2-p.p. $\rightarrow S + V_1, V_2$-p.p.

省略對等連接詞，並將動詞改為 V-ing 或者 p.p.。

- The smart student raised his hand and answered the difficult question.
  → The smart student raised his hand**, answering** the difficult question.
  這聰明的學生舉手並回答出困難的問題。
- The girl turned off the TV and started to do her homework.
  → The girl turned off the TV**, starting** to do her homework.
  這女孩關掉電視並開始做功課。
- Ron seriously delayed the project and was yelled at by his manager.
  → Ron seriously delayed the project**, yelled at** by his manager.
  Ron 因為嚴重耽誤企劃而被經理大罵一頓。

$S + V_1$, and + $S + V_2 \rightarrow S + V_1 \ldots, \begin{cases} V_2\text{-ing} \\ V_2\text{-p.p.} \end{cases}$

省略對等連接詞與相同主詞，並將動詞改為 V-ing 或者 p.p.。

• The boss slammed the door, and he walked out of the office.

→ The boss slammed the door**, walking** out of the office.

老闆用力甩上門，走出辦公室。

• Fiona was looking for her missing child, and she looked nervous.

→ Fiona was looking for her missing child**, looking** nervous.

Fiona 正在找她走失的孩子，看起來很焦慮。

• Alison broke the window, and she was scolded by her father.

→ Alison broke the window**, scolded** by her father.

Alison 打破窗戶，被她爸爸責罵。

2. 由從屬子句簡化而來：用於主要子句和從屬子句的主詞相同時。

Step 1 省略從屬子句中的主詞。

Step 2 若句意清楚可省略從屬連接詞；反之，則保留。

Step 3 將從屬子句的動詞改為分詞：

(1) 表示**主動**或**進行**意義的動詞改為現在分詞 (V-ing)；

(2) 表示**被動**或**完成**意義的動詞，一般將 be 刪去，只保留過去分詞 (p.p.)。

以下分成幾種情況來說明：

$$\text{Conj.} + \text{S} + \left\{\begin{matrix} \text{V}_1 \\ \text{be} + \text{V}_1\text{-p.p.} \end{matrix}\right\}, \text{S} + \text{V}_2 \rightarrow \text{Conj.} + \left\{\begin{matrix} \text{V}_1\text{-ing,} \\ \text{V}_1\text{-p.p.,} \end{matrix}\right\} \text{S} + \text{V}_2$$

保留連接詞讓句意清楚，並將動詞改為 V-ing 或者 p.p.。

• After the student turned in her assignment, she felt relieved.

→ After **turning in** her assignment, the student felt relieved.

這學生交完作業後，覺得鬆了一口氣。

Note turn in 為主動動作，故用現在分詞形 turning in。

• After the child was punished, he cried loudly.

→ After **(being) punished**, the child cried loudly. 這孩子被處罰後，大聲哭泣。

• If Victoria is asked, she will tell the truth.

→ If **(being) asked**, Victoria will tell the truth. Victoria 如果被問，就會說出實情。

Note 「被處罰」和「被詢問」均屬於被動的動作，故用過去分詞。

$$\text{Conj.} + S + \begin{Bmatrix} V_1 \\ be + V_1\text{-p.p.} \end{Bmatrix}, + S + V_2 \rightarrow \begin{Bmatrix} V_1\text{-ing,} \\ V_1\text{-p.p.,} \end{Bmatrix} S + V_2$$

當句意清楚時，可省略連接詞，並將動詞改為 V-ing 或者 p.p.。

- Because the man was drunk, he took a taxi home instead of driving by himself.
  → **Being** drunk, the man took the taxi home instead of driving by himself.
  因為喝醉，這男子搭計程車而非自行開車回家。
- Since Barbara had enough time, she volunteered to help in the nursing home.
  → **Having** enough time, Barbara volunteered to help in the nursing home.
  因為有足夠的時間，Barbara 自願到療養院幫忙。
- After Gabe was encouraged by his teacher, he regained his confidence.
  → **Being encouraged/Encouraged** by his teacher, Gabe regained his confidence. 受到老師鼓勵之後，Gabe 重拾信心。

3. 獨立分詞構句：用於前後二句的主詞不同時。

Step 1 保留前後句的二個主詞。

Step 2 省略從屬連接詞。

Step 3 將從屬子句的動詞改為分詞：

(1) 表示**主動**或**進行**意義的動詞改為現在分詞 (V-ing)；

(2) 表示**被動**或**完成**意義的動詞，一般將 be 刪去，只保留過去分詞 (p.p.)。

- Since it was getting dark, the children rushed home.
  → **It getting dark,** the children rushed home. 天黑了，孩子們趕緊回家。
  Note 前後二句的主詞不同，必須保留。
- After the work had been done, Larry went home.
  → **The work having been done,** Larry went home.
  工作做完後，Larry 就回家了。

4. 分詞構句的否定形：在分詞構句之前加上 not 即可形成否定形。

- Because Hank didn't have enough cash, he paid the bill with a credit card.
  → **Not having enough cash,** Hank paid the bill with a credit card.
  Hank 沒有帶足夠的現金，所以他用信用卡付帳。

• As the visitor didn't know the way to the train station, he asked for help.
→ **Not knowing the way to the train station**, the visitor asked for help.
因為那遊客不知道往火車站的路，他開口求助。

Try it! 實力演練

I. 選擇

_____ 1. After _____ a shower, Dylan felt refreshed.
(A) take (B) taking (C) took (D) taken

_____ 2. _____ in simple English, this story book aims at pre-school children.
(A) Written (B) Writing (C) Writes (D) To write

_____ 3. Choose the **wrong** sentence.
(A) Before entering the house, you should take off your shoes.
(B) Being late for the date, Tommy apologized to his girlfriend sincerely.
(C) Being hit by a car, the ambulance sent the injured man to the hospital.
(D) Not knowing how to solve the problem, Ed asked his teacher for help.

II. 句子改寫

1. { The thief threw away the stolen wallet.
The thief ran away in a hurry.
(1) (以 and 改寫) ______________________________
(2) (改為分詞構句) ______________________________

2. { The weather is sunny today.
I feel like going biking.
(1) (以 Because 改寫) ______________________________
(2) (改為獨立分詞構句) ______________________________

3. { Nora isn't feeling well.
Nora will take a sick leave.
(1) (以 As 改寫) ______________________________
(2) (改為分詞構句) ______________________________

Chapter 13 子句

子句是包含於一個句子中的另一個句子或字串，通常含有主詞與動詞。依據結構不同，可分為**獨立子句**與**從屬子句**。

13-1 獨立子句與從屬子句

1. 獨立子句即所謂的主要子句，表達句子的核心意義，意思完整且能單獨存在。
2. 相較於獨立子句，從屬子句不能單獨存在，必須由一些字詞引導。依據**功能**不同，可分為**名詞子句**、**形容詞子句**和**副詞子句**。

子句	範例
獨立子句	• Olivia hung up the phone. Olivia 掛上電話。 （Olivia hung up the phone：獨立子句） • The student stayed up last night; therefore, he dozed off in class. （The student stayed up last night：獨立子句；he dozed off in class：獨立子句） 這學生昨晚熬夜，因此在課堂上打瞌睡。
從屬子句	• That the sun rises in the east is true. 太陽真的從東邊升起。 （That the sun rises in the east：名詞子句） Note that 引導的子句當主詞用，不可以單獨存在。 • Issac is a man who has a strong sense of responsibility. （who has a strong sense of responsibility：形容詞子句） Issac 是個責任感很強的人。 Note who 引導的子句當形容詞用，不可以單獨存在。 • After the patient took the medicine, he felt better. （After the patient took the medicine：副詞子句） 吃了藥後，這病人覺得好多了。 Note after 引導的子句當副詞用，不可以單獨存在。

Try it! 實力演練

將畫底線的子句標示 P (Principal Clause 獨立子句) 或 S (Subordinate Clause 從屬子句)。

1. [ ] This story book that has many illustrations is mainly for children.
2. [ ] The man returned the kettle to the supermarket.
3. [ ] Do you know what happened to the famous singer?

13-2 名詞子句

1. 名詞子句是將子句當成名詞使用，意即在此用法中的子句具有名詞的功用，可以當主詞、受詞、補語或同位語。
2. 名詞子句常用 **that**、**疑問詞 (如 what、who、when、where、why、how 等)** 或 **if/whether** 引導。
3. 以 that 引導的子句當作受詞或補語時，可以省略 that。

名詞子句的主要用法，統整如下：

用法	範例
名詞子句當主詞時，其後接單數動詞，that、疑問詞或 whether 均不可省略	• **That** Tim has passed the final exam surprises everyone. 大家對 Tim 通過期末考一事感到驚訝。 • **What** these protesters want is justice. 這些抗議者要的是正義。 • **Whether** the rumor is true or not is still unknown. 這謠言的真假還是個未知數。
名詞子句當補語時，可以省略 that，但不可省略疑問詞或 whether	• The club members' opinion is (**that**) the membership fees should be reduced. 俱樂部會員認為會員費應該降低。 • The engineer's suggestion is (**that**) the hard drive should be formatted. 工程師建議硬碟格式化。 • Daniel's problem is **whether** he can find an ideal job. Daniel 的問題在他是否能找到理想的工作。 Note whether 引導的名詞子句當主詞補語，不可省略 whether。

名詞子句當受詞時，可以省略 **that**，但不可省略疑問詞或 **whether**、**if**	• I think (**that**) we had better discuss this project as soon as possible. 我認為我們最好盡快討論這個計畫。 • The mayor claims (**that**) he has nothing to do with the scandal. 市長宣稱他和這個醜聞沒有關係。 • No one understood **what** the drunken man was saying. 沒人聽得懂這個醉漢在說什麼。 Note 不可省略 what。 • Sue wonders **whether/if** her boyfriend has free time this weekend. Sue 想知道她的男朋友這週末是否有空。 Note 不可省略 whether/if。
名詞子句當同位語時，可用於補充說明前面的名詞	• Despite the fact **that** parrots can imitate human speech, they may not understand its meaning. 儘管鸚鵡會模仿人類說話，牠們可能不了解其中意義。 • Many people are excited about the news **that** the superstar is going to hold a concert. 大家對於這位超級巨星要開演唱會的消息都感到很興奮。 (1) 在此用法中通常不省略 that。 (2) 常出現於此用法的名詞有 fact、news、thing、belief、idea、report 等。

Try it! 實力演練

I. 引導式翻譯

1. Cindy 有男朋友這件事不再是個秘密。

   ______ Cindy has a boyfriend is no longer a secret.

2. 醫生建議病人盡可能多喝水。

   The doctor suggests ______ the patient should drink as much water as possible.

3. 這老人說的話聽起來很荒謬。

   ______ the old man said sounded ridiculous.

II. 句子合併

1. { Scientists can clone sheep. / It is not a fiction anymore. } (That . . .)

→ ____________________

2. { Ian would give us a hand. / Ian promised it. } (Ian promised . . .)

→ ____________________

3. { When did Sam leave? / We don't know it. } (We don't know . . .)

→ ____________________

4. { Father left a message. / He made some sandwiches for our breakfast. }

→ ____________________

13-3 形容詞子句

形容詞子句也就是關係子句，它們所修飾的先行詞可以是主詞、受詞或補語 (請參考 CH 10)。

形容詞子句的主要用法，統整如下：

用法	範例
修飾主詞	• People **who** are optimistic tend to live longer. 樂觀的人往往會比較長壽。 • The ring **which** Teddy bought for Helen is a Valentine's Day gift. Teddy 買給 Helen 的戒指是情人節禮物。 • The man **whom** we came across yesterday is the owner of the factory. 我們昨天遇到的男人是這家工廠的老闆。 • The park **where** we used to play hide-and-seek is near the post office. 我們以前常玩捉迷藏的公園在郵局附近。

修飾受詞	• David is standing next to a statue **which** is 30 years old. David 正站在有三十年歷史的雕像旁。 • The customer bought many products **that** were on sale. 這顧客買了許多特價的產品。 • Joe bought a second-hand car **whose** condition was still excellent. Joe 買了一輛車況仍然良好的二手車。 • Nobody knows the reason **why** Mr. and Mrs. Pitt sold their house. 沒人知道 Pitt 夫婦賣房的理由。
修飾補語	• Adam is a man **who** has great enthusiasm for volunteer work. Adam 是個對義工服務很有熱忱的人。 • The leopard is a kind of animal **which** can run very fast. 豹是一種可以跑得很快的動物。 • This is the most popular song **that** the composer has ever written. 這首歌是這個作曲家寫過的歌中最受歡迎的。 • In the musical, the Phantom was a character **whose** twisted mind drove him to do crazy things. 在音樂劇中，魅影這角色扭曲的心理使他做了許多瘋狂之舉。

Try it! 實力演練

I. 句子改寫

1. { The fountain is next to the bench.
   The fountain doesn't work.

   The fountain ______________________________

2. { Jessica received a parcel.
   The parcel was sent from Australia.

   Jessica received a parcel ______________________________

3. { Dave is the person.
   You can depend on the person.

   Dave is the person ______________________________

II. 句子合併

1. { Hugh's face turns red whenever he sees the girl. / Hugh has a crush on her. } (. . . whom . . .)

→ ______________________________

2. { My family are talking about the day. / My parents got married on this day. } (. . . when . . .)

→ ______________________________

13-4 副詞子句

1. 副詞子句是以**從屬連接詞**引導的從屬子句，在句子裡扮演副詞的作用，表示「時間」、「原因」、「結果」、「目的」、「條件」、「讓步」等 (請參考 CH 9)。
2. 副詞子句置於主要子句前時，需加逗號；反之，則不需要。

副詞子句的主要用法，統整如下：

用法		說明
表示時間		常用於表示時間的連接詞有 before、after、when、while、as soon as、since、until 等。
	範例	• **After** the athlete drank some iced soda, he felt refreshed. → The athlete felt refreshed **after** he drank some iced soda. 喝下一些冰汽水後，運動員恢復精神了。 • Nora called her boyfriend **as soon as** she got home. Nora 一回到家就打電話給男朋友。
表示原因		常用於表示原因的連接詞有 because、as、since 等。
	範例	• **Because** the baby's diaper was wet, she cried. → The baby cried **because** her diaper was wet. 因為尿布濕，這嬰兒哭了。 • **Since** it is windy and chilly, you had better put on your coat. 因為風大又冷，你最好穿上外套。

<table>
<tr><td rowspan="2">表示
結果</td><td colspan="2">常用於表示結果的連接詞有 so、so . . . that 等。</td></tr>
<tr><td>範例</td><td>• The train was delayed, so these passengers could not get to their destinations on time.
火車誤點，所以這些乘客無法準時到達目的地。
• The fog is so heavy that all the flights have been canceled.
霧太濃，導致所有班機停飛。</td></tr>
<tr><td rowspan="2">表示
目的</td><td colspan="2">常用於表示目的的連接詞有 so that、in order that 等。</td></tr>
<tr><td>範例</td><td>• Matilda lowered her voice so that she wouldn't disturb her roommate.
Matilda 降低聲音，如此才不會打擾到室友。
• Mom put the fruit in the refrigerator in order that they could stay fresh.
媽媽把水果放在冰箱裡，以便保鮮。</td></tr>
<tr><td rowspan="2">表示
條件</td><td colspan="2">常用於表示條件的連接詞有 if、unless、even if 等。</td></tr>
<tr><td>範例</td><td>• If you want to apply for the scholarship, you have to fill in the form.
如果你想要申請獎學金，你必須要填表格。
• Rebecca won't forgive her husband unless he apologizes to her.
除非她丈夫道歉，否則 Rebecca 不會原諒他。</td></tr>
<tr><td rowspan="2">表示
讓步</td><td colspan="2">常用於表示讓步的連接詞有 although、even though 等。</td></tr>
<tr><td>範例</td><td>• Although the scarves were expensive, the wealthy woman bought a dozen.
雖然這些圍巾很貴，這貴婦買了十二條。
• Even though it is autumn, the weather is still hot.
儘管現在已經是秋天，天氣仍然很熱。</td></tr>
</table>

注意

在副詞子句中，若要表達未來式的時態，必須以**現在式的動詞代替未來式**。

• [O] I will ask Stuart to fix the computer when he **comes** home tonight.

[X] I will ask Stuart to fix the computer when he **will** come home tonight.

當 Stuart 今晚回家時，我會叫他修理電腦。

Note 在副詞子句裡，以現在式 comes 表達未來式。

Try it! 實力演練

I. 選擇

______ 1. ______ Ed got home, he found that he had left his book on the bus.

(A) Unless (B) If (C) As soon as (D) Now that

______ 2. The starving man kept eating ______ there was nothing left on his plate.

(A) if (B) unless (C) since (D) until

______ 3. The girl applied some suntan lotion ______ she wouldn't get sunburned.

(A) so that (B) as long as (C) now that (D) as if

II. 句子合併

1. { The boy shouted at his mother. / The boy felt guilty. } (After . . .)

→ ____

2. { The woman doesn't make much money. / The woman lives a luxurious life. } (. . . even though . . .)

→ ____

3. { The driver was fined. / The driver was caught speeding. } (. . . as . . .)

→ ____

Chapter 14 假設語氣

假設語氣用於表達「與事實相反的事情」或「與事實不符的願望」。依照時態可分為與**現在**事實相反的假設語氣、與**過去**事實相反的假設語氣、和與**未來**事實相反的假設語氣。

14-1 與現在事實相反的假設語氣

表示與過去事實相反的事情：

If + S + were/V-ed, S + would/could/should/might + V . . .

與現在事實相反的假設語氣，主要用法整理如下：

用法	範例
在與現在事實相反的假設語氣中，**if** 子句的動詞用過去式，主要子句的情態助動詞也用過去式	• If Johnson **had** enough money, he **would travel** around the world. 如果 Johnson 有足夠的錢，他就會環遊世界。 Note 事實上，Johnson 沒有足夠的錢，故不能環遊世界。 • Eric **might call** the girl if he **knew** her telephone number. 如果 Eric 知道那女孩的電話，他可能會打電話給她。 Note 事實上，Eric 不知道那女孩的電話，故不能打給她。
不論主詞的人稱為何，**if** 子句中的 **be** 動詞一律用 **were**	• If I **were** a bird, I **could** fly. 如果我是鳥，我就會飛。 Note 事實上，我不是鳥，所以不會飛。 • If Teddy's parents **were** here, they **could** share his joy of winning the talent show. 如果 Teddy 的父母在這裡，他們可以分享他贏得達人秀的喜悅了。 Note 事實上，Teddy 的父母不在現場。 • What **would** Nancy **do** if she **were** a millionaire? 如果 Nancy 是百萬富翁，她會做什麼？ Note 事實上，Nancy 不是百萬富翁。

	• If **there were** no electricity, our lives **would be** very inconvenient. 如果沒有電，我們的生活會很不方便。
將 if 子句中的一般動詞改為否定意義時，使用 didn't	• How nice it **would be** if I **didn't** have to take the final exam! 如果我不必考期末考，那該有多好！ • If Kate **didn't** have to work today, she would go to watch a movie with her friends. 如果 Kate 今天不必上班，她會和朋友去看電影。

Try it! 實力演練

I. 選擇

______ 1. If Victoria ______ here, she ______ tell us what to do.

(A) is; would　(B) was; might　(C) were; would　(D) were; may

______ 2. If the weather ______ fine today, the boys ______ go roller-skating.

(A) was; would　(B) were; will　(C) are; will　(D) were; would

______ 3. If Nelly ______ to do the report, she ______ to those mails earlier.

(A) has; will reply　(B) didn't have; could reply

(C) doesn't have; could reply　(D) had; won't reply

II. 引導式翻譯

1. 如果 Peterson 先生有正面積極的生活態度，他就不會老是感到沮喪。

______ Mr. Peterson ______ a positive attitude toward life, he ______ not ______ so depressed all the time.

2. 如果沒有空氣和水，很多生物就不能活。

If ______ ______ no air and water, many living things ______ not live.

14-2 與過去事實相反的假設語氣

表示與過去事實相反的事情：

If + S + had + p.p., S + would/could/should/might + have + p.p.

在與過去事實相反的假設語氣中，if 子句用**過去完成式 (had + p.p.)**，主要子句使用**過去式的情態助動詞 + have + p.p.**。

- If Ron **had studied** hard, he **could have passed** the exam.
  如果 Ron 之前讀書認真點，他就能夠通過考試。
  Note 事實上，當時 Ron 讀書不認真，故沒通過考試。
- If the boy **had caught** the bus, he **would not have been** late for school.
  如果那個男孩有趕上公車，他上學就不會遲到。
  Note 事實上，當時那男孩沒有趕上公車，故遲到了。
- If Mrs. Brown **had locked** the door, the thief **would not have broken** into her house. 如果 Brown 太太當時有鎖門，小偷就不會闖進她家。
  Note 事實上，當時 Brown 太太沒鎖門，故遭小偷。
- Angela **could have won** the game if she **had had** more time to prepare for it.
  如果當時 Angela 能有更多時間準備，她就可以贏得比賽。
  Note 事實上，當時 Angela 沒有更多時間準備，故沒贏得比賽。if 子句中的第一個 had 為過去完成式的 had，第二個 had 為 have 的 p.p.。

Try it! 實力演練

I. 選擇

______ 1. Mrs. Wright ______ their anniversary if her husband ______ her of it.

(A) forgot; didn't remind
(B) will have forgot; didn't remind
(C) would have forgot; had not reminded
(D) forgot; could have reminded

______ 2. Tim ______ a headache this morning if he ______ up so late last night.

(A) hadn't had; would not stay
(B) wouldn't have had; had not stayed
(C) won't have; didn't stay
(D) hadn't had; won't stay

_____ 3. If these students had started their project earlier, they _____ it in time.
(A) could finish (B) can finish
(C) could have finished (D) can have finished

II. 翻譯

1. 如果 Greg 那時再三考慮 (think twice)，他就不會做了後悔的事。
If Greg _____ _____ _____, he _____ _____ _____ _____ something regrettable.
2. 如果 Laura 那時解釋清楚，她和 Derek 之間就不會有誤會了。
If Laura _____ _____ clearly, there _____ not _____ _____ misunderstanding between her and Derek.
3. 如果 Ray 沒花那麼多時間看電視，他就不會變近視了。
If Ray _____ not _____ so much time watching TV, he _____ not have _____ near-sighted.

14-3 與未來事實相反的假設語氣

1. 與未來事實相反：
If + S + were to + V, S + would/could/should/might + V
2. 表示「萬一」的假設語氣：
If + S + should + V, S + {would/could/should/might | will/can/shall/may} + V

1. If + S + were to + V, S + would/could/should/might + V

此用法表示未來不可能發生或者可能性極低的事情。if 子句的動詞用 **were to + V**，主要子句用**過去式助動詞 + 原形動詞**。

- If the sun **were to** rise in the west tomorrow, I **would tell** you the secret.
如果明天太陽從西邊升起，我就告訴你秘密。

Note 事實上，太陽不可能從西邊升起，所以我不可能告訴你秘密。

- If Shawn **were to** win 10 million dollars in the lottery, Helen **would marry** him. 如果 Shawn 中了一千萬樂透，Helen 就會嫁給他。

  Note 說話者認為 Shawn 不可能贏得千萬美金樂透，所以 Helen 不可能嫁給他。

2. If + S + should + V, S + {would/could/should/might | will/can/shall/may} + V

此用法表示未來有可能發生的事情，可能性比 were to 高，意為「萬一」。if 子句用 **should + V**，主要子句用**過去式情態助動詞 + V** 或**現在式情態助動詞 + V**。使用**現在式**時，表示可能性較高。

- If Ian **should be** late, he **could take** the next train to catch up with us. 萬一 Ian 遲到，他可以搭下班火車趕上我們。

  Note 說話者認為 Ian 有可能遲到，但可能性不高。

- If the library **should be** closed, Benson **may go** to the bookstore to buy the books he needs. 萬一圖書館沒開，Benson 可能會去書局買他需要的書。

  Note 說話者認為 Benson 很可能去書局買書。

Try it! 實力演練

I. 選擇

______ 1. If the sun ______ rise in the west, Roger ______ get rid of his bad habits.
(A) shall; should (B) had; shall (C) may; were to (D) were to; would

______ 2. If the pop singer ______ cancel his concert tonight, his fans will feel disappointed.
(A) should (B) could (C) might (D) would

______ 3. If the waiter ______ break another plate, the manager ______ fire him.
(A) will; may (B) can; might (C) should; might (D) will; were to

II. 引導式翻譯

1. 如果水從地球上消失，所有的生物就無法生存。

If water ______ ______ disappear from the Earth, all the living creatures ______ not survive.

2. 如果時光倒流，你會做什麼？

If time ______ ______ turn back, what ______ you do?

III. 句子合併 (用未來假設的句型合併)

1. { The seasons do not stop changing.
People's lives are not greatly affected. } (. . . were to . . .)

→ ______________________________

2. { The weather is bad.
The ball game may be postponed. } (. . . should . . .)

→ ______________________________

14–4 假設語氣中省略 if 的用法

1. if 引導的從屬子句中若有 **were**、**had** 或 **should** 時，可以省略 if。
2. 此時，必須將 were、had 或 should 移到主詞之前，形成倒裝結構 (V + S)。

were、had 與 should 的假設語氣，省略 if 時的結構如下：

Were	+ S +	N/adj.,	+ S +	would/could/should/might	+ V	與現在事實相反的假設語氣
Had		p.p.,			+ have + p.p.	與過去事實相反的假設語氣
Should		V,			+ V	與未來事實相反的假設語氣

• If Carol **were** rich, she could move to the metropolitan area.

→ **Were** Carol rich, she could move to the metropolitan area.

如果有錢，Carol 就能搬去都會區。

• If Amy **had** submitted her report on time, she would not have lost some scores.

→ **Had** Amy had submitted her report on time, she would not have lost some scores.

如果 Amy 準時繳交報告，她就不會被扣分。

- If the flight **should** be canceled, the secretary would inform the manager immediately.
  → **Should** the flight be canceled, the secretary would inform the manager immediately. 萬一班機取消，秘書會立刻通知經理。

Try it! 實力演練

I. 依據文意，在空格中填入 were、had 或 should

1. ______ Eunice good at English, she could communicate with foreigners easily.
2. ______ Ben not talked so loudly, he would not have awakened the baby.
3. ______ the manager's plan fail, he will be fired.

II. 句子改寫 (省略 if 並改寫下列各句)

1. If George were here, he might know how to get to the supermarket.

____

2. If the man had driven a little slower, he would not have missed the post office.

____

3. If you should need any further information, please contact me.

____

14-5 表示「但願…」的假設用法

本句型用來表達「不可能實現的願望」，意為「但願…」。在用法上，分為「與現在事實相反的願望」和「與過去事實相反的願望」。

1. wish 表示「但願…」，其兩種用法的結構比較如下：

主要子句	that 子句	意義
S + wish	(that) S + were/V-ed . . .	願望與現在事實相反
	(that) S + had p.p. . . .	願望與過去事實相反

2. 表示「但願…」的兩種用法，整理比較如下：

	說明
表示「與現在事實相反的願望」	that 子句的動詞用 **were** 或**過去式動詞**。
	範例
	• I wish (that) I **were** 180 cm tall. 但願我有 180 公分高。 Note 事實上，我沒有 180 公分高。 • Daniel wishes (that) he **could read** people's minds. Daniel 但願他會讀心術。 Note 事實上，Daniel 不會讀心術。 • The girl wishes (that) she **could travel** to the space. 這女孩希望能去太空旅行。 Note 事實上，這女孩無法去太空旅行。
表示「與過去事實相反的願望」	說明
	that 子句的動詞用過去完成式 (**had + p.p.**)。
	範例
	• Mike wishes (that) he **had applied** for the Australia Working Holiday Visa last year. Mike 但願自己去年有申請澳洲打工渡假。 Note 事實上，Mike 去年沒有申請澳洲打工渡假。 • Judy wishes (that) she **had bought** that watch for her mother. Judy 但願自己之前有買下那隻錶來給媽媽。 Note 事實上，Judy 之前沒有買下那隻錶來給媽媽。 • Ellen wished (that) she **had not been** so stubborn. Ellen 但願自己之前沒有那麼固執。 Note 事實上，Ellen 之前很固執。

Try it! 實力演練

I. 填空 (依提示字填入正確動詞形式，不限填一字)

1. The lady wishes she ______________ (know) what to do now.
2. The little boy wishes that he ______________ (have) a toy car.
3. The girl wished that she ______________ (have not argued) with her parents yesterday.

II. 引導式翻譯

1. 但願我知道怎麼修電腦。

   I wish I ______ how to fix the computer.

2. 但願我去年耶誕節時在德國。

   I wish I ______ ______ in Germany last Christmas.

3. Amanda 但願自己沒寄出那封信。

   Amanda wishes that she ______ not ______ the letter.

14-6 as if 與 as though 引導的假設用法

1. as if 與 as though 用來表達「彷彿」或「好像」之意。
2. 視語氣上的不同，as if/as though 引導的子句可使用**直說法**或**假設語氣**。

根據用法與搭配動詞的差異，整理比較如下：

<table>
<tr><td rowspan="4">表示「可能發生的事情」</td><td>說明</td></tr>
<tr><td>as if/as though 引導的子句使用直說法。</td></tr>
<tr><td>範例</td></tr>
<tr><td>• That man dances as if he is a professional dancer.
那個男人跳起舞來彷彿是個專業的舞者。
• That lady sounds as though she has read the novel.
那個女士聽起來彷彿她讀過那本小說。</td></tr>
<tr><td rowspan="4">表達「與現在事實相反」</td><td>說明</td></tr>
<tr><td>as if/as though 引導的子句動詞要用 were 或過去式。</td></tr>
<tr><td>範例</td></tr>
<tr><td>• Kate talks as if she knew how to solve the problem.
Kate 說得彷彿她知道如何解決這個問題。 Note 事實上，Kate 不知道如何解決問題，與事實相反，屬於現在假設法，故子句動詞用過去式 knew。
• Lance dresses as though he were from a wealthy family.
Lance 穿著彷彿他是來自豪門。 Note 事實上，他並非來自豪門，與現在事實相反，故子句用過去式動詞 were。</td></tr>
</table>

	說明
表達「與過去事實相反」時	as if/as though 引導的子句動詞要用**過去完成式 (had + p.p.)**。
	範例
	• May looked as if she **had seen** a monster. May 當時看起來好像遇見怪物似的。 Note 事實上，May 當時沒有遇見怪物，與過去事實相反，故子句用 had + p.p.。 • Oscar sounded as though he **had visited** New York before. Oscar 聽起來好像以前造訪過紐約似的。 Note 事實上，Oscar 以前沒有去過紐約，與過去事實相反，故子句用 had + p.p.。

注意

1. 主要子句與 as if 引導的子句為同時發生的事情時：**S + V + as if + S + were/V-ed**。
   - The patient felt **as if** her head were going to explode.
   這病人覺得她的頭痛得快爆炸了。
2. as if 引導的子句比主要子句早發生或已持續一段時間：**S + V + as if + S + had + p.p.**。
   - After an exciting game, these basketball players smelled **as if** they had not taken showers for a week. 在激烈的比賽後，這些籃球選手聞起來彷彿已經一個星期沒洗澡。

Try it! 實力演練

I. 填空 (依提示字填入正確動詞形式，不限填一字)

1. The old lady talks as if she ______________ (be) a queen.
2. The student sounded as though he ______________ (be admitted) to a top university, but in fact, he was still waiting for the result.
3. The careless young man drove as if he ______________ (be) drunk.

II. 引導式翻譯

1. 該名記者聽起來彷彿他知道很多名人的秘密。
   The reporter sounds as if he ______ many celebrities' secrets.
2. 昨晚 Jason 說話的樣子，彷彿他已經嚐遍天下的美食。
   Last night Jason talked as if he ______ ______ delicacies around the world.

3. 這小孩吃東西的樣子，彷彿他已經餓了三天。

The child ate as though he ______ ______ hungry for three days.

14-7 表示「要不是…」的假設

表達「要不是…」的意思時，因為其內容常與實際情況相反，故須使用假設語氣。

1. 與現在事實相反的假設語氣

If it **were** not for	+ N,	S + would/could/should/might + V. . .
But for		
Without		

- **If it were not for** the glasses, the old man **could not see** clearly.

  → **But for** the glasses, the old man **could not see** clearly.

  → **Without** the glasses, the old man **could not see** clearly.

  要不是有眼鏡，這老人就看不清楚。

  Note 事實上，現在有眼鏡，所以這老人看得清楚。

- **If it were not for** air, human beings **would die**.

  → **But for** air, human beings **would die**.

  → **Without** air, human beings **would die**.

  要不是有空氣，人類就會死。 Note 事實上，現在有空氣，所以人類不會死。

2. 與過去事實相反的假設語氣

If it **had** not **been** for	+ N,	S + would/could/should/might + have p.p. . . .
But for		
Without		

- **If it had not been for** the rain water, the mountaineer who got lost **might have died** of dehydration.

  → **But for** the rain water, the mountaineer who got lost **might have died** of dehydration.

→ **Without** the rain water, the mountaineer who got lost **might have died** of dehydration. 要不是有雨水，那個迷路的登山客當時早就脫水而死了。

Note 事實上，那個旅者當時有雨水喝，所以他沒因脫水而死。

• **If it had not been for** the teacher's encouragement, the student **would have given** up learning.

→ **But for** the teacher's encouragement, the student **would have given** up learning.

→ **Without** the teacher's encouragement, the student **would have given** up learning. 要不是有老師的鼓勵，那個學生本來會放棄學習。

Note 事實上，那個學生當時有老師的鼓勵，所以他沒放棄學習。

Try it! 實力演練

I. 選擇

______ 1. If it were not for his tight schedule, Phil ______ French and German.

(A) may learn (B) might be learning

(C) may have learned (D) might have learned

______ 2. If it ______ for the man's timely rescue, the lady ______ hit by the car.

(A) were not; will be (B) was not; would be

(C) were not; would have been (D) had not been; would have been

II. 引導式翻譯

1. 要不是有鹽，食物就會食之無味。

______ ______ salt, food ______ be tasteless.

2. 當時要不是有 Nick 的提醒，我可能會忘記繳電話費。

______ Nick's reminder, I ______ ______ ______ to pay the telephone bill.

Chapter

15 特殊句構

此單元介紹具有特殊用途的幾種句型：祈使句、感嘆句、強調句與倒裝句。

15-1 祈使句

祈使句用於表達說話者對聽話者的請求、命令、指示、建議或勸告。

祈使句的主要用法，整理說明如下：

用法	範例
主詞為第二人稱 **you** 時，通常被省略而以原形動詞開頭。要強調語氣時，會保留 **you**	• **Stand** up. 起立。 • **Speak** louder。 說話大聲點。 • **Let** me give you a hand. 讓我來幫你。 • **You turn down** the volume! 你把音量轉小點！
若句中動詞是 **be** 動詞時，以原形表示	• **Be** quiet. 安靜。 • **Be** patient. 有耐心點。 • **Be** a good boy. 當個乖孩子。
欲表示禮貌時，可加入 **please**，置於句首、句中或句末	• Please **be** seated. 請坐。 • Please **pass** the salt to me, Hank. → Hank, please **pass** the salt to me. → Hank, **pass** the salt to me, please. Hank，請把鹽遞給我。
欲加強語氣時，可在句首加上助動詞 **do**	• **Do** have some more juice. 再多喝點果汁。 • **Do** take my advice. 一定要聽我的忠告。 • **Do** show me your pictures. 一定要給我看你的照片。

可在句首加上 **don't** 或 **never**，以形成否定。用 **do not** 時，語氣更正式、更強烈	• **Don't** believe him. 別相信他。 • **Don't** be so noisy. 別這麼吵。 • **Do not** be late. 別遲到。 • **Do not** lean against the wall. 別靠著牆。 • **Never** tell a lie. 絕對不要說謊。 • **Never** be late for school. 上學絕對不要遲到。

學習便利貼

No + V-ing 可表達強烈命令對方不要做某事，意思為「禁止…」。
- **No** talking in class! 禁止上課說話！
- **No** parking! 禁止停車！

Try it! 實力演練

I. 句子改寫 (將下列句子改為祈使句)

1. You can make yourself at home.

____

2. I want you to leave me alone.

____

3. I hope that you can be quiet for a few minutes. (. . . , please.)

____

II. 翻譯

1. 此處禁止亂丟垃圾 (litter)。

____

2. Ian，別把你的錢包放在桌上。

____

3. 絕對不要闖紅燈。

____

15-2 感嘆句

感嘆句用於表達強烈的情感，如驚奇、讚美、高興等，句尾用驚嘆號。

What + a (+ adj.) + N (+ S + {be 動詞 / V})!

強調「形容詞 + 名詞」，有時只接名詞，使用上經常省略主詞與動詞。

- **What** a nice day (it is)! 天氣真好啊！
- **What** a mess (it is)! 怎麼那麼髒啊！
- **What** a wonderful world (it is)! 多美好的世界啊！
- **What** a lovely girl Laura is!
  Laura 真是個漂亮女孩！

How + {adj. / adv.} (+ S + {be 動詞 / V})!

強調「形容詞」或「副詞」，使用上經常省略主詞與動詞。

- **How tall** the tree is! 這棵樹好高啊！
- Look at the baby! **How adorable**!
  看看這個寶寶！多可愛啊！
- **How fast** Phelps swims! Phelps 游得好快啊！
- **How swiftly** the leopard moves!
  這隻豹的動作真敏捷啊！

Try it! 實力演練

I. 在空格中填入 what 或 how

1. ______ a hot day!
2. ______ hot the tea is!
3. ______ sweet the apples taste!

II. 句子改寫

1. Jolin is a talented singer. (What . . .)

____

2. These novels are interesting. (How . . .)

____

15-3 強調結構

在英文中，可用字詞或句型來加強語氣。

依照強調內容不同，整理介紹如下：

<table>
<tr><td rowspan="4">強調名詞</td><th>說明</th></tr>
<tr><td>(1) 句型：the very + N
(2) 其後的關係代名詞必須用 that。</td></tr>
<tr><th>範例</th></tr>
<tr><td>• This is the very novel that Yvonne wants to read. 這正是 Yvonne 要讀的小說。
• Angelina is the very woman that Brad loves. Angelina 正是 Brad 愛的女人。
• Steak is the very dish that my brother likes. 牛排正是我弟弟喜歡的料理。
• Mr. Yang is the very man that they are looking for.
楊先生正是他們在尋找的人。</td></tr>
<tr><td rowspan="4">強調動詞</td><th>說明</th></tr>
<tr><td>(1) 句型：do/does/did + V
(2) 此用法僅用於肯定直述句中。</td></tr>
<tr><th>範例</th></tr>
<tr><td>• Do make sure that you have brought your passport. 務必確認你帶了護照。
• Alex's wife does like the Valentine gift he gave her.
Alex 的老婆很喜歡他送的情人節禮物。
• These members did support their new chairman. 這些會員十分支持新主席。</td></tr>
</table>

<table>
<tr><td rowspan="4">分裂句</td><td>說明</td></tr>
<tr><td>(1) 句型：It + is/was + 被強調部分 + that + 句子剩餘部份
(2) 可強調主詞、受詞、副詞。使用此句型時，要注意 be 動詞的時態。</td></tr>
<tr><td>範例</td></tr>
<tr><td>• Chloé plays badminton with her colleagues every Friday.
Chloé 每週五和同事打羽球。
→ It is <u>Chloé</u> that plays badminton with her colleagues every Friday.
Note 強調主詞 Chloé。
→ It is <u>badminton</u> that Chloé plays with her colleagues every Friday.
Note 強調動詞 play 的受詞 badminton。
→ It is <u>every Friday</u> that Chloé plays badminton with her colleagues.
Note 強調副詞 every Friday。
• It is <u>Father</u> that washes the dishes every day. 每天洗碗的是爸爸。
• It was <u>Alice</u> that mailed a parcel to me. 寄包裹給我的是 Alice。
• It is <u>noodles</u> that Mom is cooking for dinner. 媽媽正在煮麵當晚餐。
• It is <u>cartoons</u> that these kids love to watch. 孩子們喜歡看的是卡通。
• It is <u>in spring</u> that these flowers bloom. 這些花是在春天綻放。</td></tr>
</table>

Try it! 實力演練

I. 填空 (填入適當的字來加強語氣，不限填一字)

1. That is ________________________ purse that Miriam is looking for.

2. ________________________ listen attentively to your teacher in class.

3. Generally speaking, girls ________________________ like to share their feelings.

II. 句子改寫 (將下列句子改為分裂句)

Samuel dressed himself like Spiderman on Halloween.

(1) (強調 Samuel) ____

(2) (強調 on Halloween) ____

15-4 倒裝句

在英文句中，一般語序是主詞在前，動詞在後 (即 **S + be/V/助動詞**)。有時要強調某部分或修辭上的需要，可變動字詞的位置，形成動詞在前，主詞在後的倒裝語序 (即 **be/V/助動詞 + S**)。以下介紹幾種常見的倒裝句。

1. 地方副詞片語在句首的倒裝句

地方副詞 (here/there) +	be/V + S (名詞)	倒裝
地方副詞片語 (如 under the table) +	S (代名詞) + be/V	不倒裝
介副詞 (如 away、up、down、off) +		

(1) 此句型將地方副詞 (片語) 或介副詞置於句首，以作為強調。

(2) 在此句型中，需使用倒裝語序，直接將動詞移至主詞前。

(3) 在此句型中，主詞為**代名詞**時，**不用倒裝**，使用正常語序 S + V 即可。

學習便利貼

常見的地方副詞有 a. here、there，b. 表示方向的介副詞，如：in、out、up、off、away、down 等，以及 c. 表示位置的副詞片語，如：at sea、in the living room、under the table。

- A witch (S) is (be) **in the forest**. 在森林裡有一位女巫。
  - → **In the forest** is (be) a witch (S). Note 主詞為名詞，須倒裝。
  - → **In the forest** she (S) is (be). Note 主詞為代名詞，不須倒裝。
- The bus (S) comes (V) **here**. 公車來了。
  - → **Here** comes (V) the bus (S). Note 主詞為名詞，須倒裝。
  - → **Here** it (S) comes (V). Note 主詞為代名詞，不須倒裝。
- The balloon (S) flew (V) **away**. 氣球飛走了。
  - → **Away** flew (V) the balloon (S). Note 主詞為名詞，須倒裝。
  - → **Away** it (S) flew (V). Note 主詞為代名詞，不須倒裝。

2. 否定詞在句首的倒裝句

	動詞	主詞	
否定詞 +	be	+ S	
	can、will、may、should 等		+ 一般動詞
	do/does/did		+ 一般動詞
	have/has/had		+ p.p.

(1) 為了加強語氣，可將否定詞置於句首，此時必須使用倒裝語序。

(2) 此句型與地方副詞在句首的倒裝用法有些差別，是將句型改為疑問句 (V+S) 的結構：

a. 主要動詞為 be 時：將 be 移到主詞前。

b. 有情態助動詞 (can、will、may 等) 時：將其移到主詞前。

c. 主要動詞為**一般動詞**時：在主詞前加上助動詞 do、does 或 did。

學習便利貼

常用的否定詞有：no、not、never、seldom、rarely (很少)、hardly、scarcely (幾乎不)、little、nowhere (任何地方都不)、in no way、by no means (絕不) 等。

- Teresa is **seldom** late for school.

→ **Seldom** is Teresa late for school. Teresa 很少上學遲到。
(is = be, Teresa = S)

- The news was so shocking that Wendy could **hardly** believe it.

→ The news was so shocking that **hardly** could Wendy believe it.
(could = aux., Wendy = S)

這消息太驚人，Wendy 幾乎不敢置信。

- The residents of this community talked **little** about the strange man.

→ **Little** did the residents of this community talk about the strange man.
(did = aux., the residents = S)

這個社區的居民很少談論那個奇怪的男人。

- The public had **never** seen such an interesting architectural design.

→ **Never** had the public seen such an interesting architectural design.
(had = aux., the public = S)

大眾從未看過這麼有趣的建築設計。

3. only 在句首的倒裝句

	動詞	主詞	
Only + 副詞片語/子句	be	+ S	
	can、will、may、should 等		+ 一般動詞
	do/does/did		+ 一般動詞
	have/has/had		+ p.p.

(1) 為了加強語氣，可將 only 引導的副詞片語或子句置於句首，此時必須使用倒裝語序。

(2) 此倒裝用法是將句型改為疑問句 (V+S) 的結構：

a. 主要動詞為 be 時：將 be 移到主詞前。

b. 有情態助動詞 (can、will、may 等) 時：將其移到主詞前。

c. 主要動詞為**一般動詞**時：在主詞前加上助動詞 do、does 或 did。

- The diligent employee is relaxed **only after work**.

→ **Only after work** is (be) the diligent employee (S) relaxed.

只有在下班後，這勤奮的員工才覺得放鬆。

- These fruits ripen **only in summer**.

→ **Only in summer** do (aux.) these fruits (S) ripen. 只有在夏天，這些水果才會成熟。

- The busy manager is able to take a rest **only when he is at home**.

→ **Only when the busy manager is at home** is (be) he (S) able to take a rest.

只有在家時，這個忙碌的經理才能休息。

- One can realize the importance of health **only when he loses it**.

→ **Only when one loses his health** can (aux.) he (S) realize its importance.

只有當一個人失去健康時，他才知道其重要性。

- Greg felt relieved **only after he finished his oral report**.

→ **Only after Greg finished his oral report** did (aux.) he (S) feel relieved.

做完口頭報告後，Greg 才覺得鬆了口氣。

4. so/such/neither/nor 起始的倒裝句

(1) so、neither 或 nor 起始的句子必須用疑問句結構的倒裝語序。倒裝句中的動詞與時態取決於前句。

(2) **so** 與 **neither** 為副詞，無連接的功能，與前句之間須用 and 連接；**nor** 為連接詞，不須加 and。

句型 1. 附和句

肯定句 +	, and **so** +	be	+ S	表示「也…」
否定句 +	, and **neither** +	modal verb (will, may 等)		表示「也不…」
	, **nor** +	do/does/did		
		have/has/had		

• The model is fashionable, and **so** is her mother.
be S

這模特兒很時髦，她的媽媽也是。

• Kylie has a sweet voice, and **so** does her sister.

Kylie 的聲音很甜美，她姊姊的也是。

Note 在此句中，has 表示「有」，是一般動詞，用助動詞 does 形成倒裝句。

• I have been to Scotland, and **so** has my classmate.

我去過蘇格蘭，我同學也去過。

Note 在此句中，have 是助動詞，用助動詞 has 形成倒裝句。

• Hannah is not addicted to Korean dramas, and **neither** are her friends.

→ Hannah is not addicted to Korean dramas, **nor** are her friends.

Hannah 不迷韓劇，她朋友也不著迷。

• Derek will not go cycling this weekend, and **neither** will his brother.

→ Derek will not go cycling this weekend, **nor** will his brother.

Derek 這週末不會去騎自行車，他弟弟也不會。

句型 2. 「如此…，以致於…」

So +	adj./adv.	+ be	+ S		that . . .
		+ modal verb (will 等)		+ 一般動詞	
Such +	(a) (+ adj.) + N	+ do/does/did		+ 一般動詞	
		+ have/has/had		+ p.p.	

- The speaker's words were **so convincing** that everyone believed him.

  → **So convincing** were the speaker's words that everyone believed him.

  (were = be; the speaker's words = S)

  這演講者的話很有說服力，以致於大家都相信他。

- The museum has **such a large collection of antiques** that many people like to visit it.

  → **Such a large collection of antiques** does the museum have that many people like to visit it.

  (does = aux.; the museum = S)

  該博物館收藏許多古董，所以很多人喜歡去參觀。

- The student walked **so slowly** that he missed the bus.

  → **So slowly** did the student walk that he missed the bus.

  這學生走得很慢，所以他錯過公車。

- Nathan is **such a responsible person** that he is elected the class representative.

  → **Such a responsible person** is Nathan that he is elected the class representative. Nathan 很盡責，所以他被選為班級代表。

5. 假設語氣中省略 if 的倒裝句

$$\text{If + S +} \left\{ \begin{array}{l} \text{were} \\ \text{had} \\ \text{should} \end{array} \right\} \ldots \rightarrow \left\{ \begin{array}{l} \text{Were} \\ \text{Had} \\ \text{Should} \end{array} \right\} \text{+ S} \ldots$$

在假設語氣中，若 if 引導的子句含有 were、had + p.p.、should 時，可省略 if，並將 were、had、should 移至主詞之前，形成倒裝句 (請參見 CH14)。

- If I **were** a bird, I could fly.

  → Were I a bird, I could fly. 如果我是鳥，我就會飛。

- If Nicholas **had** paid more attention, he would not have made this mistake.

  → Had Nicholas paid more attention, he would not have made this mistake.

  如果 Nicholas 多注意點的話，他就不會犯這個錯。

- If a theme park **should** be built here, many tourists will swarm into this area.

  → Should a theme park be built here, many tourists will swarm into this area.

  萬一主題樂園建在這裡的話，很多遊客會蜂擁而至。

6. 讓步子句的倒裝句

$$\left.\begin{array}{l}\textbf{Although}\\ \textbf{Though}\end{array}\right\} + \textbf{S} + \left\{\begin{array}{l}\textbf{be + adj.}\\ \textbf{be + N}\\ \textbf{V + adv.}\end{array}\right\} + \textbf{S} + \textbf{V} \ldots$$

$$\rightarrow \left.\begin{array}{l}\textbf{Adj.}\\ \textbf{N}\\ \textbf{Adv.}\end{array}\right\} + \textbf{as} + \textbf{S} + \left\{\begin{array}{l}\textbf{be}\\ \textbf{V}\end{array}\right\} + \textbf{S} + \textbf{V} \ldots$$

(1) 在讓步子句中，若要強調形容詞、副詞或名詞時，可將其置於句首，改為含 as 的句型，形成倒裝句。

(2) 注意，在此句型中，名詞移到句首時，冠詞要省略。

- **Although**/**Though** the boy is young, he is brave.
  (the boy = S, is = be, young = adj.)

  → Young **as** the boy is, he is brave. 雖然這男孩年紀小，但是他很勇敢。
  (Young = adj., the boy = S, is = be)

- **Although**/**Though** Mr. Cunningham is a billionaire, he lives a frugal life.
  (Mr. Cunningham = S, is = be, billionaire = N)

  → Billionaire **as** Mr. Cunningham is, he lives a frugal life.
  (Billionaire = N, Mr. Cunningham = S, is = be)

  雖然 Cunningham 先生是億萬富翁，但他生活節儉。

- **Although**/**Though** Ed drove fast, he failed to attend the meeting on time.
  (Ed = S, drove = V, fast = adv.)

  → Fast **as** Ed drove, he failed to attend the meeting on time.
  (Fast = adv., Ed = S, drove = V)

  雖然 Ed 開車的速度很快，但仍沒能準時出席會議。

Try it! 實力演練

I. 選擇

( ) 1. Timothy is superstitious, and so ______ her mother.

(A) does (B) is (C) will (D) has

( ) 2. ______ as Barbara is, she makes much money.

(A) Freelance writer (B) A freelance writer

(C) Although a freelance writer (D) Freelance writing

( ) 3. _____, he would come with us.

(A) Is Charles free (B) Had Charles been free
(C) Should Charles to be free (D) Were Charles free

II. 句子改寫 (將下列句子改為倒裝句)

1. The train goes there.

(1) There ______________________________

(2) There it ______________________________

2. Timmy never had the nerve to try bungee jumping.

Never ______________________________ the nerve to try bungee jumping.

3. You will understand your grandfather only when you are in his shoes.

Only when you are in your grandfather's shoes ____________________

實力演練解答

Chapter 1 英文句子的基本概念

1-1 I. 1. I am pleased to meet you.
主語 述語

2. The doctor suggests that the patient should quit smoking.
主語 述語

II. 1, 2

1-2-1 I. 1, 3

II. 1. The nervous man spoke very fast.
S vi.

2. The diligent worker works six days a week.
S vi.

3. My brother goes to school by bus.
S vi.

1-2-2 I. 1. Tim's answers are unexpected.
S vi. SC

2. Everything looks fine.
S vi. SC

3. After the show, the audience remained seated until the lights were on.
S vi. SC

II. 1. A 2. C

1-2-3 I. 1. The thirsty athlete drank much water.
S vt. O

2. Many people believe that the mayor will make a wise decision.
S vt. O

3. The angry mother didn't know what to say.
S vt. O

II. 1. Grandma told a ridiculous story.

2. Judy forgot to bring an umbrella.

3. Do you know where your brother is?

1-2-4 I. 1. Remember to show the security your ID.
IO DO

2. Victoria left her husband some food.
IO DO

3. The president's speech brought the people some hope.
IO DO

II. 1. Remember to show your ID to the security.

2. Victoria left some food for her husband.

3. The president's speech brought some hope to the people.

1-2-5 I. 1. We consider Tina suitable for the job.
S vt. O OC

2. They kept themselves warm by using hand warmers.
S vt. O OC

3. The members elected Eric president.
S vt. O OC

II. 1. The teacher's explanation made the question easier.

2. The workers painted the room pink.

3. Angela left her purse on the bus.

1-3 Have you ever visited Hualien __?__ Hualien is a wonderful place for sightseeing __.__ In recent years __,__ more and more people have traveled to Hualien for a relaxing weekend __.__ There __,__ tourists can visit Taroko National Park __,__ where they can see amazing cliffs and gorges __.__ In addition __,__ hiking down the path is something that tourists should not miss in Taroko National Park __.__ An exciting alternative that Hualien offers the tourists is whitewater rafting along Hsiukuluan River __.__ Rafters may enjoy the excitement while appreciating the gorgeous sights __.__ What a joyful trip it seems __!__

Chapter 2 名詞

2-1 I. 1. My sister boyfriend won the lottery! → sister's

2. Mr. Jones teaches music in a boys high school. → boys'

II. 1. Nobody; girl's 2. window; house

2-2-1 I. 1. a 2. a 3. The, the

II. 1. Max is a honest man. → an

2. Charles keeps three pets, including a dogs and two turtle. → dog, turtles

3. A comic book I borrowed from Frank is interesting. → The

2-2-2 1. mosquitoes 2. persons/people 3. branches 4. women 5. activities
6. sheep 7. teeth 8. children 9. puzzles 10. boxes

2-3-1 I. 1. C 2. B

II. 1. Air; water 2. a piece of; two cups of

2-3-2 I. 1. difference 2. silence 3. evaluation 4. deletion 5. expression 6. argument

II. 1. B 2. A 3. B

2-3-3 1. Middle East; pork 2. Chinese; Chinese New Year's Eve 3. Hayao Miyazaki; Japanese

2-4 I. 1. C 2. A 3. D

II. 1. My sister's class consists of forty students.

2. Different peoples have different cultures and customs.

2-5 I. 1. The couple are just passer by; they don't know what happened. → passers-by

2. Adam goes hiking with his father in law every weekend. → father-in-law

3. Fiona is already a grown up, but she acts like a child. → grown-up

II. 1. fireflies 2. mothers-in-law 3. policemen 4. push-ups

2-6 I. 1. Ben; Cindy's 2. Ben's; Greg's 3. Helen's; Meg's

II. 1. C 2. B

Chapter 3 代名詞

3-1-1 I. 1. He 2. His 3. him

II. 1. Hank; I 2. You; he; I 3. we; you; they

3-1-2 I. 1. yours 2. mine 3. his

II. 1. B 2. A 3. C

3-1-3 I. 1. C 2. C 3. B

II. 1. himself 2. themselves 3. myself

3-1-4 I. 1. it 2. It 3. it

II. 1. it 2. It 3. It

3-2 I. 1. A 2. B 3. D

II. 1. these/those 2. those 3. this; that

3-2-1 I. 1. B 2. D 3. B

II. 1. that 2. those 3. It

3-3-1 I. 1. one 2. one 3. one 4. the other 5. It 6. it 7. it

II. 1. one; the other 2. one; another; the other 3. the others

3-3-2 1. some 2. any 3. any 4. some

3-3-5 1. anyone; familiar 2. something; important 3. someone; special

3-4 I. 1. Who 2. What 3. Which

II. 1. What did Helen lend to her classmate?

2. Whom/Who did the boy ask about the history of the church?

3. What had made the residents suffer from various diseases?

Chapter 4 助動詞

4-1 I. 1. is/was; are/were 2. Does; does 3. have

II. 1. Is the baby sleeping soundly in the room?

2. The typhoon didn't cause serious damage to the village.

3. Has the man's speech moved all the audience?

4-2 I. 1. B 2. D 3. D

II. 1. should 2. must/should 3. should; can/may

4-3 I. 1. C 2. B 3. D

II. 1. must be 2. must have taken 3. could have joined

Chapter 5 動詞的時態

5-2-1 I. 1. starts 2. washes 3. relies

II. 1. spends 2. has; has; begins 3. Does; goes

5-2-2 1. were 2. gets; has 3. used; goes 4. arrived 5. put; sat

5-2-3 I. 1. Maggie will go to a hair salon to dye her hair this Saturday.

2. The government will take action to fight against piracy.

II. 1. C 2. D 3. B

5-3-1 I. 1. are flying 2. are lying 3. are shopping

II. 1. C 2. B 3. D

5-3-2 I. 1. were taking 2. was cooking 3. was using

II. 1. D 2. A

5-3-3 I. 1. will be baking 2. will be discussing 3. will be singing; meet

II. 1. Sarah will be bathing her baby at eight o'clock tonight.

2. Caroline will be watching a soccer game at six o'clock this evening.

3. The students will be reading the poems on their textbooks when their teacher comes.

5-4-1 I. 1. B 2. A 3. D

II. 1. has been 2. Have; been 3. has gone to

5-4-2 I. 1. had finished 2. had happened 3. found; had lost

II. 1. invited 2. found 3. had forgot 4. left 5. felt 6. had

5-4-3 I. 1. will have read 2. comes; will have been 3. get; will have tidied

II. 1. A 2. D 3. B

5-5-1 1. Since Andrew updated his Facebook status, he has been playing video games.

2. The artist has been painting for five hours.

3. Mia has been working in the bakery across the street since she moved to this town.

5-5-2 1. had; been; walking 2. had; been; trying 3. had; been; driving

5-5-3 1. will have been teaching 2. will have been raining 3. will have been running

Chapter 6 主動與被動語態

6-2 I. 1. is performed 2. was fixed 3. will be held

II. 1. The baseball game was canceled because of heavy rain.

2. The technology company's new products will be introduced at the trade fair tomorrow.

6-3 I. 1. is being heated 2. was still being investigated

II. 1. The new concert hall is being built in the city center by the workers.

2. The software was being updated by the engineer when the phone rang.

6-4 I. 1. has been solved 2. had been caught 3. will have been delivered

II. 1. The boy's pencils had been sharpened before the boy went to bed.

2. Jack's house has been painted white.

3. By this May, a million dollars will have been donated by this kind-hearted lady.

6-5 I. 1. must be sent 2. was made to move 3. was seen to play

II. 1. The suspect was made to tell the truth.

2. The runner was seen to fall in the race.

Chapter 7 動名詞與不定詞

7-1 I. 1. C 2. D 3. B

II. 1. playing 2. swimming 3. turning

7-2 I. 1. A, B 2. D 3. A

II. 1. to raise 2. to do

7-3 I. 1. B 2. D 3. B

II. 1. having replied 2. to return 3. talking

Chapter 8 形容詞與副詞

8-1-1 I. 1. B 2. B 3. A

II. 1. either 2. another

8-1-2 I. 1. six; second 2. first

II. 1. many 2. few 3. little

8-1-3 I. 1. C 2. A

II. 1. sunny 2. creative; colorful 3. meaningless

8-1-4 I. 1. My mother bought me a beautiful pink dress.

2. The long boring movie makes the audience sleepy.

II. 1. B, close public attention 2. A, a strange old man 3. B, something positive

8-2 I. 1. suddenly 2. truly 3. patiently 4. possibly 5. naturally 6. scientifically

II. 1. Patricia always delays doing her work.

2. The students are nervously waiting for the exam result.

8-3-1 I. 1. as tall as 2. as well as

II. 1. as expensive as that necklace.

2. as diligently as Sean.

3. English as hard as Carol/she.

8-3-2 I. 1. fiercer 2. healthier 3. better 4. most cautious 5. slimmest 6. worst

II. 1. harder 2. earlier 3. more 4. best 5. worst 6. most skillfully

8-3-3 I. 1. much/even/far; better; than 2. more; intelligent; than; less; efficiently; than

II. 1. (1) better (2) superior (3) worse 2. is the lighter of the two

8-3-4 I. 1. C 2. D 3. D

II. 1. No other type of car is as expensive as this one in this car company.

2. (1) No other man/person/employee speaks English as fluently as Shawn in this department.

(2) Shawn speaks English more fluently than any other man/person/employee in this department.

8-4 I. 1. A 2. C 3. B

II. 1. The longer Ms. Wang stayed in the department store, the more she bought.

2. This lake is three times as big as that swimming pool./This lake is three times bigger than that swimming pool./This lake is three times the size of that swimming pool.

Chapter 9 連接詞

9-1 I. 1. and 2. but 3. or

II. 1. My father bought a bicycle and a smartphone for me.

2. The patient took the medicine and felt better after that.

3. Which does Jake like, coffee or tea?

9-2 I. 1. B 2. C 3. D

II. 1. Both sweaters and scarves are necessary in winter.

2. Either you or your sister has to clean the room.

3. Yolanda speaks not only English but also Japanese.

9-3 I. 1. B 2. C 3. D

II. 1. The guest took off her shoes before she entered the house.

2. Although the soccer team lost the game, they were not discouraged at all.

3. As long as you show friendliness, you can make friends easily.

9-4 I. 1. C 2. A 3. B

II. 1. Frank wrote a love letter to Sandra; moreover, he sang a love song to her.

2. The teacher has explained the theory several times; however, the students still can't understand it.

3. Dry your wet hair; otherwise, you will catch a cold.

9-5 I. 1. not; but 2. or 3. and

II. 1. Put on your coat, or you will catch a cold.

2. Have some more cake, and you won't feel hungry.

3. Doris is not afraid of cockroaches but dogs.

Chapter 10 關係詞

10-1-1 I. 1. who/that 2. which/that 3. that

II. 1. The tourist who/that has a map in her hand is looking for the train station./The tourist who/that is looking for the train station has a map in her hand.

2. The words which/that are written with a pencil are blurred./The words which/that are blurred are written with a pencil.

10-1-2 I. 1. whom/that 2. which/that 3. whom

II. 1. The cyclist whom/that the careless driver hit was sent to the hospital.

2. The stray dog the animal rescue team saved was adopted.

3. The science fiction about which Sharon is talking appeals to young readers.

10-1-3 I. 1. whose; membership; cards

2. of; which; tires

II. 1. The earthquake victim whose leg was bleeding was saved by the rescue team.

2. Donald will work in a Canadian company whose logo is a maple leaf.

10-2 I. 1. B 2. D 3. A

II. 1. who/that lives in Los Angeles

2. , which was made in Switzerland,

3. , which is the capital of France,

10-3 I. 1. C 2. A 3. C

II. 1. that objected the proposal.

2. that live in a house with a beautiful garden welcome their neighbors and share the garden with them.

3. that can solve this problem.

10-4 I. 1. B, C 2. A, D 3. A, B

II. 1. (1) Many people like to go camping in spring when the weather is comfortable.

(2) Many people like to go camping in spring in which the weather is comfortable.

2. (1) Philip is looking for a quiet room where he can take a nap.

(2) Philip is looking for a quiet room in which he can take a nap.

Chapter 11 疑問句

11-1 I. 1. Was everyone in the room surprised at the news?

2. Should the patient change his diet?

3. Does Adam get up early every morning?

II. 1 When will your uncle and his family leave for San Francisco?

2. What did Nancy eat for lunch?

11-2 I. 1. Let me know if you can join us.

2. We are curious about what Richard bought for his wife for their anniversary.

II. 1. where Cathy's foreign friend comes from.

2. when the sit-in protest was finished.

3. what you have been doing lately?

11-3 I. 1. C 2. A 3. D

II. 1. is 2. didn't 3. haven't they 4. is there

Chapter 12 分詞

12-1 I. 1. B 2. C 3. D

II. 1. interesting; interested 2. spilt/spilled 3. stored

12-2 I. 1. C, D 2. C, D 3. A, C

II. 1. Cherry's son is a spoiled child, always having his own way.

2. Sebastian works in a computer company set up by Bill Gates.

3. (1) On the baseball field, there are many baseball players who/that are practicing for the upcoming game.

(2) On the baseball field, there are many baseball players practicing for the upcoming game.

12-3 I. 1. B 2. A 3. C

II. 1. (1) The thief threw away the stolen wallet and ran away in a hurry.

(2) The thief threw away the stolen wallet, running away in a hurry.

2. (1) Because the weather is sunny today, I feel like going biking.

(2) The weather being sunny today, I feel like going biking.

3. (1) As Nora isn't feeling well, she will take a sick leave.

(2) Not feeling well, Nora will take a sick leave.

Chapter 13 子句

13-1 1. [S]

2. [P]

3. [S]

13-2 I. 1. That 2. that 3. What

II. 1. That scientists can clone sheep is not a fiction anymore.

2. Ian promised that he would give us a hand.

3. We don't know when Sam left.

4. Father left a message that he made some sandwiches for our breakfast.

13-3 I. 1. which/that is next to the bench doesn't work.

2. which/that was sent from Australia.

3. whom you can depend on/on whom you can depend.

II. 1. Hugh's face turns red whenever he sees the girl whom he has a crush on.

2. My family are talking about the day when my parents got married.

13-4 I. 1. C 2. D 3. A

II. 1. After the boy shouted at his mother, he felt guilty.

2. The woman lives a luxurious life even though she doesn't make much money.

3. The driver was fined as he was caught speeding.

Chapter 14 假設語氣

14-1 I. 1. C 2. D 3. B

II. 1. If; had; would; feel/be 2. there; were; could

14-2 I. 1. C 2. B 3. C

II. 1. had; thought; twice; would; not; have; done

2. had; explained; would; have; been 3. had; spent; would; become

14-3 I. 1. D 2. A 3. C

II. 1. were; to; could 2. were; to; would

III. 1. If the seasons were to stop changing, people's lives would be greatly affected.

2. If the weather should be bad, the ball game may/might be postponed.

14-4 I. 1. Were 2. Had 3. Should

II. 1. Were George here, he might know how to get to the supermarket.

2. Had the man driven a little slower, he would not have missed the post office.

3. Should you need any further information, please contact me.

14–5 I. 1. knew 2. had 3. had not argued

II. 1. knew 2. had; been 3. had; mailed/sent

14–6 I. 1. were 2. had been admitted 3. were

II. 1. knew 2. had; tried/ate 3. had; been

14–7 I. 1. B 2. D

II. 1. But; for; would 2. Without; could; have; forgot/forgotten

Chapter 15 特殊句構

15–1 I. 1. Make yourself at home.

2. Leave me alone.

3. Be quiet for a few minutes, please.

II. 1. No littering here.

2. Don't put your wallet on the table, Ian.

3. Never go through/run a red light.

15–2 I. 1. What 2. How 3. How

II. 1. What a talented singer Jolin is!

2. How interesting these novels are!

15–3 I. 1. the very 2. Do 3. do

II. 1. (1) It was Samuel that dressed himself like Spiderman on Halloween.

(2) It was on Halloween that Samuel dressed himself like Spiderman.

15–4 I. 1. B 2. A 3. D

II. 1. (1) goes the train. (2) goes. 2. did Timmy have 3. will you understand him.

基礎英文字彙力2000

丁雍嫻 邢雯桂
盧思嘉 應惠蕙　編著

◆ **最新字表！**

依據大學入學考試中心公布之「高中英文參考詞彙表 (111 學年度起適用)」編寫，一起迎戰 108 新課綱。單字比對歷屆試題，依字頻平均分散各回。

◆ **符合學測範圍！**

收錄 Level 1~2 學測必備單字，規劃 80 回。銜接國中內容，奠定日後英文實力的基礎。
Level 1：40 回
Level 2：40 回

◆ **素養例句！**

精心撰寫各式情境例句，符合 108 新課綱素養精神。除了可以利用例句學習單字用法、加深單字記憶，更能熟悉學測常見情境、為大考做好準備。

◆ **補充詳盡！**

常用搭配詞、介系詞、同反義字及片語等各項補充豐富，一起舉一反三、輕鬆延伸學習範圍。